AUGUST IN THE VANISHING CITY

a novel by

Lakis Polycarpou

To Jim and Nancy,

Thanks for your support!
Best,
Lakis

City of the Future Publishing

Tarrytown, New York

Book cover design by Ira Golberg.

ISBN: 978-1-943870-03-5
ISBN-13: 978-1-943870-03-5

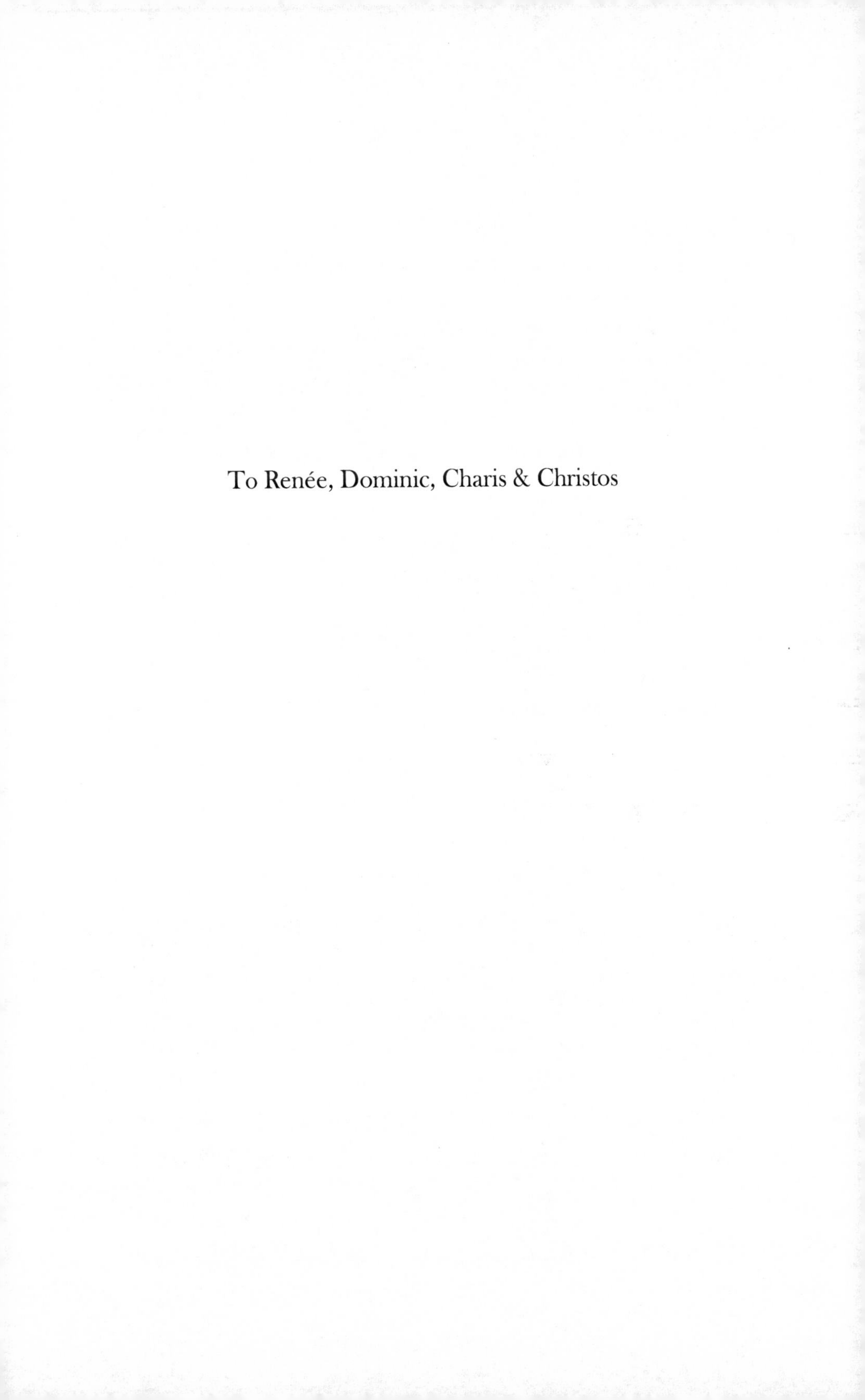

To Renée, Dominic, Charis & Christos

O, beware, my lord, of jealousy!
It is the green-eyed monster
which doth mock
The meat it feeds on.

—William Shakespeare, *Othello*

Truth, where's the truth?
I too was an archer in the war;
my fate: that of a man who missed his target
. . .
The nightingales won't let you sleep in Platres.

—George Seferis, "Helen"

Acknowledgements

Researching and writing this novel would not have been possible without the support of my family, friends and many others who have helped me over the years.

In particular, I would like to thank my parents, who never stopped believing in me.

A very special thanks to my aunt, Maria Matsi, who indulged my research and went out of her way so many times to help me find the right people to talk to every time I visited Cyprus.

Finally, thanks to my wife Renée, who has helped and supported my writing in more ways than I could mention.

Historical Note

August in the Vanishing City takes place on the Mediterranean island of Cyprus. In ancient times Cyprus was known as the birthplace of Aphrodite, the goddess of love. According to Homer, the great archer Teucer moved to Cyprus and founded the city of Salamis near Famagusta after the Trojan War. In the Bible, Cyprus is mentioned as the birthplace of Saint Barnabas, and as the place of Paul's first mission.

Cyprus was a province of the Roman and Byzantine Empires for more than a thousand years. In 1191 it was captured by King Richard the Lionhearted during the Third Crusade. A year later Richard sold the island to the Knights Templar, who in turn sold it to Guy de Lusignan, a French noble.

In 1473, the island fell to the Venetian Empire. Shakespeare's Venetian tragedy Othello was set "in a Seaport in Cyprus," presumably Famagusta. In the story, Othello leads a garrison to Cyprus to defend it from the invading Turkish navy, only to find when they arrive that a storm has sunk all of the enemy's ships. In reality, Venetian forces weren't so fortunate. In spite of the impressive fortifications the Venetians built in Nicosia and Famagusta, the Ottoman Turks conquered the island in 1571.

Cyprus remained a province of the Ottoman Empire until it was ceded to Britain in 1878, in return for the British help during the Russo-Turkish war.

Throughout a succession of different empires and a revolving ruling class, the peasant Greeks of Cyprus maintained their identity and their Orthodox Christianity. In 1955, after many years of protest, Greek Cypriots (comprising 80 percent of the population) started an armed insurrection with the aim of throwing off British rule and uniting the island, at long last, with Greece. In suppressing the insurrection, the British Colonial government fomented inter-communal strife between the Greek Cypriots and the Turkish Cypriots, who comprised 18 percent of the population.

By 1959, the Greek revolutionaries successfully threw off British rule, but were denied the long-sought union with Greece. Instead, a hastily drafted and ultimately unworkable constitution was imposed on them. Within three years, constitutional government had fallen apart, leading to a short, bloody civil war.

Over the next decade, the two communities of the island grew increasingly embittered, with Turkish Cypriots withdrawing into isolated enclaves, as Greek nationalists attempted to undermine the Greek Cypriot government and unite the island with Greece.

In 1974, Greek nationalists staged a coup against the elected Greek Cypriot government of Archbishop Makarios. In response, Turkey invaded, pushing 200,000 Greek Cypriots from their homes and de facto partitioning the island.

August in the Vanishing City takes place in the mid 1990s, some two decades after the invasion. As of this writing, Cyprus remains partitioned.

Rizokarpaso
Kyrenia
Guzelyurt
Nicosia
TURKISH OCCUPIED TERRITORY
Lefka
Famagusta
Polis
Deryneia
Ayia Napa
Protaras
Kakopetria
Platres
Larnaca
REPUBLIC OF CYPRUS
Paphos
Kourion
Limassol
UN Green Zone
Dhekelia UK sovereign base
Akrotiri UK sovereign base

August in the Vanishing City

Chapter One

THREE MONTHS BEFORE PETROS' RELEASE from the army, the Turks kill a Greek soldier on the Green Line in Nicosia. The boy bleeds out in the weedy Dead Zone near Ledra Street, behind sandbags and rows of barbed wire, where boarded-up brick buildings from colonial days stand mute as they have for decades, their doorframes and shutters rotted away by the passing years.

Greek medics try to go in, but the Turks shoot over their heads, refusing to let them move forward. Forty minutes pass from the moment they cut him apart with machine gun fire to the arrival of the United Nations troops to retrieve him. In his hand they find a brown bag holding a carton of cigarettes and a bottle of Cyprus brandy, and everyone just shakes their heads. What was he thinking, the poor boy, that he had made friends with the other side?

It is not the first time that soldiers arranged to exchange gifts across the Green Line, their judgment clouded by the boredom of those long, hot brown hours—stale, fly-infested hours that stank of tired nationalism, pointless waiting and absurdity.

It is of course the Greeks who bring gifts. The Turks have nothing, especially the boys from deep Anatolia, who, they say, are literally starving when they come to occupy this foreign land that they are told is Turkish.

The Turks say the boy had ignored an order to halt—and who knew what was true?

Correctly speaking, the Turk who shot him was doing his duty. Petros' uncle Michalis says this, one day when Petros and his cousin Elias are on leave, eating roasted chicken and potatoes, salad and pickled caper greens—the ones with thorny stems that stick in your throat—at Michalis' hotel by the beach. Never trust a Turk, he says.

It is at that moment that Petros realizes how impossible it is to die significantly anymore. Once, he thinks, no one forgot a hero, and all soldiers were heroes, but that has not been true for a long time. Now a soldier's death has no more meaning than that of a reckless boy on a fast motorcycle who tries to pass a lumbering fruit truck too quickly and runs headlong into oncoming traffic.

~~~~

But that conversation comes later. In the days immediately after the killing, when death is still fresh in the air, Petros and Elias are still stationed near the Famagusta border, along a different part of the Green Line. The barracks and observation point are in an old building that seems to sweat blood and leak strange memories; Petros sleeps poorly.

Unlike in old Nicosia, here the Dead Zone stretches for hundreds of meters between the two sides, across dry rolling hills—scrub that could have been anywhere in this part of the world. Beyond that, from the building's roof one can see all of Varosha, the city of the vanished—a coastal suburb south of Famagusta, now a modernist mausoleum, the largest ghost
~~~~

town in the world. Looking from a distance, at first you don't see it. The city looks like many others in this part of the world, a mix of apartment high-rises and coastal hotels and low, one- and two-story, flat-roofed, cinder-block buildings—buildings, to be sure, that have seen better days. It is only through binoculars that you realize there is no traffic, no movement, that the windows are broken and the streets are swallowed in weeds.

Unlike the rest of northern Cyprus, they say the Turks took Varosha by mistake during the invasion—a giant accidental bite—when they called in airstrikes on Greek artillery positions in the city. They called in airstrikes and flattened buildings, and the children screamed and the people fled, yelling "they will kill us all." And the tanks rolled in, and in a few months the whole city was wrapped in cyclone fencing and barbed wire and abandoned to lizards and feral cats, a rotting "bargaining chip" that the other side hoped to give back in return for the stubborn world finally admitting that Northern Cyprus was Turkish and pretending the rest hadn't happened. Now, it lies empty still, a testament to the madness of war—a grand, accidental experiment to see what strange things happen to human places when all the humans leave.

Petros sleeps poorly. It has been three weeks since they arrived, and every night since, he lies awake thinking about how close he is. There is a house, he thinks, a few kilometers from here, where my parents lived. He closes his eyes as if he can remember the place; but all that his memory delivers him is a smell, musty at first and then salty, like the smell of seaweed and the ocean.

It isn't a real memory (Petros was born after the invasion); it comes from a picture of his mother and father when they were young, which lies among dozens of others in the old chest at the house in Nicosia. In it, his father is wading knee deep in the water, carrying Petros' mother out to sea. Behind them there is a building, right on the beach, and a row of sunbathers. His father gazes out toward the ocean, and his mother's mouth is half open as if about to laugh. Then he pitches her into the water, and she jumps up, chasing him. Petros imagines this part, even though his parents had always been too old for that kind of roughhousing. It is possible that the picture itself is imaginary—has he ever really seen it?

Hours go by. Finally he pulls the single sheet back and rises, standing at imaginary attention for an imaginary moment and stares into the darkness. Then he drops to the floor and begins: one, two, three ... thirty, forty, fifty. At one hundred pushups, he pauses for ten seconds to control his breath so as not to wake the others, and then he begins again. Two hundred later, he stops again, his triceps aching. He is no longer the skinny, sweet boy with the sunken chest and sheepish eyes, and never will be again.

Images rise in his mind as he continues, causing him to lose count—images of his mother, his father, Famagusta as he imagines it—images and the ghosts of bad feelings and bad moods that he pushes away, again and again. When the morning wake up call comes he springs up, a satisfying pain rippling through his torso, not even remembering when he had finished or what his new record is.

Hours pass in dull rotation. Petros sits in a dark shaded room, smoking a cigarette, sipping a shot of red *zivania* from the bottle his fellow soldier Antonis brought from the Kykkos monastery a few days earlier. His face and chest are damp from the heat.

At the next table, the other soldiers—his friends—are playing *pastra*. How many times have they asked him to join in? But Petros has lost his taste for card games. Across from him, he stares at a cracked wall, its white paint peeling, a line of ants running down its face. It is past lunch time—when will Kostas get back with the damn food? It's too early to drink, someone says.

"What?"

"Hey *malaka*," says Antonis, "it's too early to drink."

Leave it to the alter-boy—rule-bound, sincere and religious, in spite of the cursing—to cut off the mid-day drinking.

Petros takes another sip and rubs his forehead.

"Petro," says Kostas suddenly, "Your cousin tells us you knew the boy?" He speaks with ferocious urgency, as if knowing the answer to this question is an emergency, which, Petros thinks, it is not.

Elias speaks without looking up from his cards. "What kind of an idiot would do such a thing?"

Petros looks for a moment at his cousin—his cousin, his best friend, practically his brother—and feels the old nauseating knot of resentment churn and tighten in his stomach, as if trying to ring the *zivania* out like a sponge. He recently heard a rumor about Elias—a rumor about his cousin and a girl—*the* girl, the one thing that means more to Petros than his hatred of Turks.

Antonis puts his cards down, stands up and, without asking, takes the bottle of *zivania* and Petros' glass off of the table and goes away to the kitchen. He is right—at some point, it will be time to switch tower duty, better not to be drunk—but how realistic is that? Minutes pass before Antonis returns with a tray of four *demitasse* of Cyprus coffee and tall glasses of water.

"Did you know him?" Kostas asks again.

Petros refuses even to shrug, lifting the cup to his lips and sipping the bitter mud, feeling the grains in his mouth, on his tongue. The room is bare and they are waiting, waiting for what, no one is sure—food, yes, but what else? The next order, the next assignment, the next location, which could come along at any minute, or not. Petros doesn't want to think about any of it anymore. Soon he and some of the others will be on leave, getting drunk and maybe lucky with the foreign tourist girls in Ayia Napa. He closes his eyes and imagines it ... the beach, the half-naked bodies, lying on the sand ...

"Stop asking him," says Antonis. "How would he know him? He would have said something anyway."

Petros stares at the wall, but he is no longer thinking about the boy—he doesn't want to think about the boy. No—now he is thinking about the girl, his girl—or at least the one he has sworn to make his own.

Elias wonders aloud why a soldier would do such a thing.

"He must have had sympathy for them," says Kostas. He means the Turks.

"I have sympathy for them," says Elias. "That doesn't mean I would commit suicide to deliver them a bottle of brandy."

Memories rush to Petros' mind—of Elias on one of those fast motorcycles, running off the road, flying through the air into a wheat field near Astromeridis; of Elias almost falling off a sheer rock face he was scaling near the birthplace of Aphrodite while trying to impress a Danish girl he met on the beach.

"Maybe he was lonely," says Antonis.

"Maybe he was ugly," says Elias, "too ugly to get a girl ..."

"Even ugly boys can get girls in Cyprus!" Kostas protests. He himself is heavyset, thick around the midsection and committed to the view that he has as much opportunity with women as his friends.

"Okay, he was ugly and fat," says Elias, "shy and scared of girls." Elias himself is never scared of girls, but he has sympathy for boys who are—he is always concocting elaborate schemes to get one of them laid, introducing them to the latest Swedish or German or English tourists he has picked up on the beach. He tries to help Petros too—he has tried so many times.

"So what if he's fat," says Antonis. "That's no reason to kill yourself. Doesn't he have a family who loves him?"

"His family—let's say—died in the war, and the only ones left are communists who he can't talk to, because he hates communists."

"He hates communists but loves Turks?" says Kostas.

"He doesn't love Turks," says Elias, "but he has sympathy for them, because his father once told him a story—wait, wait, let me finish—a story about how he was saved by a Turkish family in the war."

There is clamor and shouting at the sentimental absurdity of this speculation—sentimental not because such things had not happened, but in spite of the fact that everyone knew they had.

"Hey Petro, tell us something," says Elias. "Tell us something about this boy who got himself killed to give the Turks a cigarette."

Petros slams his coffee on the table hard enough that chunks of thick, wet sludge leap from inside it, splattering themselves on the table like a brown bloodstain. "I knew him," he says. Each seething word creeps slowly off his tongue—each word a wild animal, provoked and dangerous. "I knew him. He was not fat, he was good looking, a good looking boy—a sweet-faced kid, with a family—my mother knows them, we used to see them sometimes in Kakopetria."

No one speaks for a moment; everything stops, even the breeze. Sweat collects in armpits, running in beads down ribcages. Every one of them feels for a moment as if he is burning, they are like living *kleftiko,* slowly roasting in a sealed-up furnace, as Elias described it a while back.

Elias speaks first. "You're a liar," he says. "You didn't know him. He's not even from Kakopetria." He swallows heavily. "But you're right about everything else, he wasn't fat, or bad with girls, he was a charming kid."

So there it is—it is Elias who had known the boy; Elias who is looking for something by making up stories and trying to bait them into saying something, God knows what or why.

"Tell us," says Kostas. But at that moment there is a clamor from the tower and an officer shouts down that it is Elias' turn on watch, and that he'd better move his ass, he is being watched, no doubt about it.

The moment passes, and none of the boys bring up the dead soldier again. A sweet-faced boy died for a reason they can't understand, and the days creep by like sleepy wild animals.

Chapter Two

This is Ayia Napa: open-air bars, music, drinks, beaches and banana-boat rides. In the sky, skinny-legged girls in bikinis dangle softly from quiet parasails, tugged along by motorboats driven by sinewy, well-bronzed boys. On the beach, the all-but-naked bodies bake, reveling in the mysterious marriage of innocence and debauchery that seems embedded in the startling beauty of this place.

Night falls, and the pale, translucent sea whispers. You can hear it even now, underneath the chest-rattling bass-thump of techno music from the clubs, music that spills forth and shakes the streets; even now, behind the sound of stumbling, drunken voices, rolling down the narrow alleys; even now, when the mute neon lights scream their joyous kitsch to the world, as if they could shout out the dark. But even they cannot drown out the sea's peaceful whisper.

It is here Petros sees her, not far from the beach. A glimpse of her in profile, as she turns away into a streaming mass of people, the soft sway of her hips disappearing in the crowd outside of Starsky's club.

It is here he sees her, and for the first time that day he is truly awake; truly awake for the first time in weeks. He throws the half-smoked cigarette to the ground and rushes forward, rushes to follow her, not caring that he is leaving his friends and fellow soldiers back inside the club, that they will wonder where he is. Nothing matters—he races down the street, the muscles of his legs and chest straining against his tight, recently sunburned skin.

She is not supposed to be here; she is supposed to be in that tiny village in the mountains past Platres, where the air is cool and the nightingales never let you sleep; where rich, young kings once ran to escape the heat and drink brandy sours; where the poet claimed to have met Helen and she told him she never went to Troy.

She is not supposed to be here; she is supposed to be standing in front of that one-room school, trying to convince poor mountain village kids of the importance and nobility of Greece, the reality of local saints and their miracles, how to multiply fractions. She is supposed to be there, because that is where he imagines her, day after day when he falls asleep. He imagines her there, just after the bell rings and she steps out of her room and is surprised and happy to find him waiting for her there. He falls asleep imagining it, wakes up believing that it will someday be true. In truth, he is not even sure when the school year ends. Is it June again already?

She is supposed to be there but now she is here and he cannot wait to catch her, see her, look into her eyes again.

~~~~

She has occupied a place in his heart for as long as he can remember.

Petros' love for the girl Joanna is woven into his earliest memories. She, his sister's best friend, the girl with light-brown
~~~~

hair and watery eyes (eyes, he thinks, that you could swim in; eyes you could drown in). An unusually fair girl among the dark Cypriots; a fair-haired girl who carried her own darkness inside.

They were refugees together, in those early years after the war—living at first in tents, and then on the living-room floors of one relative, friend, or another. At a little house in Strovolos, Petros and his sister and a half-dozen cousins and friends lay splayed out and sweating on mattresses on the living room floor—Joanna among them. She was his sister's age, not quite five years older than Petros; old enough to see and remember things that Petros forgot.

During the day they played hide-and-seek in the back alleyways, or, if it was too hot, Monopoly inside on the floor, with the shades shut and fans blowing while the adults took their afternoon naps or snapped beans in the kitchen for dinner. Joanna helped him count the money, trade properties, build hotels, when he was still too little to understand. She took his side, told his sister Anna to be nice to him.

At night Joanna and Anna sat up and talked, shadows and faint light on their faces, gossiping in hushed whispers, about things he didn't understand. He would drift off and then wake with a start; convinced he would never sleep, he rushed out crying to his mother and uncles—all of them still awake on the veranda smoking cigarettes and watching subtitled reruns of *Charlie's Angels* on a little, thick-screened, black-and-white television.

Irritated, one of the uncles would stand up, come in and shout at the girls, and Petros would feel sorry—sorry because even then he could see how sad and confused Joanna was, how much she needed and clung to those whispered conversations with her best friend.

Joanna's father was not there; he had gone missing when the Turks came. Like so many others, he picked up a rifle and marched out to face them, even though after the coup there was no government and barely an army to tell them where to go and fight. After the war, Joanna talked about her father as if he would return—as if he were just about to come back, tomorrow or next week. All of the adults cried when she said this, especially Joanna's mother. Joanna said it was because they didn't understand. In fact, she said with a whisper, she had seen him—he had come to her in the night, touched her face, told her that he was okay, but that she mustn't tell anyone.

Shortly after that she disappeared then too—for eight years with her mother, off to the cobblestone streets of Salonica, Greece, the city of the white tower, where they had family of some sort. By the time Petros saw her again, her illusions were gone; there were none left alive, she said, and anyone who thinks differently lives in a dream. There was a terrible look on her face as she told Anna these things—a hollow blank look, like a blackboard wiped clean, with only the faintest residue of chalk dust in the corners.

By then Petros' own father was gone, dead of heartbreak and sadness and too many cigarettes and ouzo. Now we understand each other, he thought. We know life without fathers. No, her eyes said. It is not the same.

Eight years; and then one day Joanna and her mother walked back into his life—into their tiny courtyard in Kato Lakadamia's refugee housing and she smiled at him—that soft, gentle smile, the way she had when they were young. Without thinking he jumped up, and threw his arms around her, only to feel the shock in his gangly, 14-year old body that underneath her pink oversized sweater she was now a woman, overflowing with soft curves. He pulled back, surprised, and spoke rapidly, to cover his embarrassment. "I know you missed me," he said.

She smiled and adjusted her sweater, to hang off one shoulder again.

Joanna, he rushed to tell her, there's so much you missed! Color television, new roads, a Pizza Hut! She nodded, her earnest, kind eyes open wide, as if to reassure him that what he was telling her was important, even as he was suddenly aware only of a stain on his shirt and a constellation of red bumps on his gleaming adolescent face.

Then she heard the voice: her best friend, Anna, coming down the stairs. Both of them cried out at the same time, rushing into each others arms. Later Petros stood silent outside Anna's room, his ear to the door, heart racing as the girls gossiped and played the recent hit songs—"Live is Life" , "Suzana"—on the cassette player.

In the years that followed, he spent many evenings that way, his ear to Anna's door, listening for the thin sweet sound of Joanna's voice, waiting for the rare and precious moments when she would laugh at something Anna said—truly laugh, a wild squeal bursting forth before she could choke it off—and Petros would smile, breathing shallowly, praying they didn't hear him and at the same time wishing they did; wishing that they would call him to come sit with them, even for a few minutes.

Anna accused him often of spying but he denied it with such conviction that he almost believed himself. He was not eavesdropping—just pausing for a moment between here and there. Was it his fault if they were so loud that he overheard?

In those next few years, he saw her often; she and Anna were fellow students, training to be teachers at the pedagogical academy. They would spend hours together studying and listening to music and talking about things that Petros pretended not to care about. He only thought he loved her then; he knew for certain later.

~~~~

There: he sees her again.

I am searching for you, he thinks. *Searching for you in Ayia Napa.*

A glance, from the side, she turns a corner and he follows. She looks for a moment as if she is laughing in a crowd of other boys and girls whom he does not know. She is arm in arm with someone, a boy, but he cannot see their faces. It is her—it must be, he thinks, but why would she be here, with people he does not know? The crowd turns the corner, passes under the dusky glow of the lights, her name rises in his throat, to his lips, but is choked out against the relentless beat of the music. It cannot be her, but he is sure that it is. He is sure in the way you are sure when you want something so badly, so fiercely, that the desire for it to be true makes it so.

And yet—why is she here? The question fills him with dread. If she is here, it is not to see him. Someone else.

There is a rumor. There is a rumor about the girl and his cousin Elias, and Petros believes it. He believes it because he knows his cousin; knows his cousin's faith in passion and recklessness and in following his heart, whatever damage it does. It is, after all, these things that Petros loves most about
~~~~

him; these are the qualities without which Elias would not be who he is.

It was Elias who gave Petros the courage to grow his hair long and pierce his ear when they were both still in high school, even after their mothers broke down and cried and yelled at them, begged them and swore that they had destroyed them, ruined their lives. It was Elias who took him on a motorcycle ride for the first time, smuggled him cassettes of Bob Dylan, old *Rembetika* music and Pink Floyd's "The Wall" as if they were precious contraband. Petros listened and understood, and the world had meaning again. They played backgammon and chess in the cafes, read Seferis and Cavafy, argued about philosophy, complained that Cyprus had lost it's soul to American culture and greed (never mind that Elias' father, uncle Michalis, was getting rich in the hotel business). It was Elias who taught him how to drink and play cards. It was Elias who taught him that there were more important things in life than money.

And, it was Elias who taught him how to pick up women—how to scan a tourist bar and see opportunity, how to seize the moment and walk up to a foreign girl, smile at her and pretend you barely speak English.

No. There must be another reason.

He thinks he has caught sight of her again: a girl in a crowd of friends. He sprints toward the crowd, pushes through the angry boys and grabs her arm, but it is not her: the stranger he touches turns around and recoils, her strange, foreign face shocked and disgusted, and Petros backs away. "Sorry," he breathes, his chest heaving.

"Sod off!" she spits. "Greek plonker!"

The drunken British soldier who stands next to the girl shoves Petros gratuitously, and then puts his arm around the girl's waist—as if to declare ownership. "Country full of window-lickers," he says.

It is all Petros can do to refrain from punching him in the face, but that would suggest that he cared about this foreign stranger girl, when all he wants to do is erase the memory of her face from his mind forever.

He realizes now that he must return and find his friends, not an easy task in the overrun, drunken night. He pushes back through the crowd—for some reason everyone seems to be going the opposite way, he feels like a fish swimming against an undertow, swept off-course. He has to loop around to get back to Eclipse, and when he gets there the bouncer won't let him in. I was just here, he says, no you weren't. Fuck this place, he shouts—he doesn't want to go in anyway; he doesn't want to be here at all. He turns and walks back into the alcohol-drenched alleyways. *I am searching for you,* he thinks. *Searching for you in Ayia Napa.*

~~~~

A few weeks earlier Petros confronted Elias about the rumor, on a day when they were in Protaras, sitting outside under the tiki-style thatched roof of Uncle Michalis' open-air, beachfront restaurant.

Tourists were already crowding the beaches. Unlike in Ayia Napa, here it was families—fat, middle-aged men and their leather-baked wives, women with still-attractive bodies and deep-wrinkled, sun-damaged faces. With them, diffident teenage children tuned out on their walkmans, wishing they
~~~~

could escape. The smell of deep-fried calamari and octopus in lemon juice walks by as if it, too, is a tourist.

"Joanna?" said Elias. "A girl like that? For me?" His tone was soothing, almost hypnotic, and Petros felt his rage evaporating, as if by magic or hypnosis. The sound of his cousin's words, as smooth as the sun and the sea. "Of course she is beautiful," he said. "For a Cypriot girl. But you know me —I need a girl who is ..." he trailed off and made a gesture with his hands.

"...willing?" said Petros.

"No," says Elias. "No, not exactly. I need a woman who makes me feel like life is bigger than I imagined it. Not one of the sad girls who are chained to the past." He pauses, tosses a pistachio shell over the edge of the veranda, and then continues. "The question is: why are you still going on about her? What is it about this weary village girl—who can never be yours anyway?"

"Why do you put it like that?" Petros spits.

"Don't take offense, cousin. You know I don't mean it that way. But think about it. Think about the responsibility! She's a girl who has spent her life drinking bitterness; a girl who only wishes for the bad things of this world to go away, to be able to forget that war and loss and abandonment are not only part of life, but that they are at the center of her life."

He paused, looked out toward the sea.

"You're not like her. You're like me—you have a lust for the larger world. You are meant for bigger things. No—she needs a quiet boy, someone who will always be there for her. Someone with a good, boring job who takes her to church and gives her the quiet family she always wanted. Someone who helps her accept her loss, not someone who reminds her of how bad it was. Not a man of passion. Even if she marries an ordinary man she'll cry every morning when he leaves for work and curse at him when he comes home and has forgotten to buy eggs, and he will not understand that it is not about eggs; that she is furious that he abandoned her, even for a few hours, and he will not understand why, not understand that there is really nothing he can do to make her happy."

"I would never leave her." *She is too good for you*, Petros thinks.

"Even if she would have you, how long would it last? A moment or two of passion and bliss, and then what? You get bored, or look at another woman, even for a moment. You think of other places, other possibilities for life, and she knows it. All you have to do is think it, for a moment, and she will know, and she will hate you even if she is not sure why. She will demand that you reassure her. And you will, and it will work for a while and then—bam!—it happens again, maybe this time for no reason. And you feel guilty and sorry even though you are doing nothing. And you remember that you love her and then it happens again. And this becomes your life, and yes, you never leave her, because you love her and can't bear to damage this fragile flower of yours, even if it means you spend your life rotting away inside."

~~~~

I don't care, Petros thinks. *I don't care how damaged she is, how much work. I would take it all, if she would have me.*

In his pocket, he carries photographs. Some of them are old; prints of family from decades ago, prints of history, of nobler times. Some of them are new: ones he has taken himself with his father's old Nikkormat FS. The most important one is of
~~~~

Joanna; a snapshot he took of her lying on a beach towel in Ayia Napa; a rare day when he had the courage to photograph her. It was on one of those blistering weekends in August, when those old friends of the family, Yiorgos and Eleni Zenios, took the four of them—Joanna, Petros, Elias and Anna—to the shore.

In the photograph her eyes are shut. She is still damp from a dip in the sea; she and Petros had been in the water together, he flirted with her with unusual confidence. She jumped on his back playfully and dunked his head under the water.

Wasn't it that same night—or was it some nearby evening—when the four of them sat on the rooftop terrace of his uncle's apartment drinking lemonade and she had asked for ice cream?

Wasn't it that night—that night, when the silhouettes of Paralimni's famous windmills creaked and moaned, and the sun sank into the ocean and spilled color and luminescence into every corner of the world—this was how he remembered it—and she said you know what I want right now? *Pahit Ice.*

It was the best idea he had heard in a long time. *Pahit Ice*—Italian-style Cyprus *gelato,* made from local fruit and Cyprus milk. I'll get it for you, he said.

Anna rolled her eyes. "Where are you going to get *Pahit Ice* now?" she asked.

"Trust me," he said. "I know a place."

He left quickly, his chest vibrating with excitement. It was only when he was downstairs and outside that he realized he had a problem. He did know a place—but it was at least a couple of kilometers away, and he didn't know how to drive. Eleni and Yiorgos Zenios were there of course, resting in a bedroom on the second floor, but asking them for help would destroy the moment entirely.

The only other option sat smartly against the side of the house—Elias' Lambretta. A black and gold beauty, with a boxy body and art deco style chrome stripes—an old-school bike that looked like it was built to be ridden by a dark man with a five o'clock shadow and a lit cigarette in his mouth, with a skinny girl in a 1960s shirt-dress clinging to his waist. Petros' had admired it since the first time he saw it.

Unfortunately, unlike most of his friends, Petros' had still never ridden a motor scooter. After his uncle Sotiris was flipped off his Vespa through the windshield of a Volkswagen, Petros' mother had made Petros swear never to ride one. Until that moment, promises to his mother still meant something; until that moment when the great force of desire and the glimpse of opportunity obliterated all sense of promise and obligation. He looked at the scooter now, thought of the girl on the roof who was waiting for ice cream, and imagined what his uncle Sotiris might tell him to do if he could talk. Petros wished he had a cigarette, but smoking was something else he had promised his mother he would never do.

Years later, after the army had made a man of him (or so he thought) he would look back at that moment and wonder what had taken him so long—what had taken him so long to stop fawning over life like a boy looking through a shop window; what had taken him so long to finally reach out to grasp it, to feel it, to taste it.

After a moment he slipped his leg over the saddle and took the handlebars into his hands. How hard could riding it be? He thought about going back upstairs and asking Elias to help him, but highlighting his ignorance to his cousin at that moment would have been a crushing defeat.

He gripped the handlebars firmly, grabbed the clutch, turned the throttle and pressed the starter as he thought he was supposed to. The machine sputtered to life and then roared, sending a tingling vibration through his chest. He smiled and turned his head, as if she were already that girl, sitting behind him, arms wrapped around his waist, holding on for dear life.

He turned the throttle. The bike reared up and shot forward out from underneath him as if it could escape its master; Petros refused to release the handlebars and yanked backward, as if he could convince the machine to heel by asserting his dominance. The bike rose up, and for an instant was above him; he landed hard on his back, the bike on top of him, its rear wheel still kicking ferociously. For a good three seconds it spun against his naked leg, until he realized that he could release the throttle. He pushed it off him, tears and fury in his eyes.

For a long moment he lay bleeding in the dirt, wondering who would come rushing to him first, and how and what he would explain to them. It was all over; all hope with Joanna was lost. There would never be a day, a moment like this again. She would see him and pity him, and smile at him sweetly, and think of him as she always had, as her best friend's little brother. She would be sorry that she had suggested the idea of ice cream, and guilty that she had in some way helped cause this bloody misfortune. She would pity him, but she would not be impressed.

But then, strangely, minutes passed and no one came. It occurred to him that no one had heard him crash—or if they had they were unable to distinguish it from the random sounds of the evening. He moved his legs and his arms, and began thinking that all might not be lost. Once more, he thought. He stood up, looked down at his leg; it was scraped raw from the thigh to the ankle, streaked with blood. A voice told him to forget it, to go inside, get help, she would understand, but something in him refused.

He climbed onto the bike again. Pain seared through his leg, and he could feel thin cool lines of blood running down his calf into his sandal. Let it out slowly, he said to himself, turning the throttle again. This time, the bike behaved as he pulled out into the street.

In line at the ice cream shop, a round-bellied man in front of him yelled a conversation at his friend next to him. In front of them, a couple of young English tourist boys pushed each other in front of a haggard mother. Behind the counter, a beautiful Greek girl scooped ice cream in slow motion, as if she were creating a work of art with each cone. Come on, thought Petros. The man with the big belly glanced down, and caught a glimpse of Petros' leg. "Hey!" he said. "You're bleeding!"

"It's nothing," said Petros, flicking his head back as if to look casual.

"No," said the man, "You're really bleeding, what happened? Come here!" he grabbed Petros arm and pulled him toward the front of the line, shouting for help. The line parted; an older woman appeared from behind the counter. He's bleeding the man said. "*Panayia mou*!" said the woman. "What happened?"

The woman was a classic *Yiayia*—one of a million grandmothers of Cyprus, living and dead, who we, the ungrateful, callously ignore until our time of need, when we call upon them and they miraculously appear, and then we take them for granted. He of course said thank you, as she wiped his leg with iodine and dressed it in gauze, but what he felt was irritation as she grilled him on who he was, what he was doing alone here, who were his parents, why did he not call them—the long arm of mothering-by-proxy was inescapable, even here. It was not until years later—at a moment when he realized in terror that there were places in the world that the loving, protective arms of the collective *Yiayias* could not reach—that he would think and remember and be grateful.

Time passed; night fell. Anna went to her room to read; Elias wandered off, God knew where. Joanna was still sitting on the roof, peering out intensely at new stars of the rapidly darkening night, as if she might at long last find something she had been looking for.

"I'm back," he said, and she jumped, startled. "We should eat quickly, it's melting."

This was how he remembered it: that somehow, in spite of everything, he had managed to bring her an ice-cream cone, though he could not imagine how he carried it with a wrapped up leg on that scooter he could barely ride.

She gave a short delighted gasp. You found it! she said. He handed her the cone—three mixed flavors, chocolate, vanilla and rosewater. She took it from him, and took a long soft bite with her thick, tender lips, smiling as the white and pink ran down the cone over her fingers.

He stepped back, raised his camera to take a picture—she put her hand up as if to say stop, but it was too late, he had snapped the photo.

It was only then she noticed his leg and her eyes widened—what happened? she asked.

He shook his head. It's nothing, a little scrape, that's all. His heart was racing. This was it, his one moment. Whatever happened, nothing would be the same after this.

Unsure what to do, she passed the cone to her left hand, and reached out to give him a bite. The melted ice cream had now run through her delicate little fingers past her thumb to the fleshy base of her hand. He reached over, took her arm and gently put his lips to the place where the rosewater ice cream was now running onto her wrist, and kissed it gently, never breaking her gaze.

Her face, which had for an instant finally relaxed, fell suddenly back into it's usual solemn demeanor. She pulled her hand away, and then, with a second thought, reached up and touched the side of his face.

This was how he remembered it: the sticky feeling of her soft small hands on his face, her smile, returning for an instant. "You got me ice cream," she said. "Sweet boy."

And then, pulling away, half turning toward the vast dark horizon, she paused. "You are too young," she said.

"No," he said.

"You are too young, you are my best friend's brother ..."

The rest, in his memory, was muddled by the sudden rising black cloud of shame, bitterness and self-hatred that spilled out from him. Forgive me—did he say it or just think it? Something in her words about nice boys, how he will find a good girl, there is time, he is only 16.

Her rejection was so gentle, so sweet and so thorough that it would have destroyed any man.

That was how he remembered it.

~~~~

Hours before he thought he had found Joanna in Ayia Napa, Petros met a pretty British girl on the beach. He had seen her from across the sand and he wanted her: flat stomach, perfect legs, little breasts and freckles, light brown hair bleached blonde by the sun. Go then, and get her, Elias said.

So he talked to her, and told her she was pretty, and she drank and drank and drank, and he touched her arm, touched her hips, drew in so close that he could smell cheap suntan lotion. She was wearing a thin little pink bikini. Tomorrow she will win the bikini contest, he told her. He put his hand on her hips—she was still in the bikini under the pullover. Where are you staying, he asked? She told him that she would meet him at a karaoke bar that evening.

He hates karaoke—so much that he decided to forget about the girl and go with his friends to Eclipse. Now though, alone and bitter, locked out of the club, he decides to give it a try.

Fortunately he is acquainted with the bouncer at the karaoke bar—the son of the local pastry chef in Lakadamia near his mother's house—so he has no problem getting in. He is greeted with the sound of off-key wailing to the tune of "Like a Virgin." He looks to the stage and happily sees the girl there, with her friend. She sees him, smiles brightly and waves. He grins back at her and for a moment his irritation and loneliness is forgotten.

It takes two more shots and twenty minutes of pleading by the girl before he agrees to go on stage and sing with her, but he does it, and they all laugh at each other.
~~~~

Later, in her room, he wonders where the girl's roommate is, as she unties her swimsuit and pushes his hand up under her pullover to her soft, small breast. There is a blank, alcohol-addled look on her face as he pulls off the rest of her clothes and his own, and proceeds with the awkward ceremony of copulation—new bodies, smells, mysterious callouses.

Just as she draws him into her he looks down for an instant at her feet, and realizes that they are not pretty and he is repulsed; for a moment all desire leaves him. Elias always said that the longer you drank, the prettier the girls got—not that he would know; he always caught the best looking one in the room. Now Petros discovers again that it is a lie; a line his cousin uses to push his followers toward the also-ran girls while he seizes the best ones for himself. No, Petros thinks. The longer you drink the more likely you are to suddenly notice just the wrong thing about her; the thing that reminds you that you and she are and would forever be strangers.

In the middle of the night, the girl's roommate stumbles in, laughing ridiculously, a middle-aged, balding Greek on her arm. Petros' girl curses at her, and Petros keeps his eyes shut and tries to sleep through whatever happens in the next bed. In the morning he and the girl shower together.

It is beautiful and horrible. As with the others, he will remember it differently each day, depending on his mood.

He leaves before breakfast. She doesn't bother to ask if she will see him again, but just smiles and waves. "Bye," she says.

He leaves the hotel. The little seaside tourist village of Ayia Napa is not quite awake, but the sun is up, the sky is blue and the world is once again illuminated.

~~~~
~~~~

He decides to head back to Protaras, to the little apartment he and Elias often shared when they had leave. It is one of a half-dozen rental properties that Uncle Michalis owns, a two-minute walk from the beach, but quiet; he looks forward to closing his eyes and shutting down his swimming mind for a few hours.

He had told Elias that he planned to stay with Antonis in the hotel room they'd pitched in for in Ayia Napa, but he is in no mood to be here anymore.

He wonders now where Elias is. In spite of his suspicions and bitterness, he has missed his cousin. Going out is never the same without Elias. He was the kind of friend who could instill confidence in anyone in any situation; the kind of friend who, with a couple of lines, could turn the most boring moment into something hilarious and unforgettable; the kind of friend who brought the party with him wherever he went. Petros hopes that he will find him at home, that they can while away the morning at his uncle's cafe talking about nothing, playing backgammon and drinking their morning *frappe*.

He gets to his Vespa and decides to take a moment. He reaches for his saddlebag and pulls out the old Nikkormat, opens the aperture as wide as possible and tries to hold the camera still as he clicks shots of the street. The intense brightness of the summer morning light and odd shadows it casts bother his eye more through the view-finder; the photographs will not turn out, he knows this. They will bleed colors and movement and light into a swirling mess that someone else might label artistic, but for Petros it will just be a record of his disappointment.

He takes the drive back, slowly, there is still alcohol in his head, more than he would like to admit. It is only a 15-minute drive, down the coast, cutting across the cape before the turn to Cape Greco—one of the most beautiful drives in the world, especially in the evening when the sun sets and everything is draped in indescribable, sweet light. During the daytime the trip is mostly dry brown scrub—the color of the dryness in Petros' throat—interspersed with rocky outcroppings and soul-quenching views of the sea.

And then, on to Protaras, a glittering citylet of more garish hotels that rises suddenly along the shore. If it weren't for the Turks, there would still be nothing here, Petros thinks. Nothing but romantic windmills and hoop houses growing winter tomatoes and cucumbers, and the once-unspoilt beaches only the locals knew about.

When his parents had honeymooned here at Fig Tree Bay in the late 1960s, the only thing there was a single, seaside restaurant and a few rickety shacks selling Cokes and lemonade. Now there are dozens, and more built each day; soon, he thinks, you will not be able to see the sea from the road because of the hotels.

It is still the frontier, in a way. It is almost as if there is an invisible line where the hotels and restaurants end, where you can step over and walk in old Cyprus again, land of the simple, hardy survivors who scrape out their living from potatoes and sheep's milk. No—more than a living; a life, a good life, a life suffused with meaning and spirit, a life connected with the Earth and the sky, with the cycles of birth and love and death. Year by year, it washes away.

None of this would have happened without the Turks—if they hadn't taken Varosha, and driven the tourism entrepreneurs south, Protaras and Ayia Napa would still be quiet, best-kept-secret places. In that way, the invasion was a blessing for his uncle Michalis. It was sheer luck that he inherited that bare land in the Paralimni district. Ambition led him to seize the opportunity, to build a real estate empire when the widows and orphans were still grieving.

Petros turns on the unpaved, sand-grooved street slowly, just in time to see her there, in front of his apartment building, in a white summer dress, up on her toes, arms around Elias' neck.

He pulls over, turns off the bike a block away. They still haven't seen him, they embrace for a long time. Perhaps just a friendly hug, he thinks. American-style, the way that comrades or close friends embrace. Yes, that is all it is, but if so, why doesn't he approach?

Instead, he slowly takes his camera out of the bag, focuses it and begins taking pictures, as if he is secretly gathering evidence of a crime. Why should it be a crime, or even a betrayal? She made her lack of feelings for Petros clear to him years ago, and as far as he knows, nothing has changed. What right does he have to feel this fury?

They are just friends, he thinks. This is a misunderstanding. But if that is all, why does she look so forlorn when she turns to leave; if that is all, why does Petros wait until she is gone and Elias is back inside to approach; if that is all, then why does he walk into the apartment without speaking?

Elias says nothing as well; Petros crawls straight into his bed with his shoes on, and thinks of Ayia Napa and determines that he will forget what he has seen. *I am searching for you in Ayia Napa*, he thinks.

Chapter Three

Their short leave ends; Elias and Petros return to the army, this time on different rotations.

Petros can't stop thinking about it—that brief glimpse of the two of them, together. He refuses to believe it is true, that it means what it appears to mean; he takes the undeveloped film from his camera and hurls it into the sea, as if by destroying the evidence he can destroy the truth.

Even so, he can't convince himself. He is ashamed; then infuriated, then ashamed again—each emotion in turn overrunning the other, each emotion colored and framed by deeper ones: sadness, depression, despair.

He has not seen Elias for days; they are on different rotations, by accident or design, he is not sure. He is relieved, because their separation delays the inevitable confrontation that is coming. Petros knows this: he must confront his cousin, confirm the truth, ask him why. Why, of all the girls in all the world that could be his did Elias choose the one unrequited love of Petros' life?

Days go by, his discharge date growing closer by the minute; with a sickening feeling in his gut, Petros must think about the next step in his life. He has been accepted to university in Athens, but has deferred for a year. His uncle Michalis has offered him a job at his hotel, a not-unpleasant job, a way to unwind from the military grind—sun, beach, girls. But the tourist season will be ending soon, so how much will there be to do? The thought of working for his uncle turns his stomach.

Finally, he gets a message from his cousin, a slip of paper, suggesting they meet in Limassol, where Elias has an errand to run. "Come with me. We can take a couple days off—unofficial."

He agrees to meet, unsure of what he will say. The feeling in his heart terrifies him. It is over, he will say. You will always be my cousin, but never again my *koumbaros*, never again my friend. The thought fills him with rage and sadness and relief. Never again to live like that, as supporting cast for more courageous men with bigger lives. He will make his own life big.

Still, the thought makes him sick. In a few weeks his whole future has come apart—dreams and fantasies of dreams of his life with the one woman. Dreams accumulated for so many years like sediments of sandstone, suddenly dissolved, crushed and violently expelled. Now he will sever the last link to his present and past, to the one person who understands him, who made him understand himself. As if it were possible, his loneliness grows more profound. Loneliness and rage. Of all the women in the world, all the rich bounty of Cyprus and Europe who would offer themselves naked at his doorstep, Elias had to choose her?

~~~~

Limassol: a major port, a city that is in some ways even more cosmopolitan than the capital, Nicosia; and yet, somehow, also one of the most romantic, with its legacy of empires come and
~~~~

gone. Ancient amphitheaters. Imposing medieval castles and drawbridges, the fortress where Richard the Lionhearted was married; the stark white minaret of the Grand Mosque in the old Turkish quarter.

Petros arrives an hour early, walks between the palm trees along the promenade by the shore, watches a departing tanker on the horizon as it slips silently over the edge of the sea.

They have arranged to meet in the old town. A relic of languid colonial days, it is the one part of the city that will not capitulate to the bustling rush of the post-invasion boom. Built when the ornament of buildings was not yet dispensable, it exudes the dignity and civility of earlier ages—a civility made visible in the smallest details of elegant balusters, fanlight windows, wrought-iron balconies, wooden shutters, white and blue and yellow awnings, brick pavers—becalming architecture at war with honking cars and whining motorbikes that sputter and squeeze through the narrow streets.

The restaurant is nondescript but familiar. Petros and his friends have met here before, many times, not for the food or the service but because it was usually quiet when they had quiet matters to discuss. But those discussions have ended—faded away a long time ago. So why did Elias want to meet here now?

He gets there early, tells the waiter that he has a friend coming, asks for a glass of water. Annoyed, the waiter rolls his eyes and gestures vaguely toward a table in the corner, as if he can park the boy there and forget him, even though there's not another soul to serve.

Soon, though, a group of men enter, voices booming. Four of them wear Armani suits, gold rings, necklaces; the fifth wears a traditional *thwab* and *keffiyeh* headscarf. Arabs, Petros thinks, probably Lebanese, rich refugees left over from the civil war. It sounds as if they are in a heated argument, but they are just talking. Groups of Arabs are even worse than Greeks that way; all conversation is shouting. The waiter comes quickly and gives them a large table; almost at once the proprietor comes out and begins taking orders.

There is no air conditioning. A swamp cooler in the front of the room spins quietly and does nothing, especially for the table in the corner where Petros is sitting. "Excuse me," he says. "Can I get a glass of water?" It is suddenly too hot to breathe.

The proprietor doesn't even look up at the sound of Petros' voice; the waiter, a short, skinny man of about 40, stands quietly at attention in the corner.

Where the hell is Elias? Petros pulls out a cigarette to calm himself—to look calm—and stares across the room. It's no good—his dry throat suddenly feels as though it will close up. Why won't anyone just bring him a bottle of water?

When he glances over at the table of Arabs, he sees that their drinks have appeared already, as if by magic, and the proprietor is taking their order, both sides communicating in broken English.

"Excuse me," Petros says more loudly. Neither looks at him; they each disappear into the kitchen. One of the Arabs glances over at Petros, and then turns back to his table.

Are they deaf? Petros throws the cigarette on the floor. Time to leave; screw Elias.

Just then, his cousin appears, but to Petros' chagrin, Antonis is with him. This is unexpected; now Petros will have to make a public scene. He feels a rush of nervousness, unsure of what to do.

"Cousin!" Elias grins, blissfully happy to see Petros, completely unaware that Petros knows about his disloyalty; and yet, Petros can't help smiling. "How's it? Have you ordered?"

Petros shrugs, and gestures toward the kitchen. "They don't serve our kind here," he says.

The others sit. "What do you mean?" says Elias.

"I've been here for 15 minutes," Petros says, "And they won't even bring me a glass of water."

"Eh." Elias waves his hand. "We are here," he says with a wink. "And we have things to discuss."

"Ya." Antonis punches Petros' shoulder, hits him on the back and pulls up a chair.

"Ya," Petros responds, grudgingly. "What brings you here? What brings you both?"

Elias holds up a finger. "A moment," he says. He looks toward the front door; a second later, it opens, and here is Stelios.

Petros smiles now, broadly, in spite of himself. It has been a long time.

Stelios smiles too, as he saunters over, and at this Petros shudders imperceptibly. The scar on Stelios' upper lip is still there, of course, and though it has faded over the last year, it still gives his smile a twisted, vicious look, a reminder of arbitrary cruelty and stupidity.

Has it been only a year? I seems like a lifetime. When they met, Stelios was a new recruit, fat and baby-faced. Petros and Elias were by then "old soldiers"—a designation one got about a year or so in, halfway through the compulsory service period.

At the time, Petros and Elias were on duty as military ambulance drivers, a position they enjoyed, racing through the streets with pretty foreign girls or just to pick up lunch for the boys. On this night, though, they received a late, panicked call: some fellow old soldiers had been hazing a couple of new recruits in the middle of the night, and something had gone wrong.

Tradition held that the old soldiers would haze the new ones, toughen them up for battle. The idea: make them suffer now that they might endure suffering later; inflict pain now that they will be prepared to deliver it later; be cruel now that they may be hardened to cruelty. Make them men, that they will be men, when men are needed. Stelios, a fat boy from a village outside of Paphos—a province of a province—was more vulnerable than most.

On that night, they came after one o'clock, dragged the new recruits from their cots by their ankles, unceremoniously dropping them on their backs and sides and stomachs onto the cold concrete, kicking their ribs until they jumped up or pissed their underwear or both. They made them do pushups, stood on their backs. Slapped their faces; berated them with boring words, made them feel bad, made them feel afraid—the usual.

But then, one of the old soldiers thought of a cruel twist; he made Stelios pull his shirt up over his head and then he tied it tight, so it covered his mouth and eyes, keeping his arms tangled inside. "Spin," he said.

At 30 rotations, Stelios told the soldier he was going to be sick; at 50, his ankles crossed and he fell, hands still tangled, unable to catch himself, face first into the bent iron corner of the cot, splitting his lip in two, like a melon. They said he didn't even cry out—he just tore the bloody shirt off his face and got on his feet again to take more punishment.

It was of course Elias who drove the ambulance; Elias, who never had any taste for hazing rituals. They reached the hospital, the boy was given stitches; the tooth they couldn't put back. In the end it could have been worse.

After they dropped him at the hospital, Petros and Elias went back and gave the hazing soldiers a beating, a taste of what they had dished out. It was a rough, asymmetric kind of justice, but something that Stelios never forgot. He attached himself to them—made himself ready for the moment he could repay them.

After the incident, one might have expected a boy like Stelios to just keep his head down and try to survive; instead he applied for the Special Forces. Even Petros and Elias laughed at this ("what is this, the *souvlaki* brigade?") but to everyone's surprise he was accepted. Now, only a year later, he wore a Green Beret and their insignia: "Fortune Favors the Bold."

Now he is changed; his bulk transformed from fat to solid mass. A transformation not of loss, but gain of control; his body moving now not as a loose collection of wobbling parts, but as a careful unit. Without looking physically much different, he has gone from a person who was picked on to one who could pick on anyone.

Petros rises; they grab hands, slap each other on the back. He feels his resolve to confront his cousin slipping.

Why has Elias brought them? Only then does Petros realize that with his fixation on the girl—on forcing Elias to admit what he has done—he has forgotten that Elias called the meeting and has an agenda of his own. The four of them are of course old friends, but they have other things in common, secret things that Petros had almost forgotten. And this was the place they usually met.

But Petros cannot think about those things yet. His throat is dry and his anger is rising. He raises his hand to flag the waiter but is still ignored.

"Maybe we should just go somewhere else," says Stelios coolly. Petros can tell he doesn't relish the idea. Beads of sweat are already forming on his temples; it would be nice just to have some water.

"They'd better come soon," says Antonis, "if they don't want trouble."

Petros smiles. Someone who didn't know him better might find those words funny coming from Antonis. Of the four of them he is the one who comes off as the most straight-laced. Tall, thin, clean-cut. Plans to be a doctor. The kind of kid who already looks as though he might be a doctor. Not the type you would expect to be involved in political rallies and street protests. *Exactly why we need him,* said Elias.

"Calm yourself," says Elias. "Let's see what happens. Anyway, we have business to discuss."

This, now. By now Petros has figured out where Elias wants to go with the meeting, and the thought agitates him; he simmers, on the edge of a rolling boil. He has been muzzled by circumstances—or by design, who knew how many steps ahead of him Elias was? He could say nothing now, not in front of the others. Lunch would be a wasted opportunity, and for the first time in years, he has no patience with wasted opportunities. The pointless waiting and time-biding of the army has infected his soul, but he is about to be free, free in so many ways, if the circumstances of his life will just allow it!

The owner of the cafe appears with bread and bottles of water for the table of Arabs.

"Hey," says Antonis loudly. "Can we have some service here?"

For the first time, the proprietor glances over at them. He puts his hand up, as if to say "okay, okay," but also "calm down." He goes back.

Antonis curses under his breath.

Elias tries again to bring the conversation back to the topic he wants to discuss. "I have talked to the others. They want to take action. Retaliation."

He is referring to Takis and Kostas, the other members of the *Filiki Eteria*—the "Friendly Society"—that the six of them formed together a year ago. They named it after the secret 19th century group of heroes that organized to successfully throw off 400 years of Turkish slavery and create the first nation of Greece in modern times. ("We are humble in origins," Elias would say dramatically, "but we are inspired by giants.")

It began with Petros and Elias, the summer before they entered the army—that summer when the Kyrenia mountain forest burned. No one knew how the first fires started, but the Turks couldn't stop them, and they wouldn't ask the Greeks for help, so all they could do was watch, looking north at the smoke-plumes and cry as if the flames were burning their own flesh.

"We have to do something," Elias said to Petros. "The politicians are corrupt, they do nothing. It is up to the ordinary people."

They began hatching plans, and slowly, quietly, feeling out potential members. By late spring they were six. Stelios was the last. Petros couldn't believe it when Elias suggested they recruit him, but Elias insisted: the boy has heart, he said. You wait and see.

They met, in various places and times, but most often in Limassol; often enough in this very restaurant.

"Let's go somewhere else," says Stelios under his breath. Usually he is the calm one, but he too can be pushed. Petros has an impulse to provoke his friend to rage and see what happens.

"Forget about that!" says Elias. "We have more important things to talk about!"

"What," says Antonis with irritation. "What do they want to retaliate for?"

Elias sits up, taken aback. He bangs his hand suddenly on the table. "For the soldier!" he shouts. "For *our* soldier! Did you forget so soon?"

Antonis rolls his eyes. "All I'm saying," he says, "Is that there are plenty of things to retaliate for. Like the invasion. The partitioning of our country. The thousands they killed. Shall I go on?"

"I'm not saying it's a good idea," says Elias.

"What do they have in mind?" asks Stelios.

"One-for-one," says Elias. "No: actually two for one. They kill one of ours, we kill two of theirs."

The idea hangs numbly in the air, mingled in the thick plumes of cigarette smoke that they poured into the corner of the room in the absence of food or water.

~~~~

It seemed a sad decline from their grandiose ambitions a year ago. They had come up with a number of ideas, most of them dramatic, foolish and impossible. The most developed one involved a return to Varosha, Famagusta. The plan: slip past the barbed wire of the ghost-city in the middle of the night, and raise the Greek flag from the roof of the tallest hotel. The *Filiki Eteria* would take credit for it, anonymously.

They had actually gotten quite far in their planning. The secret was that the special forces often sent reconnaissance teams across the border into Varosha at night. They just needed to get more information on how to go about it. Petros was tasked with this; he started asking around, quietly, posing hypothetical questions.

"Yes, I can tell you," said the soldier. He had been; a handful of times, only at night—they only went at night. The soldier pointed toward the flat, open fields that lay between their observation post and Famagusta. "There. Do you see it? A crease in the landscape."

Petros didn't see it; from there in Deryneia, the contours of the Dead Zone are barely rolling, brown dirt, thin grasses, patches of shrubs. Behind it, a line of scattered hotel high rises; behind them, the sea.

"Take the binoculars." The soldier handed them to him, and they looked again. Then he saw it—the small ridge the soldier was talking about. Not quite a ravine—barely a ditch, an indent. "Follow that," said the soldier, "and it takes you all the way to the city. He spat. "For what it's worth." The soldier made no secret of his impressions of Varosha: weeds, snakes, decay. Nothing worth fighting for.
~~~~

That is where you are wrong, Petros thought.

Slowly, the plan came together, and actually seemed feasible. They discussed routes, equipment, times of day. They gathered maps. They steeled their nerves.

And then, other events intervened.

Even as the *Filiki Eteria* came to the final stages of their plan to raise the Greek flag in Varosha, other events were unfolding. The bikers, someone said, were planning another protest.

The Cyprus Motorcycle Federation had organized two previous protests, a few years earlier, which lead to skirmishes with the U.N. and Turkish troops on the Green Line, but had barely registered a blip in the international press. This time, though, Hadjicostas, the president of the Federation, was determined that cameras would be on them. The idea: to ride from once-divided Berlin, to Cyprus, up to the Green Line, and attempt to cross—to show the world how Cyprus was the only partitioned land left in Europe.

It was a good plan: the boys of the *Filiki Eteria* had to admit that. Better, perhaps, than their own. "Who's going to notice a Greek flag in Famagusta?" Takis wondered.

They agreed to put their own plans on hold and to join the protest if they could, as their own "Friendly Society Contingent"—though as active-duty soldiers they wouldn't be able to start in Berlin; it would be challenging enough to get them to join in Cyprus.

It should have been electrifying: the idea of a thousand bikers pushing past the troops of the Green Line to finally reach home. But the idea just made Petros feel numb; he realized he didn't want to go. *Am I a coward?* he wondered. Or was it something else? What were the chances that the Turks would let them cross? And if they didn't cross, what then?

"The best we can hope for," said Antonis, "is to force the Turks to start another invasion. At least then we will know where we stand."

So those were the choices, Petros thought: empty gestures, or total defeat. Surely, there must be more to life than this?

~~~~

It is not so much the poor service alone that embitters them; it is the contrast with the fawning attention paid to the rich foreigners at the other table—Arabs, no less.

Even Antonis looks ready to make a scene.

"Okay," says Elias. "Maybe we should just leave then."

"Why should we?" Petros booms. "This is our country! Why should we not be given the same service as these foreigners?"

"The Turks took half the country," says Antonis. "And now we're losing the other half!"

Two of the men at the table glance over now. It could be discomfort, but Petros interprets the man's expression as impudence—every place these Arabs go, they think they are the natives. Petros considers punching that expression—whatever it means—off the man's face.

The waiter appears again; he must have heard the soldiers' comments, because now he doesn't even look up when Antonis practically shouts to get his attention, as if he and the table of Arabs are behind a glass wall.

Petros leaps up suddenly, grabs his chair and hurls it toward the back of the room, into a glass-framed print of the Rock of the Roman, the Birthplace of Aphrodite, with text that reads "Welcome to Cyprus, the Island of Love!" The glass shatters on
~~~~

impact, and the print falls to the ground. Antonis is up now, too, turning over the tables around him. Petros grabs the nearest chair, raises it over his head and smashes it into the ground until its legs snap off.

The waiter is yelling, grabbing his hair, calling for the owner now. "Police, police, call the police!"

The owner appears, shouting full force. "Stop, stop, you crazy fucking …"

Stelios stands, backs against the wall, pressing himself into it as if his impressively stocky body could disappear into it. Elias remains seated, legs crossed, grinning his old Cheshire grin.

The owner's eyes dart back and forth, from Petros to Antonis and back. Finally his plaintive gaze lands on Elias, appealing for him to intervene. Elias raises his hand and smiles, as if to say "by and by ..."

The owner hesitates and steps forward as if to grab Antonis. Antonis raises his fist; Petros lifts what is left of the chair over his head. "No no!" pleads the owner. "Stop!"

Antonis kicks the last table over.

The owner runs now, toward the kitchen. "I'm calling the police!"

"Okay kids!" says Stelios. "Time to go now!"

On the street: walking briskly, through the narrow alleys; a few seconds to dissolve into the lazy summer before the police arrive. "Where are you parked?" Elias asks.

Petros can't stand it anymore: he grabs Elias' shirt, shoves him against a wall, pushes his forearm across his cousin's throat. Their gazes meet; anguish in both their eyes. There are no longer any secrets between them. *I want to know, how it is that you have everything and I have nothing—not just Joanna but everything.*

Stelios and Antonis, a few paces ahead, spin around, the confusion on their faces another irritation to Petros. He pushes harder; Elias barely resists, pulls back on the arm just enough to keep breathing. "Not now!" he chokes.

Antonis grabs Petros from behind, yanking him away, too violently—they both stumble backward into the street, a car squeals to a halt, the driver shakes his fist at them like a cartoon.

Elias puts his hands up, conciliatory. "I don't know what you think you saw …" he says.

"There's no time for this!" Stelios shouts.

Petros surges forward. This time, Stelios surprises them all with a punch to the side of Petros head, knocking him into the street.

Petros scrambles, tries to get up, but his head is buzzing and Elias is already backing away.

"This isn't over!" Petros shouts, but he knows, of course, that it is.

They hear the police car pulling up at the end of the street, and they scatter.

Later, he finds himself smoking and walking alone along the waterfront, watching the pretty young couples, the happy families, and feels a choking bitterness in his throat. The seed of the impulse has grown, and is ready to flower. *I must go home,* he thinks.

Chapter Four

IMAGINE HIM NOW: ON LEAVE from the army again, sitting at the table in that second-floor apartment up from the beach in Protaras—the one that Uncle Michalis owns, the one that on still, humid nights is infested with bats.

He turns on the light by the bed and there they are—little black balls of fur, a half dozen or so, curled up on the walls, the ceiling, the doorframes. He tries to catch them—but only when there is someone there to impress, a foreign girl who wakes screaming in the bed beside him, screaming as if she has had a limb removed. He tries to catch them, but how? Find a bucket, slam it over them—and then what? The windows have no screens, and they come from that dark tree over there, the one with the black limbs just outside. What else lurks there?

Now he is chasing them and they dart around the room in a frenzy and that beautiful girl he brought home is still screaming. He picked her up not far away, at that ridiculous bar, the one with the light-show and giant dancing fountains. Who was she anyway? How did he of all people—he, with the crooked nose and pock-marked face, he who cannot catch a bat in a bucket—find such a creature, one of those perfect-shaped statuesque beauties who in a just world wouldn't give a second glance to a thousand better-looking men? It didn't happen often, not like with Elias. But this is Cyprus, the island of love, and he is a mysterious, dark, Greek man, and sometimes that is all that matters.

No; better to leave those damn bats alone; better yet don't even turn on the light, even if it means leaving that cute thing alone in the dark while you bang your shins on the stupid coffee table trying to get to the bathroom . . . (are you still drunk? Most likely, time to take an aspirin).

No—not then. Another night, alone.

Imagine him there, not giving a shit about bats, eating a loaf of bread, a loaf of perfectly fresh semolina that soaks up olive oil like a sponge. It is all he eats, sometimes, for days on end, olive oil and bread with some dates and raisins, a hunk of *halloumi* here and there, washing it down with the taste of ouzo or retsina. On this night, there are no bats and no strange women, only the soldier and his bread and olive oil and retsina and melancholy reflections as he thinks of her, the girl, the girl he has known and lost—the one he cannot live without.

He has just finished his evening pushups. On the table: a stack of loose-leaf papers and an old fountain pen—a light brown, marbled Waterman he had been told was given to his great grandfather for services rendered to the British colonial authority. He loves it not for its history but for what it provides him—an excuse to put his hand to the page and write things that have meaning and depth, though his subject is always the same.

Dear Joanna, what can I say to you? I am thinking of you every day.

It goes on like this. Year in, and year out, he puts his pen to the page and writes to her, writes long letters, even when he has nothing to say. When he was younger it was notes about school

—about what he was studying, who his teachers were, how his friends planned to travel the world, though he meant to go only as far as Athens. When he was younger he would write her, and then look at himself in the mirror, thin arms and pock-marked face—he believes she is disgusted by his face—and do pushups obsessively, a cigarette hanging from the corner of his mouth.

Later he wrote about the army; told her how the officers were incompetent, described to her what Famagusta looked like up close—as soldiers, they were allowed to get much closer than anyone else. He told her how he could still see the spirit of the place in the shells of its buildings, even though the buildings themselves would have to be torn down entirely if they ever returned.

He wrote to her about how much he wanted to return—how much he wanted to take her by the hand and walk her across the Dead Zone, past the barbed wire, to home. He told her how he imagined her, the smile on her face, when he walked her through the front door of the house—a new house, a house rebuilt, one that could be theirs. He described it: whitewashed, with blue wooden shutters, grape arbors and lemon trees, thick and overflowing with fruit. He told her that he dreamed of that moment on humid summer nights, and in his dream it was so real it was as if he could taste the salt air of the Famagusta shoreline; smell the bougainvillea, taste the fresh loquats straight from the tree. From there, they would walk hand in hand to the beach, five minutes away, splash in the water, and hold each other as dusk fell.

The first letter he wrote to her he burned, then rewrote and then burned again. After the tenth he stopped burning them, paperclipping them instead and sliding them into a nondescript manila envelope he kept at first by his bed, and later, among the few personal effects he was allowed to have when he joined the army. He liked to have them close by, so he could reread them often and wait for the moment when he received a sign of what to do.

He no longer believes he will actually send them; too much time has passed, and he has disappointed himself too often. At first he was sure it was only a matter of time before he had the courage to do it. At any given moment he had her address, and usually had written it out on an envelope. As he wrote each letter, he convinced himself that this one he would send; but always there was something wrong, something awkward, something stupid. A man knows when he will be rejected. Petros knew. And yet, once the cruel animal of desire has sunk its claws into a young man's mind, it only lets go when it chooses. What to do then? Take a risk and be told never, once and for all? Or find a way to pretend and hope and dream, that at some moment—the right moment—something would change, and he would have courage and courage would be rewarded?

The pen hovers over the paper. Something has changed.

Something has changed. This ritual—at first frightening, then comforting, is suddenly revealed to him for it's obvious absurdity.

Something has changed. It is Elias; the rumor, and now the reality, of him and her. For the first time he realizes there must be others—that she is not sitting and waiting for him, frozen in time, an ever-present possibility. There are others, there will be others. At the moment it is Elias, a misadventure that will end badly for her, as it always did for women who came into his sphere—unless it wouldn't, who knew? Perhaps they would be different together, perhaps Elias would suddenly decide she was 'the one' and reform himself and marry her. The shadow of this thought passes long enough for Petros to imagine it with a brief and terrifying vividness, and then to see himself on his motorcycle, morbidly hurtling over the side of one of the cliffs near Paphos at the Birthplace of Aphrodite.

The nib of the pen touches the paper. *Something has changed*, he writes. *This is the first letter I have written you that I truly mean to send.*

He finishes the letter; finishes and starts and finishes again. Then he finishes his retsina, and folds up the paper. Then he unfolds it, and lays it on the table; then he rises, goes to his little leather valise—another thing that once belonged to a long-lost relative—opens the outer sleeve and pulls out a stack of some thirty loose-leaf pages—what remains of the letters he has written her, a six-year, one-way narration of his life. He puts them underneath his most recent letter; then he pours himself another glass.

In spite of the late hour, it is still sweltering here; the thick humid fingers of the night wrap themselves around his torso and squeeze, as if to wring every drop of moisture from his body. Nevertheless his fingers are cold, his feet numb. Somewhere he has a large envelope. I should go to sleep, he thinks. I can find it in the morning. He goes to the bathroom, turns off the light, bangs his shins again and lies down on the lumpy mattress. In the darkness his head buzzes pleasantly, but he dreads the feeling; he knows it means he will sober up in the middle of the night and not be able to sleep for hours after. It's okay, he thinks.

He stands up and turns on the light. He must find the envelope, tomorrow is too late; tomorrow is a liar and a cheat, tomorrow always betrays you. How many times before he learns? You are not the same person in the morning; tomorrow the bravery of now is reduced to simpering cowardice and regret.

The envelope is where he thinks it is, the same outside pocket of the valise. He realizes that it is pre-addressed to her, correctly, to the little house in the little village in the mountains where she and his sister Anna live. All he has to do is put his stack of papers in—his life—and seal it. He looks at the pile of words; ridiculous words. He laughs at himself, puts his hand on his forehead. Time to burn them all, finally. He picks up the stack, walks to the small gas stove and picks up the box of matches to light it. A match ignites; he holds it in one hand, the stack of papers in the other; he brings the corner close. At long last, it will be over, he thinks. He can write her another note in the morning, a sane, sober note. He can always write another note.

Instead he blows out the match, turns off the stove, turns, turns again and walks back to the little table. He picks up the envelope, slides the letters in and seals it. There is a post box at the end of the street—a bright yellow cylinder that looks like a funny man with a strange-looking hat waiting for him. I will take it in the morning, he thinks. Then he thinks better of it and goes immediately.

The street is only slightly cooler than the apartment. No one is out; a peacefulness has settled on the area, though in the distance the sounds of club music still spills out in the night air. The yellow post box smiles at him. He doesn't hesitate, not at this point; the envelope slides in, and he turns toward home, a strange, surreal giddiness rising through his body. He has taken charge, everything will be different now.

He returns, turns off the light, bangs his shins again, lies down in bed, and dreams of bats on the walls.

Chapter Five

THE AIR BURNS HOT ON his face on the road to Platres, even at 65 kilometers per hour on a motor scooter; even in the foothills, elevation rising, where things usually begin to cool. Petros curses through his teeth. He still has hope that he can reach the girl before the letters do; before his humiliation is complete.

He is in a foul mood, having spent the morning yelling at the post office clerk in Paralimni, trying to get back the letters he had mailed two nights before. He began calmly, but when the weasel clerk with the ridiculous mustache refused to listen, Petros started shouting that he was a solider and it was a matter of national security, that he would have them all arrested, but the man just closed his window. "At least tell me when it will arrive," he pleaded. But by then the man refused to even acknowledge his presence. Petros started pounding on the counter, yelling that the man must tell him, he had to know. He only gave up when he heard the sound of the police radio as the car pulled up outside. Fortunately one of the cops was a friend's brother, someone Petros knew from high school. "Cut this *malakia* out," he said.

At the last minute as he was leaving, the post-office clerk took a kind of pity on him and shouted "anyway, they picked up the letters already on Saturday morning."

This Petros had not expected. It was Monday now. Chances were that it would take at least another day before his pile of naked confessions—his whole life—would be revealed. Petros felt at once strong and weak, heroic and exposed.

He couldn't believe it took him so long to decide to go. By the time he crawled, hung-over, out of bed on Saturday afternoon, the post office was closed.

Sunday morning he ran before the sun came up, nearly eight kilometers, more than usual. Even before dawn the air was already hot, and his skin and muscles burned, so he ran to the sea and threw his clothes off and swam to cool himself. There were girls on the beach, they saw him and pointed and giggled. "Come here!" he shouted, with a rare moment of bravado, but they just covered their eyes. He should have taken pride in his body, in the reactions he got—he didn't look like the skinny, sunken-chested boy he used to be—but no matter how strong he got, he still felt small and ugly.

Sunday he spent pacing the beach anxiously, still under the idiotic illusion that he would be able to convince them to give the letters back when the office opened again.

Only after the impossibility sunk in did he decide: he would go to her, recover the letters if at all possible before she saw them. If not, at least he would be there to see her reaction, face to face, though he didn't know what he would say.

Gradually, he rises more deeply into the mountains, the hairpins grow tighter. It is a ride that requires concentration and focus, which in turn calms him and makes him feel competent and brave. It is too dangerous to think much on these roads; dangerous to allow your feelings to distract you. His legs begin to feel sore as they grip the sides of the bike.

In the end, it is simple, he tells himself. Either the letters have reached her already or they haven't; if they have, either she has read them, or she hasn't. Three possibilities. In the first case, he will simply tell her he has come to see her—no use pretending that he is visiting his sister, who they both know is in the city. He will explain that she is about to receive a package, but that it is a mistake, that she should not open it, but save it for him and he will get it from her soon.

The second possibility: that the letters are there, but that she has not read them. In that case, he will take them from her, explain it was a mistake. She will be curious, and he will refuse to tell her anything, but she will insist, and he will say simply, I wrote you these letters because I was too much a coward to tell you in person: I am in love with you. But I don't need them now; I am here. She will be touched; she will fall into his arms, and that will be all.

The final possibility: that she has the letters and has read them. In this case, he can do nothing but hang his head and walk away in humiliation; there are sentiments in those letters that should never have been put on paper. It isn't just the terrible poetry, or the long and vivid descriptions of what he wants to do with her, to her—how he imagines the shape of her breasts, the curve of her behind, and how badly he wishes he could see her, feel her, for real, press himself against her—these are the least of the naked emotions the letters reveal. No, it is the other things—imaginary stories of them living their lives together, confessions of crying for her in the early mornings during basic training, of fantasizing about her when he meets other women in the clubs at Protaras and Ayia Napa.

~~~~
~~~~

She is a teacher, living then with his sister Anna, in a tiny village perched on a ravine, beyond Platres; a little village of almond trees and two-story stone houses, of wooden balconies and pungent odors—odors of sourdough and rising bread and over-ripe cheese—that spill forth from open doors along the narrow lanes; a little village where the sound of bells rings through the alleys, and the men drink coffee at the cafe that hangs over the river, while the women walk to church daily for Vespers; a little village where the giant brown eyes of children still stare at strangers in wonder as if they have never seen someone new in their lifetimes.

Anna is a teacher too; she has the better job, at least on paper, working in an elementary school in a larger town down the road. Joanna runs the one-room schoolhouse in the village —a school that administrators threaten to shut down every year for lack of attendance. Young teachers assigned to remote schools like these understand them for what they are: temporary dues-paying placements they will escape from as soon as a better opening arises. But Joanna loves it; the children in villages like these are the reason she has taken up teaching, the last link to lost innocence. "These children," she says, "give me hope."

The last time Petros visited Joanna and his sister it was early spring, the beginning of Lent, but it still felt like winter. They spent the afternoon drinking coffee and eating the *loukoumi* candies that are still permitted during the Lenten fast, chatting like dignified adults. As it grew dark a church bell sounded, echoing through the naked branches along the concrete walls, calling. They walked up the winding streets to where the red-tiled church rested peacefully above the village. On the way, they met villagers coming from all directions, most of whom knew and loved the girls, and smiled at them. By the time they arrived, the chants of the psalter were already crackling through the static of an old, giant speaker, which hung above the entrance to the church. The three of them squeezed inside, and took seats on opposite sides of the aisle, Petros on the right with the men, the girls opposite with the women. The air felt oily, the waxy smoke from the candles drifting all around and making his vision fuzzy; the icons of the bearded saints, which seemed glazed with it, stared from all directions.

He remembers glancing at her, across the aisle. Her face was stern as she gazed in front of her. He realized how small she was, her view just barely clearing the heads of the older women in front of her. He wondered what she was thinking; at the instant he looked over, she reached up to brush aside some of the floating strands of her light brown hair which had escaped the band in back.

He imagined himself walking with her one night, aimlessly, maybe through the streets of the village up the road. He imagined trying to convince her to have a couple of glasses of wine at dinner; then he might be able to steal a kiss from her and, out of the blue, ask her to marry him. He should have done it then; how much better it would have been.

Now he considers the possibility that she won't be there. School is out for the summer and it would be strange for a young teacher to stay alone in a small, out-of-the-way village, but Joanna is not like most teachers.

He had confirmed she was not in the city by calling his mother and asking to speak with Anna. There was no hope of subtlety.

"Hello, sister," he said. "You're back."

"I've been back for weeks," she said.

"Did Joanna come with you?"

"No," said Anna. "She stayed in the mountains. A good idea, too. It's terrible, the heat here." A pause. "Why do you ask?"

"I'm on leave," Petros continued. "I thinking of going to the mountains, so I thought I might pay her visit."

He could almost feel Anna's eyes rolling through the phone line. She knew how he felt; surely everyone did, by now. Or was it something more? The creeping cockroach of paranoia returned. If it was, after all, true what people said about Elias and Joanna, Anna would know—wouldn't she? And surely she would tell him, her brother?

"She might be at her uncle's house, in Platres."

He will have to see if she is there. He has been there before. He remembers visiting her there, the walk they took together in the woods, over the vine- and moss-covered old stone bridge that crosses Cold River and up to the waterfall. It was summer, but unlike most other rivers, the water here still flowed freely. "Come on," she said, and took him by the hand, pulling him onto a path to a place where the water tumbled over rocks above them, and the sunlight glittered on the droplets and they cooled themselves in the spray, their faces and hair growing damp in the mist. How long ago did that happen? he wonders.

~~~~

He has another reason to go to Platres—something to deliver.

Elias gave it to him that morning when Petros came to tell him where he was going. "Platres!" said Elias. "I need you to do something for me." He went into his room and came back
~~~~

with an open box. Not many things inside: a couple of icons, some worry beads, some papers, an old tourist map, a Greek flag. "I can't take it to them myself," he said. "I said I would, but I can't."

"What is it?" Petros asked.

"Personal effects."

Petros understood without another word. These were things that belonged to the soldier—the soldier who was killed on the Green Line. He was about to ask why Elias had them, but stopped himself; he knew that no explanation would be good enough. Elias had known the boy …

The request infuriated him. It had taken courage to decide to go to Joanna. It had taken courage to come tell Elias about it. He wasn't sure what he was hoping for, surprise, a reaction of some sort, but Elias had just managed to change the subject. And what could Petros say?

The thought of the boy sank into Petros, like a rock from his heart to his stomach. "Of course," he said quietly. "Where am I taking them? To his parents?"

"A relative, a great uncle, I think. I would take it myself," Elias said again. "But I can't." He sounded almost hoarse as he spoke.

What the hell was going on with Elias? He was always a mystery, yes, occasionally sullen and brooding, but not like this, not for this long. Yes, he had known the boy. But Elias knew everyone. Every time he saw Petros now, there was something else troubling him—first the fear that he had lost control of the *Filiki Eteria,* now the boy.

"Elia … tell me. What is it?" In spite of his anger and bitterness over whatever was going on with Joanna, Petros couldn't help worrying about his cousin.

Elias didn't respond for a long time. "Do you believe in God?" he asked suddenly.

"Of course," said Petros without hesitation. "Who doesn't believe in God?" The speed of his own answer surprised him.

"I believe in God," Elias said. "How can you not believe in God? How can you look over the cliffs at the *Petra tou Romiou* or through the pines at Troodos or at a beautiful village girl walking down the street in Agros or Kakopetria—her hips swaying … how can you look at these things and not believe in God?"

"Of course," Petros said, a little confused.

"But see, that's the thing," Elias continued. "That's what I don't understand. Most people who talk about God and Christ all the time say that this isn't real life, that real life comes after this one, that we'll all be judged… all that nonsense. They say the only reason this life matters is to prepare us for the next one. I mean that this life is just a rehearsal for that. Do you know what I mean?"

Petros nodded. "I'm not sure that's …"

"…But see, here's the thing," Elias continued, "I never believed that. I always thought it's about being alive now! Not being afraid of death—not because of some world to come but because being afraid of death is the thing that keeps you from living in this moment …"

"I agree with you," said Petros, "it's not about living for another world. But it's not all about hedonism either. It's about living for something more than yourself, about living for principles, because that's what makes life meaningful … ”

Elias gave Petros a sad smile. “That was the other thing I used to say. But now I'm not sure any of it's true.”

“So what are you saying, Elia? That you don't believe in God anymore?”

“On the contrary,” said Elias. “I believe in God more than ever. And for the first time, I fear Him.”

“Elia—what does this have to do with the boy? Are you suddenly afraid of dying?”

“No,” said Elias quietly. “I wish it had been me.”

Petros tried to get him to say more, to explain himself, but Elias refused to elaborate. Please just go, he said, and give the boy's family my condolences.

And so Petros just nodded, momentarily forgetting his mission to reach the girl, thinking instead about the boy and wondering what he must have been like, wondering if giving his family these things would give them any kind of solace and knowing that it would not.

~~~~

Platres: the second highest town in Cyprus—and the oldest and best resort, harkening to the summertimes of past ages when people climbed to escape the heat instead of moving toward it. From the road above, it's red-shingled roofs nestle themselves in the generous folds of the mountains amidst the wide-armed pines and blue-needled cedars, the peach and pear orchards. Nearby there are three- and four-story hotels—pleasingly symmetrical, in the old colonial style, with deep, soulful pitched roofs and wrought-iron balconies. Further back, in the
~~~~

mountains here, behind the high, hidden waterfalls, you hear the whisper of God.

But Petros comes from below, winding through treacherous curves on his motorbike. Around every blind corner, new vistas and sheer drops appear, sublime and terrifying; around every blind corner, a moment when death could appear in many forms.

In Platres at last, he pulls over to rest next to a long stone wall. An outdoor cafe sits above it; shrubs and plants and vines spill over the sides, hanging toward the road. Cars race by through the curves as if they are in Monaco, but the peace of the village is not disturbed; the people at the cafe are safe above, drinking lemonade and coffee and feeling the cool breeze and the dappled sun of a late summer afternoon in the mountains.

He decides to take some pictures. He takes his camera out of the bag, adjusts the lens and begins. It is too early in the day; the light, even here in the mountains, will be too harsh. An old woman shuffles by on the road, eying him suspiciously.

Her uncle's house lies down a narrow dirt lane, leading to a patio balcony overlooking a valley filled with grape vines. Petros knocks and introduces himself awkwardly, asks if Joanna is in. The uncle, a retired taverna owner, looks at him suspiciously, unsure who he is at first. Joanna isn't there, but a plain-looking middle-aged cousin with a sweet smile is; she is sure she has met Petros somewhere, and he is equally sure he never has.

Nevertheless, he finds himself compelled to sit for lunch and cake, just as they are compelled to invite him: the structural force of obligation exerting itself on both parties whether either wanted it or not. Petros wishes he were better at making up excuses for such situations. Time crawls by; each moment bringing the letters closer to Joanna.

They ask him what brought him to Platres, but he has no good answer. "I'm on leave," is all he can say.

The need to leave pulls at him—to get on the road, to get to Joanna, to find her, to explain himself—even though he has to make another stop, one he dreads even more.

Finally he excuses himself and heads down the road to find the dead soldier's family. He finds the boy's great aunt and uncle in a set-back cottage that hangs on the side of the mountain, behind a wrought-iron gate and a row of purple roses.

He rings the buzzer; the aunt appears first, an old woman with a sad, worn face, dressed in black, head covered in the old village style. Petros tells her who he is, what he has brought. She looks at Petros first uncomprehendingly, then suspiciously. Finally, she calls out for her husband. He comes around the corner from the back of the house, rising slowly up an outdoor staircase. He wears a Greek fisherman's cap, sports a thick, white, curled mustache.

Petros hands him the box; the old man puts it down and picks through it for a moment. Reaching the bottom, he runs wrinkled fingers over the fabric of the flag. "I bought this for him," he says.

Now the aunt begins to cry softly, and Petros is sorry. Was it necessary to open up these wounds? The pointlessness of the boy's death sits in his stomach like a rock. "My cousin Elias asked me to bring it here," Petros says. "I don't know why. Maybe so you can hold it for his mother and father?"

The old man nods. "Yes, yes," he says. He looks at Petros with gratitude. "You did the right thing," he says. He asks Petros how he knew their grand-nephew. Petros confesses that he didn't, but that Elias had. This rings a bell with the old man, who nods severely. "Yes … Elias," he says.

Long moments of awkward sadness. A few minutes of conversation, and finally, after the obligatory cake and black coffee, Petros is almost free; they are saying their goodbyes on the veranda when the uncle suddenly places Petros. "You are from Famagusta, right?"

"Yes," says Petros. "Well, my parents are."

"I knew your father," says the uncle.

Petros is surprised, and uncertain; he doubts that the old man remembers anything correctly. "You did?" he asks. "From where?"

"He … owned a hotel, with Michalis. We were neighbors. I had a hotel too. A smaller one." He smiles, his eyes misting. He gazes into the distance as if he can see it in front of him now. After a moment, his eyes come back into focus. "Your sister is a schoolteacher near here, isn't she?"

Petros nods, not quite believing the short chain of connection that seems to link all Cypriots to one another. "You're from Famagusta?" he asks. Is this a hint at why Elias' is so interested in the soldier? Another refugee from our hometown?

"Yes, yes," says the uncle, his eyes lighting up. "Of course. I knew your father well."

Petros nods. "Well … thank you," he says. "I really must be going." He knows that a quick departure borders on rudeness. "I have to see someone," he says apologetically.

"Who? Your sister?"

"Yes," says Petros. "Well, no—I'm going to visit her roommate, Joanna."

The old man smiles. "Of course," he says. "We are friends with their family as well." He seems to have a thought; he ponders for a moment, and continues. "Come here," he says, "Let me show you something."

Curses, thinks Petros. Will I never be done with this? He wants to hear what the uncle has to say, but every moment that passes brings the girl closer to opening the fateful envelope.

The uncle vanishes back into the house, and beckons Petros inside. "I'm going to show you something I haven't shown anyone in a very long time."

Petros enters again reluctantly; the uncle beckons him to sit in the living room. A few minutes later, he returns with a small, white photo album. "These are what I have to remember from those days."

Petros can barely contain his agitation, but he says nothing.

The old man opens the album and begins turning the pages. The photographs in the front of the book are mostly black and white, but as the pages turn, faded color snapshots begin to appear. The faces, Petros does not recognize, but the setting is familiar: it is Famagusta and what was slowly becoming the suburb of Varosha, from the old city walls to the beach and the beginnings of hotels; it is as if he can watch the city being built, one snapshot after another.

The old man stops abruptly: "Here is your father," he says. Petros is startled; he sees his father's face, which, through a glass darkly, could be his own. His father is wearing a fedora and leaning against a white-washed iron fence that enclosed the courtyard of a house that Petros could only assume was theirs. Standing next to them are his brother and sister—Petros' uncle Michalis and aunt Xanthe. In the photo, Xanthe looks dour, but Michalis is smiling, a half-smoked cigarette hanging from his mouth.

"This is our house?" Petros asks.

"Yes," says the old man, smiling. "I remember we used to meet there. We played cards." He pauses, and gets the same look in his eyes again—the look that old men get when the present moment turns translucent and falls away, and visions of happy memories appear, as if in a film. "I remember," he says, "Your father and Michalis worked long hours, taking care of their guests, but they always made time, after dark, to sit and drink. We talked, we talked; about movie stars and politics and what was going to happen with the damn Turks." The image of the happy memory fades suddenly, and he is back to bitterness. "If only we had known then ..." he adds.

The old man keeps turning the pages, then he hesitates, shakes his head, turns them again. "Here," he says finally. "Here is that girl's house. The other teacher who lives with your sister."

This photograph is more faded, its colors receded. Petros recognizes Joanna's mother Maria, struggling to smile, next to another woman he doesn't know. In this photograph they are inside the courtyard of Joanna's house standing in front of an outdoor table that is set with roast chicken and potatoes and salad and wine.

A little girl, barely older than a toddler, is standing on one of the chairs, leaning over the table as if she is about to dive in to the feast. Petros almost chokes as he recognizes her. "That's her," he says, incredulous. "That must be Joanna."

The uncle nods.

Petros reaches out and touches the photograph, tenderly. After several seconds of silence, he speaks. "Can I ... can I have this photograph?" he asked. He almost continues; almost promises that he will return it, or at least, bring it to Joanna, the girl who is now a woman. But he doesn't; instead he lets the question hang in the air, full of strangeness.

The uncle sits back and cocks his head to one side, as if to size up the young soldier. Behind the shadow of the old man's gray beard and his weary eyelids, his eyes shine bright and clear; his well-earned wrinkles are deep, full of life. He looks as if he is about to ask why, and then he stops. "Take it," he says. "And the other one too, of your house. I don't need them."

Petros thanks him, gets ready to leave again.

"Wait," says the uncle. The box of effects that had belonged to the man's nephew is still sitting on the floor next to the table. The uncle starts leafing through again. "Most of this, we don't need," he says.

He pulls out a beaten-up tourist map of greater Famagusta, including Varosha. "I gave him this too." The old man unfolds it and Petros sees: it is a map of the city, the city he would have been born in, the city he and Joanna would have grown up together in, if things had been different. The map is tattered, its seams cracked and tearing from too many hurried mis-folds over the years. In a glance, Petros sees its story, a hurried purchase at a kiosk somewhere, the frustrated turning and folding of the navigator in the passenger seat, the careless shoving into a glove compartment.

"This is all of Famagusta," says the old man, "and this part," he draws an imaginary line with the side of his hand and gestures to the south side of the map, "is Varosha. I can show you your house. Here is where we lived, just off of Alexander the Great." He points to a spot near a roundabout. The spot is marked, circled in pen. "He asked me for the map, you know. It was only a month or two before he was killed, God save his soul."

Petros nods, his expression numb, but his eyes transfixed. He feels suddenly as if he does know the boy, as if he can feel the boy's presence in the room with them; as if he knows the boy better than anyone living, even though they never met when he was alive.

"And here is where your family lived," says the uncle suddenly. He motions to a spot just around a corner on Victor Hugo street. "And down here, the girl's family."

"Joanna?" Petros asks.

The old man looks proudly at Petros and smiles. "Can you believe I remember?" He taps his temple. "The old brain is still working!"

Petros' heart beats faster, and his mouth feels dry, but not from rage or bitterness. It is, rather, as if, by looking at this map and the photographs—just knowing of their existence—some new possibility opens up for his life. He shudders, as if the great abstraction of the invasion—the great abstraction that hangs over his life—has suddenly become concrete and is tapping him on the shoulder. He opens his mouth to speak, but feels the words catch in his throat. Gather your courage, he thinks.

"Take it," says the old man.

"You don't need it?" Petros says stupidly.

The man laughs. "Why would I need it? To find the way back to my house after all these years?"

Petros picks up the map gingerly. "If we ever go back," he says, "I will take you there myself."

"Take the flag too." He reaches into the box and pulls out the blue-and-white-striped cloth, still folded. "This, he got from Greece when he was little," said the man. "Probably from some tourist shop, but it was important to him. He planned to raise it in Famagusta if we ever went back."

Just like us, thinks Petros. He understands now, that there was much more to the boy than the papers let on; much more that Elias wasn't telling him.

"Take it if you'd like it," says the old man. "Take it all, if you want it. May it have meaning for you."

Petros picks up the flag and the map, walks to the front door. "Thank you," he says.

The old man nods and pats Petros kindly on the back. "To the good, my boy."

Petros smiles, and glances back to say goodbye to the aunt, and sees that she is crying. By the time he reaches his motor scooter and stashes the map and the flag in his saddlebags, his own eyes are misting as well and his whole body is quivering. It takes all of his willpower to start the motor scooter and get back on the road. *Joanna, I am coming …*

Chapter Six

Back on his motor scooter: he continues up the mountain. The closer he gets, the more it seems as though this is the end —that a long line leads finally to this moment, after which all obligations and possibilities are cancelled. He realizes he has no idea what is going to happen. He expects rejection, of course. But what form will it take? He has been treading water for so long that the possibility of change seems unimaginable.

It occurs to him suddenly that he has not actually confessed his love for her since that awkward moment in Protaras years earlier; he has assumed that she, like everyone else, knows how he feels about her. But what if he is wrong?

She is waiting for him when he arrives, standing in the courtyard, leaning on the doorframe wistfully, wearing a thin-strapped, deep-plunging red sundress that falls to just above her knees. The exposed arc of her cleavage makes his hands tingle. Her thick, light-brown hair is clipped, piled up on top of her head, revealing the surprisingly long line of her neck—that same neck he used to stare at from the back seat of the car when Yiorgos and Eleni would drive them to the beach. Dangling earrings, a hint of lipstick. A provocative look except for her eyes—shy blue eyes, hiding behind small-framed turtleshell glasses.

Petros turns the bike off, and is suddenly overwhelmed by the natural silence of the world. “Good afternoon,” he says. The sound of his own, reverberating voice surprises him with its depth and resonance.

She smiles sweetly—as she always does—but with what he detects as a hint of sadness. “I’ve been expecting you,” she says. “Come in.”

He finds he is gulping for air. He hadn’t imagined it like this; he thought he would have time to catch his breath from the ride, prepare, think more about what he would say. Some pounding thing in his chest rises to his throat as if to asphyxiate him from within.

He walks toward her, gets close. She gestures him inside. He slides past her, his arm brushing against the exposed skin of her shoulder; his elbow brushing for an instant against her breast. He trembles, tries to avert his gaze by looking around the apartment.

It has been at least a year since he visited, and everything seems unfamiliar again.

The room to the left of the entrance is his sister's. A dozen posters of famous Greek and Cypriot singers—Yiorgos Dalaras, Haris Alexiou, Alkinos Ioannides—line the walls, along with a picture-board, covered with family photographs.

The living room is more ambiguous; he can’t say what belongs to whom. Stern icons cover the walls, and an odd variety of other images are mixed in: children's drawings of stick-figures, green-scribbled leaves of a giant tree, cheap magazine photograph cut-outs, including one of a little blonde boy blowing a dandelion, and one just a solid mass of daisies with a caption at the bottom in English which reads, “Believe in yourself, and everything is possible." On the wall: a strange image of a little girl with her head on a pillow, crying.

Two images at the bottom jump out. The first is a map of Cyprus with a scorpion crawling down on it from the top, over a mass of dripping blood, a Turkish star and crescent on its back. At the bottom, the words read, "When will there be justice?" Just below it, a crinkled imitation of old parchment—words that look as though they are written in blood: "Kyrenia or Death."

All of these images used to seem terribly sentimental to him; but now he feels as if there is something almost sinister about the collection. He feels an urge to rip them from the walls.

"You came," she says. "Have a seat. I was just making coffee."

Petros ignores her and follows her into the kitchen, but she doesn't hear him. For a couple of minutes he watches her back as she passes the little copper kettle back and forth over the stove's flame. She is wearing low-heeled black sandals. The muscles in her calves make his lungs ache.

"You got my letter," he says. It has taken him this long to notice it: his envelope, open on the kitchen table.

"Yes."

"Did you read it? I …"

"Stop."

He stops short, stung.

"You don't need to say more," she says.

"I had to see you," he says. "But I can go."

"Don't go. I didn't say I wanted you to go."

She motions him back to the living room to sit, and he does. She brings him a coffee and a *boureki*.

Then she sits next to him and sets her hand tenderly in his. He looks up into her soft eyes; a few hairs have come loose and float in front of her face. She is close enough to smell, a nice perfume, delicately applied; but also a hint of alcohol—wine, he thinks—on her breath. Her scent runs like fingers through his body and he feels the most visceral and painful nostalgia for some place he has never been, an experience that he will never own. It is cruel and terrifying for her to reject him like this.

"What do you want?" he asks.

Surprisingly she smiles at this. "I wish I knew," she says.

"I know what I want," he says.

She leans back to the edge of the seat, her mouth sardonic but her eyes glowing. "And what is that?"

"Do you have to ask?"

"And, what makes you think …"

"Think what?"

"That you can have me?" Her ocean blue eyes flirt with him.

He can't believe her cruelty—he has expected rejection, but not for her to toy with him this way. A disgusting bile mixed of anger, embarrassment, hurt, and bitterness rises in his throat.

"Nothing," he says quickly. He takes a breath, and sees suddenly, at long last, that there is nothing to lose. "There is no reason other than that I want you. I have wanted you since the moment I first saw you, even if it was before I could speak. No —I have wanted you since before that. I have wanted you for a hundred years—for a hundred thousand years. I have wanted you since before the stars were born. You are the sun, and I have been circling you, circling, coming back, again and again, I will always come back!" He surprises himself by shouting. "But," he adds, more quietly, "you know this. So why …" he takes one last, long look at her, sitting there in the too-revealing dress, pretending to be shy, "why are you torturing me like this?"

He has said this all and more in his letters, but she is stunned by his confession-outburst nonetheless, but only for a second. Then she surges forward, pushing her open mouth hard onto his.

It's an awkward, out-of-control kiss, a tangle of tongues and lips and banging teeth. Petros is taken aback for an instant, and then he regains control, grabbing her face with both hands to hold her still; he pulls back for a second, and then presses his lips to hers—now he kisses her—slowly, gently. The agitated tension in her body melts, and the whole room seems to sigh with relief and calm and surprised excitement. He takes a few minutes like this, exploring her mouth tentatively, and then with confidence, pushing aside the terrified voice that chatters nonsense in his head, as if it could figure out what this all means.

Now he grabs her dress at the center of her cleavage and drags her toward him violently; still holding the side of her head with his left hand, then he puts his hand over her tender, full breast. Startled, she grabs the back of his hand. "So fast … "

He doesn't stop, now moving inside her dress to run his fingers along her breast as he continues to kiss her, running his tongue along her ear, along her neck…she shudders, and then suddenly pulls away and stands up and steps back from the couch to face him.

Her hair is pulled out, a wild mess on all sides, her face and breasts are flushed her glasses somehow still on, he can see her trembling. She looks alight, enflamed and confused, her face bewildered as if she is trying to remember something important, or make a decision but is too altered to do so. But this too, only lasts a moment.

Then she rises and steps back, a faint click of her leather heel on the floor; she reaches up, unhooks the back of her dress and pulls it up over her head, tosses it into the corner of the room and stands naked before him, like a fertility goddess, a collection of perfect curves—thighs, hips, breasts—fully mature, fully woman.

At the same time, she suddenly seems younger as well. She smiles at him shyly; a girl trying to impress an older lover. "Well," she says quietly, "am I what you imagined?"

He cannot believe what is happening, his heart is racing, he feels dizzy, is thankful to be sitting down. He speaks. "Yes," he says. "You are as I have always imagined you."

She looks surprised, and then pleased. She takes a step closer to him, and then another, as his knuckles turn white from gripping the arms of the chair. It's the first time he's ever seen a woman, or it might as well be, there have been no others like this.

She stands closer, close enough to touch, but he doesn't move. "Are you surprised?" she asks.

"Yes." His answer, barely audible, croaks out like a frog.

She reaches out and runs the back of her fingers along his cheek; they make a soft scratching sound against his unshaven face. Her hands are her most mature feature—petite, but not too thin; carefully manicured but with the faint wrinkles that seem somehow both too old and too rich for the rest of her;

they are the hands of a gorgeous, middle-aged socialite, her most intimidating feature.

He is not surprised; he is shocked. The erotic charge she has built up could blow out the walls.

Finally she bends forward and kisses him again; his hands release the chair and rise as if he is under arrest; she catches his fingers in her own. She pulls him to his feet and leads him toward the bedroom. In a moment they are both naked, pressed together, bound up; in a moment they are moving together like wild animals. A cluster of sensations: his hand on the curve of her hip, the feeling of the sole of her foot on the back of his calf, the look of her half-open mouth, bright-red lips, her flushed breasts—suddenly she grasps him and rolls him over, almost throwing them both off the bed. Her nails dig into his chest, an expression something like fury on her face as she screams. And then it is over, they are lying next to each other, skin touching, damp with sweat, not caring.

"That was unexpected," he says.

He looks at her. From what has just happened, he expects to see her smile, and she does, but not before a wave of something else passes over her face—something like regret, fear or shame—and Petros is abruptly dragged back into his inner labyrinth of doubt. "Are you okay?" he asks, dreading the answer. A terrible longing takes him; terrible how one desolate glance can destroy the most perfect of moments.

He touches her face, terrified, seeing now that he has cut her strange soul loose, ripped it from whatever tenuous fibers held it in place and left it floating, tiny and adrift in some foreign sea neither of them know how to get home from.

"Yes," she says. She doesn't look at him.

Fifteen minutes later he gets up and brings her a lemonade from the homemade lemon squash in the refrigerator. They are both dripping with sweat; it is August and the house has no air conditioning. The shutters are closed, pencil-thin bands of sunlight line up along the floor.

She takes the lemonade, and drinks it quietly, not making eye contact. He sees traces of shame in the corners of her eyes. He feels ill, curses himself. It was not supposed to be like this. This woman, the love of his life. He was supposed to take her to dinner, laugh with her, tell her stories, share his dreams and aspirations. Convince her that he is a man who is worthy of her.

And who is she? Not the innocent girl he expected, and whatever innocence could have remained he has just destroyed. Unsure of what to do, he lies down next to her. At some point, they fall asleep.

Later he wakes up and looks over and sees her crying quietly. She sees he is awake too late to turn away. Suddenly she looks angry. "Have you lost respect for me?" she asks.

"No!" he says, not sure if he is lying.

"I am not who you think I am," she says quietly. She wipes her eyes.

He is afraid to respond. After a few moments she leaves to take a bath. He wants to come with her, to tell her everything is okay, even though he has no idea if it is. Midday has passed; now is the long, slow creep of evening, until the sun goes down and the earth cools, finally.

She returns from the bathroom drying her hair with a towel, wearing a dark blue silk robe that drapes itself expertly on her body, hiding and revealing every curve. She smells elegant, he thinks; they could be at a four-star hotel. He is entranced and unsettled. Where is the dour, innocent village girl he and Elias had talked about?

"Do you want some dinner?" he asks. He realizes he is hungry, famished—he hasn't had a full breakfast or lunch; or even much dinner the night before. In fact, he can't remember the last time he ate a full meal. The thought makes him feel weak. He thinks he has enough money to take her out; he starts reaching around for his pants and wallet.

"I can make something here," she says.

"I want to take you out," he says.

"No." Her answer is definitive. It makes him feel badly; this is not how the romance is supposed to happen. He is supposed to take her out, seduce her. She is supposed to be entranced but reluctant, excited but difficult. He realizes he has no idea what has just happened.

~~~~

It is still too hot to cook, so she makes a salad, fries some cheese, cuts some bread. They eat and talk, both of them slowly beginning to relax. Afterword he cuts a watermelon and they eat and laugh like children again.

Later, they go outside, sit on the veranda. Night has fallen at long last; a calming summer darkness filled with the sound of cicadas. Petros feels the cool mountain air on his chest, feels suddenly revived, full of conviction and happiness.

For a long time they sit, and smoke and sip *zivania*; for a long time they sit and talk and breathe and smell the mountain air. He thinks of showing her the photographs the old man had given him: they are in the saddlebag of his motor scooter along with the one he took of her on the beach in Ayia Napa.
~~~~

"So," she says, "You came from ... where are you stationed now?"

"Deryneia," he says. "But I came up through Platres." He hesitates to tell her that he went by her uncle's house, so he explains instead about bringing back the personal effects of the boy who was killed. "Such a waste," says Petros. "A meaningless life."

"A meaningless life? How can you say that?"

"What was the point of it?" Petros asks, "To die just to give ungrateful Turks a bottle of brandy?"

She seems offended. "Maybe a mistake," she says. "A senseless death. But you said 'meaningless life.'"

"That's what I meant," says Petros. "Look: the way we live, the way we die, what matters is what we believe in, what we stand up for. What was that boy standing up for? And if he dies that way, how meaningful was his life?"

"How can you say that! Think of the love his family had for him ... how can you say his life was meaningless?"

"The love of family ... okay, it is important to us. But in the big story of history does it really matter? Think about the people who have changed the world. People who live by principles. Kolokotronis, Grivas ... who remembers anything about their personal lives? All that matters is what they were willing to live for, to fight for, to die for! Think about Byron, the poet. A private life full of scandals! And yet he is hero to the British and even more to us because he was willing to die for Greece!" Petros realizes that what he is saying is absurd—coming from him, anyway, a man who just declared eternal love for a woman as if it were more important than anything in the world.

Joanna is shaking her head now. "No," she says. "I used to believe something like what you're saying. But I see now that it's not true. The only thing that matters is *us*. The people we love, the connections we make. In a thousand years no one will remember any of us. The only thing that will have mattered will be the people we loved. You men … you always want to make the wrong things seem important. And you convince us of it, too."

"So what then?" Petros asks. "Forget about our principles? I tell you this, nothing will ever happen in Cyprus if people don't stand up for it. And how we die … that's the only thing that tells us anything important about how we lived." He is ashamed of his words as he speaks them, they remind him of what happened at the motorcycle protest last year, his cowardice. And what is worse, he knows that she knows, that she remembers. But for some reason, he can't stop himself.

"But these days," he adds, "it feels like we all live in some kind of opium dream. They push so-called 'prosperity' on us to make us forget what they've done to us. It makes us think real things are not real, not important, and they force this pseudo-reality down our throats…"

"Pseudo-reality?" asks Joanna. "What is real then?"

"I don't know if I can even say," says Petros. "I'm drugged too, like everyone else." He thinks about his envy of Elias and his father, the hotels they own, their easy prosperity. He continues. "What are the real things? Love. God. country. Being Greek, you know? The Greekness you feel in your blood and bones. Think about it. We're Greek. We should be a part of Greece. People used to talk about it, *Enosis,* union. Everyone believed in it. Now it's a scandal to mention the idea."

"So that's it?" she says. "Being Greek?'

"Not just that," he says. "Little things, too. The smell of real food. The feeling of a woman's body in your hands." (At this, Joanna smiles, just for a second. Petros laughs at himself.) "Even when a man just looks at a beautiful woman from across the room, it makes him feel alive! The smell of real things. The smell of incense. The taste of fruit from your uncle's orchard …"

She nods. "Yes," she says, "Of course those things. But does that mean you have to sacrifice your life …"

"I'm surprised," he says with a smile. "I thought you were a patriot." He is teasing her, but is also genuinely confused. Isn't this the girl who loved her country and hated the Turks more than anyone?

"A patriot?" she says. "I used to say I would do anything for my country, that I would give my life for it, that I wished I could fight and die for it, like the men. But now? Now I only say I would give my life to see my father one last time."

This sadness again, Petros thinks. He decides it's time to change the subject. "Here," he says, "I have something I want to show you."

He stands up and heads for his motorbike, pulls his photographs and the map out of the saddlebag. "Here," he says. "Pictures from Famagusta. I have one of you and your family."

She puts her hand to her mouth. "Where did you get these?" she asks.

"From the uncle," he says. "The uncle of the boy. He knew our families. He showed them to me. I thought you might want this one." He hands her the picture of her mother and aunt, with herself as a toddler, about to fall off of the chair. She takes it and squints at it for a long time, long enough that he starts to wonder what she is hoping to find in it.

And then she starts to cry.

"What is it?" he asks desperately. Everything he says or does makes the girl cry.

"Nothing," she says. "Thank you." Tears run down her face. "I … when you said you had photographs, I was hoping one of them would be of my father. You know," she says, "when we had to leave Famagusta, we had to leave everything, all of the pictures in their frames, hanging on the walls. And now, I don't have a photograph of my father. Not even a photograph."

They sit and talk some more, and drink more. Always the topic comes back again to childhood—the fable of Joanna's childhood. He has heard it before, but the moral seems to change, as the years go by; he never tires of it.

Those images from childhood—were they real? Her father riding on a motorcycle; taking her in his arms. Going to the beach, he is holding her, rushing into the waves, and she is almost knocked over and then they run back. Would those images mean so much if he weren't gone?

"I try so desperately to remember his face, but I can't. And we haven't even got a photograph. Sometimes," she says, "when I am tired of hating them, I think about writing a letter to the Turks. I imagine giving them my address, asking them to go, find my house, and send me back a photograph." She starts to cry again. "I can see it—the place on the mantle where we kept the photographs. It is as clear as glass. How can I remember that but I can't remember his face?"

~~~~
~~~~

Tell me, he says.

I remember how it was, she says. That day when the air-raid sirens came, and she was there. As a child you hear only whispered hints and rumors that bad things can happen.

They were living in Varosha, that fashionable suburb of Famagusta.

Their house had a white-washed terrace with smooth, marble floors and a metal table, small wooden chairs and a grape vine arbor that hung thick with bunches of fruit. She remembers this, the giant bunches of grapes that were bigger than her head, and she wanted them so badly but couldn't have them, and was crying about it.

She remembers also the old safe with a combination lock; she remembers, vaguely and in snatches, how her father used to sit in front of it and stare, a drink in his hands. She remembers how the combination was taped to the back of a bookshelf, and everyone knew where it was, and yet he stared at it as if he would never get inside.

Mama, she asked in later years, what was it about that safe? What was in there that made Papa so sad? Don't ask questions, Mama said. Don't ask questions about things that should not be questioned. Don't ask questions about things that must be forgotten.

Over the years, she had grown numb to her mother's emotional churning. Unlike her aunts and uncles, Joanna had come to believe that the only rational reaction to her mother's periodic explosions and deep, reverberating sadness was to pretend it didn't exist. But she couldn't help asking questions. Even if her mother was sad, Joanna still found her refusal to say anything about so many topics strange. In Cyprus, even people who said they wanted to forget talked; even people who had things to be ashamed of eventually spoke of them. Other members of Joanna's family seemed even more reluctant, as if honoring an unspoken promise to her. Maria, they said, had gone through times that were better forgotten; more tough times than most.

Another memory: she is looking up at her father, and he is smiling at her, telling her he has to go, assuring her he will be back in a few days. He has a rifle on his back and is wearing military fatigues—anyway, that is what she remembers. And in her memory, she is crying again, asking him not to go, pounding her hands as if her tantrum could keep him there; through her tears she can see her mother crying beside her.

Don't go, she said. I have to go, *agape*, he said.

Will you be back before it's time for bed? she asked. Maybe, he said, probably not. But he would see her in a day or two.

But who will kiss me goodnight? This was their ritual—Mama would bathe her, and Papa would walk her up the narrow stairs, tuck her in and read to her. On the days when he was late from the office, she made her mother promise to send him up, and she did. He always came and kissed her. She knew he did, because she would wake up, even if they told her she had been sound asleep—she would wake up but not open her eyes.

I will kiss you from wherever I am, he said.

Now she was crying because her mother was crying. Where are you going, she asked. Her mother had already explained—there were some bad soldiers who had come to Cyprus and Papa was going to stop them. What if they shoot you? she asked, but never got an answer.

The next image, her arms around his neck, refusing to let go, tears running down her face, screaming. Then someone was pulling her off of him, but she was holding his neck fiercely, so fiercely, until he reached up, irritated, to pry her fingers apart. For an instant he was angry with her—a look she saw in his eyes, that she never forgot, and then he smiled and turned to leave quickly, swinging the little wrought-iron gate shut behind him, while she clung to her mother and sobbed.

Every day, she asked when he would return. Soon, they said, until she started complaining. You said it would be a couple of days, but it has been days and days and days.

And then the bombs fell—she remembered this too, the first one landing like distant thunder, and then like a drumbeat that punched you in the chest. Then the terrible whistling sound.

We have to go, her mother shouted. Now in the car, they had nothing but a tiny bag of clothes. Her mother at the wheel, a strange sight, it was her father who usually drove. The desperate driving, sudden turns, no seat-belts, Joanna and her brother sliding back and forth in the back seat, and the unmistakable, terrible, terrible whistling that always ended with a thump, rumble, and then a cracking-splintering sound of shattered glass, and finally sirens and screaming. And the jet planes screaming above the sound of screaming. But how will Papa find us, she cried? How will he find us if we leave?

She never fell asleep alone after that. Even when she finally grew up and lived with Anna or one of the other teachers, someone would stay up with her until she drifted off on the couch. Then they would take her arm and walk her to bed, and she would keep her eyes closed to stay asleep.

"Why did he leave us?" she asks Petros. "We say he was a hero. But why him? Why did he go when he could have stayed? Why did he go, when it didn't matter anyway?"

Christmas came, and then Easter, and then another Christmas and another Easter, and another and another. Each year the holidays were a little different, and each year they were the same. Each year they fasted and took communion, and she would pray fervently.

There were the years with Anna and Petros and their family, and then the years in Salonica, where her aunt Paula lived, and all the children talked strangely and made fun of the way she spoke Greek. There were the years when her mother took her to the footsteps of the Holy Mountain, to the point where only the men were allowed to cross. Papa, she thought, how will you find us when we are so far away?

What was it like growing up without a father? Like this: the kind of thing you would perhaps not notice so much if you weren't reminded of it always. But every time you turn around, there it is—the giant Turkish flag on the side of the mountain. There it is, in school, the class lectures about how terrible the Turks were, and the invasion, and the knowing looks cast in your direction. The other children pity you—those who have not lost their own fathers. One day you ask why your brother is not going to the army like the other boys and someone explains that he is draft exempt because his father died in the invasion. Your life, not your own—your life belonging to something bigger, your life itself just a symbol.

At the same time, there are no photographs. Her father's family was from Varosha; her mother from Kyrenia. All the family homes, every scrap of memory behind enemy lines.

She was four when it happened, just old enough to remember; but young enough to forget so much. Young enough that no memory is solid; memories shift, formless, dreamlike, but cruel nonetheless. Memories—at times she does not trust them. People would say, "do you remember when . . ." and plant an image in her brain where it would grow and become real, until she was even unsure which memories were her own.

All her life she felt sorry for herself, and then she got tired of feeling sorry for herself. When she was sixteen she swore she put it all behind herself, throwing away her old clothes and putting up pictures of European and American rock stars—as if dancing in her room with Anna could make it go away. But the gloom and self-pity always came back again anyway, until it was time to realize she would never be the carefree person she thought she should be.

People told her she was lucky; lucky to be alive, to have a loving family and friends; lucky to be smart and beautiful. She was beautiful, all the boys wanted to talk to her, until she started going on again about the war and occupied Cyprus. Some listened politely, for a while; some not at all.

Petros listens, and listens and listens, soaking up the stories, wondering briefly if she is trying to push him away, or if this is a test.

"Someday you must go back for me," she says. "Bring me something. No ... don't answer, but if you could, would you go back? To your house, to see it? See if there is anything left?"

His heart races again. I would do anything for you, he thinks, but by then she has moved on, wistfully.

"Not even a photograph," she says.

~~~~

These are the things she tells him—secret things, things so close to her heart they feel more basic than breathing.

Other things, she does not.

She does not tell him about Elias; about how he was just there, two nights earlier, slipping into and out of her house, like a thief in the night—the way he always slips into and out of her life. She does not tell Petros that this is why she stays alone in the mountains all summer—not from some sentimental love of peasant children, but to lie in wait for the promise of a quiet moment with her secret lover.

She does not tell him how she and Elias fought that night: she, the foolish village girl, demanding that he explain himself, make his intentions known. He, the wry scoundrel with his crooked smile, giving her speeches about how he is wrong for her. How she needs a quiet boy, someone who will always be there for her and look after her, someone with a good, boring job who takes her to church and gives her the quiet family she's always wanted. Speeches about how she needs someone who helps her accept her loss, not someone who reminds her of how bad it was. Speeches about how she would hate him someday, how he would hurt her just by being himself. So, why, she asked, through her tears, do you keep coming back again and again? You are a fragile wildflower, he said, of such delicate, perfect beauty—what man could ever be strong enough to look away?

She does not tell Petros how she and Elias met the second time, when she came back from Salonica: how she, a still-naive young woman, saw him at a party after a nationalist youth group rally, and didn't remember him, but was transfixed by
~~~~

his beauty. How Elias looked across the room and caught her gaze; how he strode across the floor, walked up to her without speaking and brought his soft lips to her mouth, a long, slow kiss, before he pulled back and said, "Hello, I am Elias."

She does not tell him how Elias sent her sweet postcards from all the islands, how he bought her the most delicate lace in Rhodes, a bottle of the best home made *tsikoudia* she had ever tasted from Crete (I don't drink, she said, You must drink this, he said, and then seduced her.)

She does not tell him of the first time, when they lay together in the narrow bed, and he convinced her there was nothing wrong with taking off her clothes; how he kissed her breasts, her stomach, her thighs, inside her inner folds, places she didn't know existed—kissed her in ways she never imagined, made her feel things she never thought possible.

She does not tell Petros how already she has been almost engaged twice to other men—nice boys, gentle souls, proper boys who would have treated her right. Both times Elias ruined it, showing up at her doorstep like a beggar, unshaven and wearing that leather jacket that reminded her of so many things.

She does not tell him how he made her feel the day of the motorcycle protest, after the government pressured the president of the motorcycle federation to cancel the event, and a group of bikers went anyway, Elias among them. Damn him for that, for being one of those muscular, courageous biker-boys, not afraid to face death for his country—not like the well-groomed young men her aunts and cousins were always trying to find for her. Damn him for being both brave and smart.

She does not tell Petros how she felt when she received his letters (amused, pitying, surprised, even though she knew Petros had always loved her). She does not tell him how receiving them awakened her to a new possibility—how the idea dawned on her that in one night she could finally damage Elias, as he had damaged her, again and again.

She doesn't tell Petros that she hadn't intended for things to go so far, that she thought she would just kiss him and send him on his way, but that his fervent determination had taken her by surprise and woken something in her, and she realized he was no longer a boy.

Had she had the time, she might have read more of his letters; had she done that, she might of grasped the depth, the tenacity, the persistence, the determination and ferocity of his love for her. Had she done that, she might have been more careful; she might have thought twice. But she didn't finish reading them—Anna had called her before she had the chance—and there had been no time to spare. And then it happened, and now she realizes what she has done—her best friend's brother; her lover's best friend.

Poor Petros, she thinks. And yet, wasn't she giving the boy exactly what he had dreamed of and longed for? If only for an evening or two?

~~~~

Now it is late. An uncomfortable pause has fallen over the conversation, and both of them are slipping into a dizzy haze of alcohol and exhaustion.

"I should go," he says.

"Go? Where?"
~~~~

She's correct, by now he is too drunk to go anywhere, and anywhere he could go is too far away.

He glances at her; her eyes are half-shut, her head tilted back as if staring at the stars. "Let me take you in," he says, and he takes her hand and leads her inside to her bed. She lies down; unsure what to do, he lies next to her, tries to put his arm across her. She grunts angrily and pushes him away. He is unsure now what to do, if he should say here, with her in bed, or move to the couch or sleep on the floor or leave.

"I'm going," he says finally.

"Going? Can't you stay a bit?"

He falls asleep then, but awakens at three or four in the morning with a start, a feeling of fierce urgency. He knows he can't leave, so he lies awake, staring at the faint outline of house shutters, listening to the village roosters crowing until the dawn breaks at long last.

~~~~

By the time she opens her eyes, after first light, he is already doing his morning pushups. She turns in bed and sees him on the other side of the room, moving up and down, his breath heavy but quiet.

She gets up without a word, washes and dresses without looking at him, unwilling to even ask herself if she is ashamed or confused or frightened or filled with some other unnamable emotion.

"Breakfast?" she mutters. They drink coffee and eat eggs and toast and jam and more *halloumi* without a word. She tries not to look at him, and feels lonelier than she has ever felt in her entire life.

Finally, she speaks. "I am not who you think I am."
~~~~

"Who do you think you are?" he asks.

"I think I am not a very nice person," she says. Then she shakes her head slightly. "I think I am a very confused girl."

"Maybe you're less confused than you—"

A loud knock at the door interrupts them. Joanna rolls her eyes and releases an exasperated sigh, goes to the door, tightening her robe around her. It's a neighbor woman, asking if the young lady has any jam she can borrow. Of course, madam, Joanna says, and goes to the kitchen. The woman follows her inside, sees Petros sitting at the kitchen table. He says hello, lights a cigarette and tries to look casual. Joanna hurries, fully aware that for every second the woman stands and stares at them, the potential energy of scandal is building. Soon it will ripple forth, like concentric circles. Finally the woman leaves.

Joanna sits again, looking at Petros directly for the first time. "I'm sorry—"

"Do you know what I think you are?" he interrupts.

"No, what?" she asks.

"I think that you're a fool," he says. "You're a fool to wait around for him."

So, she thinks, *he knows.* She doesn't respond, but looks away sadly, and wonders what Petros has heard. He of course cannot know the whole story, not that it would help if he did.

"Tell me," he says bitterly, "why him?"

"Do you have to ask?" she says coldly. She sees instantly that this blow has landed—his face falls, and his chest collapses. What is she doing? Why?

"Tell me," he says. "How did it start?"

"Which time?"

He grunts, almost in pain. *So,* she thinks, *he doesn't know everything.*

"The last time," he says finally.

She isn't sure how much to say, how much he can take, how much she wants to hurt him, even as he is hurting her at that moment without knowing it. "Last year," she says, "after the motorcycle rally."

When she first heard that motorcyclists were going to ride from Berlin to Cyprus and challenge the Green Line, a thrill ran up Joanna's spine. Finally, a definitive action, a gesture the world would not be able to ignore. She wanted to go with them, even though they said it was going to be dangerous, even though it was likely that no women were going, even though the only times she had been on a motorcycle was when she rode behind Elias, her arms around his waist.

She made the mistake of telling Anna she was thinking of going, and Anna told Joanna's mother, and both of them threatened to put her under house arrest to stop her.

"Don't go," Elias told her. "I will go for you." By that point, whatever had happened between them was long-since over—ever since Joanna found out that Elias had been caught sneaking two Scandinavian tourist girls into an army base.

"Go for me then," she said. And she gave him something: a little porcelain doll that her father had brought to her from Amsterdam when he went on a business trip. "Leave it for me on the other side."

In the days before the protest, the politicians and officials called the president of the Cyprus Motorcycle Federation into their offices. *What you are doing is very dangerous,* they said. *You have made your point. Move the protest somewhere else.* And when he said, no, we will not be stopped, they said *do you want to be responsible for starting another invasion?*

And so, at the last minute, he made an announcement: we must cancel. But it was too late—the boys had come too far, and waited too long. And so they went to the Green Line.

The Turks were ready. They had flown in their professional counter-protesters, ultra-nationalist "Gray Wolves" and armed them with baseball bats and metal rods. So the bikers came and they fought in the dusty Dead Zone until a pack of seven or eight Wolves beat a Greek protester to death. Two days later, after the boy's funeral, a group of relatives and friends rushed the Green Line again. This time, the Turkish army shot and killed one of the boy's cousins as he climbed a flag-pole to pull down the Turkish flag.

When Elias came back from the protest, Joanna was the first person he went to. "I left it for you," he said. There were tears in his eyes and blood on his shirt. "They killed him."

Joanna held him, and that was when it started again.

"But it's over now," said Joanna.

"Why?" asks Petros. "Why this time?"

"I ended it." She says. *He threw me away like an old shoe.*

Petros nods.

"You have to believe me, it is over," she says desperately, but she can tell that he is no longer listening, that she has lost control of an already out-of-control situation.

~~~~

The story pains him, digs into him like a knife. He had been there too, of course, at the beginning, waiting for the call to ride. But when the leader said the protest was cancelled, he had stayed behind.
~~~~

He told himself that he stayed behind for his mother; she had begged him, pleaded with him with tears in her eyes not to go in the first place. To continue after the protest was cancelled and the situation was spiraling out of control would be an additional insult, he thought.

But those were just the lies he told himself. In truth, he thought, for all of his secret plans with the *Filiki Eteria,* for all of his talk of principles and courage, he was a coward at heart.

"So," says Petros. "He went back for you." He pauses. "I never went to the protest." He speaks the words like a confession, as if she didn't know this already. He doesn't know what to expect from her.

She shrugs. "What good did it do to go?" she says. "Anyway, Elias is a liar," she says. "He told me he would go back for me ... actually go back, to Famagusta. He told me he would put a flag up for me, bring me a photograph of my father, from my house. He made me believe it too."

That was my idea, Petros thinks. The plan I came up with, for the *Filiki Eteria.*

"You have to know it's over between us!" she cries. "If it ever even began." This last part, barely a whisper.

"When?" he asks.

Now she hesitates—hesitates too long.

"When!"

"Two days ago," she says.

She is still speaking, but he has already put on his sandals and swung open the door.

"Wait!" she cries. "Petros, talk to me. You have to talk to me."

The cousin—the father of the man. His best friend, his brother. Tears in his eyes. You both have made a fool of me, he thinks.

It would have been better if she had lied; better if they woke in the morning, had breakfast, and she told him she never wanted to see him again. Then, at least, he would have those hours to hold to, memories of something real. Now even the memory of bliss was polluted, spat on. Was any part of it real? It didn't matter; even if she ran him down, held him down, pleaded with him and promised him—it wouldn't matter. Those feelings her face and body had silently cried out to him were now suspect, and he would never believe anything she, or any other woman, ever said again.

Yes, it would have been better if she had lied; but that would have missed the point. Petros had to know, and more importantly, Elias had to know, because this was the only way she could think of to hurt him, as he had hurt her. That is how it is with Elias and girls. They love him; then they hate him. Then they try to hurt him, but just hurt themselves, and anyone else who happens to be around, Petros thinks. And Elias just walks away.

Petros reaches the motor scooter, and turns toward her, one last time. "He said he would go back for you?" he spits once into the dirt. "I will go back for you. I will go to Famagusta and bring you a photograph of your father."

She is still calling after him as he starts the motor scooter; still calling after him as he pulls away, shouting after him, even though it will alert the neighbors and start a scandal. *She will start a scandal for me?* he thinks. A wise voice in his head takes heart in this, for he knows her and what she is risking of herself;

a wise voice tells him to stop, turn around, return, give her a chance to explain herself, but he has already outrun the wise voice.

He rides off into the morning light, tears in his eyes, head buzzing from exhaustion and the remnants of the wine they drank the night before. This ride will be the death of me, he thinks, but doesn't care. So many places to fly off into the abyss, so many opportunities.

He doesn't head back toward the mountains. It is too far to go that way, all the way back to Protaras, so he turns northeast, toward the city. There is a bed at his mother's house.

Twenty minutes down the road, the sky opens up between villages and a silhouette of Nicosia glitters in the distance. He pulls over, and tries to breathe, to listen, listen for anyone. This little island, he thinks, is so lonely.

Chapter Seven

PETROS KNOWS THAT JOANNA WILL forgive Elias. That she will return to him, her spirit smaller, her soul scarred and bruised; that he will appear to humble himself, to ask forgiveness, but that every time she forgives him he will just grow more powerful.

Petros knows that he himself will forgive his cousin—that is the most painful truth of all. It is for this reason that he knows he must execute his plan as rapidly as possible.

Later that evening, he returns to his station at the base, the abandoned house on the edge of free Deryneia. This time he arrives just in time to avoid being considered AWOL—but he has other problems. The soldiers are talking, word has come back: the police are looking for someone, or a group of young men—soldiers, it was said, who destroyed a cafe in Limassol. The owner apparently knew someone in the police department; the top brass in the army were playing dumb and trying to keep things quiet, but were seething.

Rumor has it that the brass already know who the soldiers are—that they are just waiting to make their move. Petros isn't sure what this means. At night, he has nightmares of court martials.

His friends are quiet and removed—they pretend to be as in the dark as anyone. In spite of the fact that they had all been there, Petros feels that all fingers are secretly pointing at him, that when it comes down to it, he will be left to hang alone.

"Don't talk about it," Antonis mutters, and Petros isn't sure which of his accumulating crimes Antonis is referring to. The threat of arrest pushes him harder.

At dusk he stands outside and looks through the old binoculars at Famagusta. A voice in his head: *go now*.

After his evening shift, he goes to his cot, scratches out three letters, seals and posts them. Then he goes to bed, waits until all is silent. After 11, he rises and slips out of the barracks, down the darkened hallway, down the stairs, greeting a groggy private at the checkpoint, who looks surprised to see him. "Someone is looking for you," he says.

"I'm not staying long," Petros responds. The private calls after him to wait, but Petros pretends not to hear, walks toward the little shed that serves as the station armory, where he has stashed his equipment. He has been waiting, preparing for this moment.

By the time the private stops hesitating and calls up for help, it is too late: Petros has left the checkpoint to begin walking north—walking toward a place where he is sure no one cares about his sad little crimes, his sorry humiliations; toward the one place that still feels like it can be called home.

Chapter Eight

Equipment list: Belgian FN-Five-seven semi-automatic pistol, Yugoslavian Zastava M-70 assault rifle, 7 magazines, backpack, radio, grenades, a steel helmet, (no … too heavy; he rejects it and takes a nylon fabric hat), two Mk 2 grenades, canteens and two bottles of water, cans of sardines, a small roll of bread, a hunk of *halloumi*, cigarettes. Flashlight, night vision goggles, small metal detector with earpiece, a pointed stick he has been whittling to flush out mines. Wire cutters. Leather gloves. And of course, his Nikkormat camera.

In his pocket, the marked tourist map of Famagusta that had belonged to the killed soldier is tucked into an envelope. Next to it, the picture of Joanna, the one he took of her on the beach, on the day he first declared his love to her. Finally: the soldier's Greek flag.

He thinks about the flag. The boy would have wanted it to fly above his own family's home, but Petros doesn't know where that is, so he will have to raise it over his parents' old house if he can find it. He consoles himself with the hope that the boy would approve, would be happy to see it fly anywhere in Varosha.

He goes through the plans in his mind again, the ones based on the research he and the others in the *Filiki Eteria* had made, updated with more recent information and the lucky find of the dead soldier's map.

The road in front of him recedes into blackness. Somewhere in the distance, the sea is visible, and the outlines of Varosha's hotels, blacked out but illuminated from behind by floodlights from the Turkish side. At the edge of the road, three plain white signs read: "STOP NO MANS LAND" but there is no gate—Petros walks past. Two hundred yards later, another warning sign, and the road turns to the right, toward the sea. Petros walks along the edge of the world.

How far will he have to travel? A little less than a kilometer to get to the first fence—not too far to walk, but a long way to crawl.

Military notes. Types of cover: logs, trees, stumps, ravines, hollows; trenches, walls, rubble, craters. Avoid outlines and shadows, silhouettes. Move position to position. Look for covered and concealed routes. Low crawl to cross flat, open areas. Otherwise, rush from position to position, unless you think there are mines.

Mines: pressure and tripwire. Crossing minefields: use the metal detector; when you get a hit, push the sharpened end of the stick into the ground. Put just enough pressure in front of you to sink it in. If it doesn't go, pick or chip dirt away. Stop probing when you touch a solid object. Avoid the mine. For tripwire mines: good luck.

Getting through barbed wire: use wire cutters, hold the loose end with cloth. Crawl through head-first, on your back, rifle on your chest.

At some point, the road just seems to end in barbed wire. Closer to the sea, the low scrub gives way to acacia trees and bushes of some sort that hang close to the edge of the road, surviving, perhaps, on the water that runs off the pale asphalt. Of course, he moves off the road as soon as he has a chance, first walking along the shoulder on the side; moving now through the weeds, crouching under the branches of the acacia trees and then into the ravine below; the sound of his movement is deafening against the almost-silent night, and he worries every second that he will be heard or seen.

He cuts southeast, about a half a kilometer. The road here hugs the Green Line—until he finds the spot he is looking for. The wire is cut here, falling down, a tangled mess. It looks like there's no way through, but on second glance he can see the gap; it's easy. From that point, it is a one-third kilometer sprint straight north to the Turkish side—there is no other way to go but running. But what of the mines? This was a question he and the others in the *Filiki Eteria* had asked the special forces soldier when they first planned this mission. *If you stay in the corridor along the furrow*, the soldier assured them, *there is no risk*. In addition, the soldier explained, for the most part fields are marked in the buffer zone and easy to avoid.

He begins pulling at the wire with his gloves, finding the places where it is already broken, cutting it where necessary. It will be easy enough to crawl through, he just needs to take the time to be careful, but at that moment, he hears a sound, a truck coming down the road. Why doesn't he see it? He realizes its headlights are off, which means whoever it is suspects something and is trying not to be seen. He looks to the other side of the road, the safe side, but there is no cover; so he takes a plunge, dives under the tangled wire into the furrow.

The truck could be Greek Cypriot or United Nations; he's not sure which one he wishes for more. It lumbers along slowly; whoever is driving is clearly looking for something. Petros realizes he is breathing furiously, his heart is pounding, he cannot control himself, something is digging into his side.

The truck slows to a stop; he hears the click of the door latch open. Voices, speaking English, but with thick, deep foreign accents, accents that mark the soldiers from far, far away—most likely Bangladeshi or Sri Lankan, he thinks. Would United Nations troops shoot him if they found him? Petros doubts it but isn't sure.

"Are you sure?" says one voice. "Tell me again what you think you saw."

"Movement," says the other voice.

"Probably an animal," says the other.

The first soldier doesn't respond, but Petros can almost hear the frustration in his silence—what animal moves like a man in no man's land?

"Shhh!" says one suddenly. Petros sees that the man is looking directly where he is lying, *I am caught, he thinks,* but instead of speaking, he closes his eyes, and holds his breath, in hopes that he will blend into the darkness.

"What?" says the other.

Now there is just sound, quiet movement. A minute passes, and Petros can no longer hold his breath, so he lets it out, slowly, slowly, through his nose, now he mustn't gasp ... the air wants to rush into his lungs, they are burning, his eyes are still shut and he hears nothing... finally the one who was sure he saw something before says "I don't see anything."

"Let's keep going," says the other.

Long, slow, breaths.

Petros hears the truck move, and opens his eyes; they are driving away. He takes in big gulps of air now.

Maybe it is time, he thinks, to give this up, to return while he has a chance. He thinks of the soldier who died so recently for less than this. The idiocy of what he is doing sinks in, but also the inevitability; the thought of returning now with nothing to show for his journey is more intolerable than death. He moves again, this time more slowly and quietly.

Further along, Petros sees the first minefield, labeled with a big white sign. On the far edge of the field, he finds the spot the solider had told him about; he reaches down with a gloved hand, pulls up the carefully pre-cut barbed wire and passes underneath. This is the open corridor the soldier has told him about—now he has to sprint to the other side and hope that the shadow of his body isn't seen.

He takes a breath, and launches himself forward, but before he takes his first full step his boot is somehow caught in the wire, and he spills forward and to the side, headlong into the minefield. He realizes what is happening as he falls; it is an instant that seems to take a lifetime. He thinks about his stupidity and wonders if there is any way to fall a different direction—he tries to throw his weight to the side—and even has time to wonder what Joanna will think when she sees the idiotic remains of his exploded body before he is buried.

He hits the dirt: for an instant, his heart explodes in his chest, a sharp pain shoots though his leg, and it takes him a minute to realize that he is still alive, that in spite of falling headfirst into a minefield, he has not set off any mines.

The worst part is that his first near-death experience has occurred so close to the beginning. It would be so easy to take this first challenge as a sign, to laugh at himself, imagine telling this story to his friends someday, a self-deprecating, comical story about something foolish he once almost did before coming to his senses and realizing that there was no reason to risk his life to visit a ghost town. It would be so easy, he thinks, to crawl backwards, untangle the barbed wire and return the way he came. So easy, and the only sensible thing to do.

He is glad he brought the small minesweeper, and the pointed stick. Shifting as carefully as he can, he unhooks the metal detector from the snap on the side of his pack, brings it around, puts the earpiece in his ear and switches it on. It begins beeping immediately with an urgent ferocity that makes Petros' heart race again—there is metal all around him, he could be lying on a mine that would have exploded had he stepped on it instead of falling, weight distributed across the dirt. But the slightest movement, he thinks, could easily blow a hole through his chest.

Start with your knees, he thinks. He uses the pointed end of the stick to poke around the edges of his legs, above his shins around his thighs, until he is convinced that there are no mines there; and then he pushes himself up, onto his knees, rising slowly into the night.

From there, it is less difficult to get to his feet; he uses the wire cutters first to make sure he is no longer tangled. It is only a few steps back to safe ground.

Now he can laugh; now he can turn around, take three steps back to safety. Now he can return, chagrined but alive.

Instead he turns again to the north. *This land,* he thinks *is my land,* and he sprints across an open field toward Turkish-occupied Cyprus.

Chapter Nine

LET US IMAGINE HIM, THEN, in the dark depths of a humid, seaside August night on the island of Cyprus, crawling on his hands and knees, under twisted lines of barbed wire, here at the edge, where the Dead Zone ends and the Turkish-enslaved land begins.

It is inevitable that he should get cut—the taut barbed wire snaps free as he snips it, whips across his face, a surprisingly deep gash, one that will scar, he thinks. It will need medical attention to avoid infection. The thought upsets him—somewhere, he held a fantasy in his mind that once through, he would never return from Famagusta, that he would hide out there, stubbornly, evading and surviving for as long as it took for the Turks to finally give in and give him back his city, his love. Until then: an uncatchable legend. Until then—or until the moment when Joanna declared her love for him, unambiguously, and called him back home.

The wire cuts his face and he bleeds. Moments later he hears a movement in the brush, not far away, voices, clattering in Turkish. Patrolmen. He sucks in his breath, but strangely, unlike before with the United Nations troops, what he feels is not panic, but despair. Despair—the sensation of hope, draining from his young body like blood from a beheaded chicken. *Watch him, now, despair, despair.*

No. He must resist the impulse—despair, he thinks, is the worst of the sins. The very unlikeliness of this return is why it matters. It is his last expression of hope against impotence.

He must be very clear: it is not suicide he seeks, but redemption; not extinction, but fame. Or rather, quiet glory; he seeks a kernel of pride, something to return home with that will live in his heart, if nowhere else. Of course, there is a good chance that when he returns the army won't let him back in. They will be forced to court-martial him for daring to return home. He will take a stand, prove a point; he will protest, even if protest accomplishes nothing.

More importantly, he is going to Famagusta to retrieve Joanna from that enslaved land: retrieve her for himself, as if she were not far away in the mountains of Troodos, crying quietly with the nightingales; as if she were still there in her seaside home, as if she had been there since 1974, lonely, waiting like a spirit for the moment when Petros, her true love, awoke and finally went out to retrieve her.

He hears Elias' voice in his head: "The Turks took Constantinople in 1453, and in the Turks' hands, Constantinople remains. You could be waiting a long time." The ghost of his cousin: haunting and irritating him even when he is alive somewhere else.

He curses to himself. He is exposed, on his back, frozen, not moving. His first thought: they will find me. His second thought: I will have to kill them.

He imagines himself in their place—how startled he would be to discover a man lying silently on his back under a fence at three in the morning. That will be his opportunity, his opening, the element of surprise. He hears the soft voices get louder, closer, and realizes he doesn't want to kill them, that for as many times as he has fantasized in his life about killing Turks, this is not why he has come. He quietly releases the safety on his rifle as his heart races in surprise and alarm.

But the soldiers don't come; the voices recede. A long time passes. He feels relief, immense, soul-freeing relief, and realizes God has given him a second chance; yet another chance to change his mind, change his ways. A chance to turn back.

That is another version of this story; a story in which he reconsiders, at this point, and decides to abandon his plan, decides to turn around and go safely home—or, perhaps, never even gets this far; perhaps, he thinks about crossing over, and realizes it is folly, and decides not to go at all. In this version of the story, he returns safely or never even leaves the safety of the base, and then discovers the truth: that Joanna loves him.

But that story is not this story. In this story, a trickle of blood runs down his cheek, and he moves forward. In this story, he decides that he will have to take his chances. In this story, he continues. In this story, somehow, he makes it across.

The UN zone was easy enough. Crossing into the Turkish-occupied territory he thought would be more difficult, but once the soldiers are gone, he is able to cut through the wire and shuffle under the fence with relative ease.

He finds another minefield on the Turkish side, but it only covers a few dozen meters, and he is able to use the small metal detector and the sharpened stick to make his way through. The sensation of resistance as the pointed end pushes into the ground makes him feel sick to his stomach the first time, and the second time and the third; but as he goes on, each moment becomes more and more surreal, and he becomes more and more surreally confident. Hear the beep of the detector in his earpiece; push with the stick, feel where the object is, move carefully past. The world was now bathed in the strange green light of night-vision goggles. Mostly, he moves with a high crawl along the edges and crevices of the landscape. In places where there is no covered route, he sprints, feeling the hand of death or mutilation on his shoulder. He prays; he survives.

~~~~

It all started before he could remember. As a little boy, his family told him about the invasion and occupation. They told him how his father had owned a fancy hotel in Famagusta where Richard Burton and Elizabeth Taylor used to stay—or so he said.

His father: a once-jovial man, increasingly tense in his later days, a man who had married old, hoping marriage would keep him young, but finding instead that it only made him older; and older still when the Turks came and dropped bombs on his beloved Famagusta.

"Look here," he had said from the observation deck at the woman's house in Deryneia, "you can see our hotel." Petros, only a boy at the time, believed him, though looking at a map later he realized it was impossible. What other things did his father say that were little more than fantasies, dreams or wishful thinking?

His father, not a man who could hold hate or outrage easily, was nonetheless drawn in to the island's collective bitterness. The hotel business lasted for three years before the Turks came. Famagusta—the robbery of the past, but also the theft of
~~~~

the future—this magnificent, glamorous future they were to have together.

His later years were either spent embroiled in legal battles against his brother Michalis over which of them should have inherited various scattered parcels of land in Paralimni and Protaras, or dreaming up schemes for what he would do when he returned to his home. Day after day he wrote letters to Richard Burton and Bridget Bardot and Elizabeth Taylor, asking them to remember Famagusta and imploring them to use their status to influence the politicians in America to do something, so they could all meet again in that fair city.

Petros once asked Yiorgos Zenios what he knew about the disputes between his father and his uncle.

Yiorgos hated Michalis—that much was clear, though Petros wasn't sure why, for certain. He gathered it had to do with his father—certain financial matters, it was said, between Petros' father and his brother Michalis were never settled, and Yiorgos blamed Michalis for it, and more importantly for the misery it brought to Petros' mother. These impressions and suspicions Petros gathered when he was still young; impressions and suspicions gathered from overheard conversations, fevered speculation with his sister and the fact that once a month or so, Uncle Michalis came by the house and handed whomever was there an envelope stuffed with 500 Cyprus pounds.

Michalis and Petros' father, Solomon, were two siblings of five. One sister died in infancy; one brother as a martyr in the EOKA period. From what Petros understood, that was how the families knew each other—Yiorgos' brother Athos had been an EOKA hero as well. The other sister, Xanthe, a sour woman with two unhappy, dowdy daughters, lived nearby in Paralimni. Petros didn't know them well.

Yiorgos, always above reproach whenever it came to gossip or criticizing others, hesitated. "I will say only this. Your father and his brother were in business together. Your uncle should have shown more loyalty."

Petros' father died in the early 1980s; as the years after the invasion went by, and any prospect of going back grew more and more remote, he seemed to lose interest in life. Petros remembered watching him sit motionless in front of their refugee house in Lakadamia, is if he could fade into the landscape and disappear.

It's hard to know if a person can will himself to die, but as Petros' father started to eat less and less, and gradually became too befuddled with life to work, it became apparent to everyone that, separated from his home, he had no desire to stay on the planet, especially when the vast expanse of the clear blue sky seemed to beckon. "The ancient Greeks believed the sky was a god," he used to tell Petros, and then he would start talking about Christ and the Resurrection. Petros was still very young when his father died.

The last memory: they were at the hospital and the room smelled of foul, deathly body odors and ammonia and bleach. Uncle Michalis was there, by his brother's bedside, holding his hand, weeping, but on his father's face was nothing but weakness; a face that had become too exhausted to express any human emotion. Michalis left; Petros' mother made him hold his father's hand, though he didn't want to.

"We must," croaked his father, "we must learn to forgive."

Petros nodded. This he had heard many times in church and in his religious education classes at school.

"You don't understand," said his father. The rasping words crawled out of his body, slowly, one by one, as if each were to be his last. "They tell us to forgive and we think we do, but we don't. Christ forgave, without even waiting for repentance. That way is the only way."

Over the years, Petros often wished he could remember these words with love and respect, but all he ever felt was bitterness—toward the Turks for taking away his homeland; toward the Greeks for their stupid machinations that led to this; and, later, toward Uncle Michalis, who had somehow managed to wrest a small fortune from it all.

~~~~

By four in the morning Petros is inside the fences; he takes shelter in the courtyard of an old house on the outskirts of Varosha. Inside the house itself would be safer, but inside the house are pitch black shadows lying upon shadows, darkness so deep even the night goggles will not penetrate it. The thought of snakes and rats and scorpions takes hold of his mind, so he remains outside where at least he can see the moon and the stars. He takes off his pack and leans against an outside wall, takes off his goggles, lets his eyes adjust to the darkness and rests.

In the predawn light, he dozes—and for a moment he is back in Nicosia, woken by a jarring voice from a truck megaphone. It is the watermelon sellers, the ones who drive around before the sun comes up, bellowing "watermelon! good watermelon, fresh watermelon, picked today!" He turns his head and Joanna is next to him; he looks at her face; she opens
~~~~

her eyes and smiles. He smiles back. "Shall I buy you a watermelon?" She laughs and wrinkles her nose. "Don't encourage them!" she says.

So strange: so many years he has shut out the noises when he slept, and returned in his dreams to Famagusta. Now that he is in Famagusta, he dreams instead of more familiar places, back home. The dream ends; he awakens, and the pain is visceral, a stabbing contraction in his chest, a longing in his loins—a sad, sad longing, a longing that makes him want to cry. He drifts off again.

Another dream: he wakes up in a haze, tussled bed sheets, clothes everywhere, the smell of boiling coffee in the *briki*, without sugar, thick muddy grounds in the bottom—an old-fashioned habit, drinking Greek-style coffee, now when all the modern kids of Athens drink only French drip. Half asleep, he wonders where the smell could possibly be coming from.

He brings his mind back to this place—back to Varosha, Famagusta. The smell of sand and sea, the gentle sound of waves on the beach—the only sound, and it fades in the distance. He wakes again; the sun is up, beating down on him, and he almost throws up upon realizing that this part is not a dream.

He gets up, and relieves himself in the abandoned courtyard and realizes he is hungry; the day yawns ahead of him. In his pack: two canteens of water, a hunk of *halloumi*, a small loaf of bread. He will have to ration it; it will be a long day, there is no way to return before nightfall. The thought worries him; soon someone will notice he is missing, if they haven't already.

At first he worries that he will be easily spotted, as he walks along the edges of the streets, trying to move in nonexistent shadows. Eventually though, the fear dissipates—the intensity of the solitude here penetrates ordinary fear and overwhelms it with a deeper, existential one. It is a fear, he thinks, that comprehends God's utter indifference to us.

Now the sun is fully out, its bright rays illuminating every corner of this desolate place, a place that was once the future. By ten o'clock, Petros is roasting in the August sun. Sweat pools under his fatigues, he lilts and wobbles, sits down suddenly. His stomach churns from days of drinking and exhaustion, but he does not vomit.

Dirt and dry sand, weeds in patches; the twisted iron hull of an old children's merry-go-round. Up, closer. He takes the Nikkormat camera out, starts taking photographs, feeling a strange satisfaction at the thought that he will have a secret record of this place.

Roofs collapsed, trees growing straight out of the corpses of homes, palm trees, flame trees, thick and stocky, like carob and olive—red, vermillion, orange, yellow flowers. Giant buildings shedding their balconies; zombie buildings shedding body parts but refusing to die a dignified death. Wild geraniums—not quite natural, flamboyant patches of orange, red, and blue, luminous mixes that escape into nature as they leap from window boxes and walk across the landscape. Climbing bougainvillea drapes entire homes in flowery shrouds.

A car dealership, filled with new-model, 1974 cars, cars that haven't moved for decades, flat tires, crusted with dirt, thick with the dry dust of twenty summers. Random chain-link fences, half-collapsed. A lone, unopened coke bottle on a shelf, gray with dust.

Strange architecture of boxes and rectangles, and buildings with curved facades. Old cemeteries, crosses, tombstones. Iron gates around houses, in the style of Nicosia. Cedars and pines. Storefront display windows with no glass. Weedy lots. Rebar out of roofs, like bizarre, punk hairstyles.

Walking down a wider boulevard: flat-roofed buildings, abandoned storefronts, a street of wildflowers and asphalt, shattered windows, shards of glass clinging to the edges, frosted with dust and age. Scaffolding, twisted signs, rusted window guards.

It is the old stone buildings that survive best: an old church, all white domes and arches, solid sandstone. In other places twisted, unrecognizable metal remnants stand alone like some strange post-modern art installation from New York.

Palm trees, thick-trunked, noble and straight, grow everywhere, gentle sentries, who do not protect so much as bear witness. Flowering yellow weeds spill forth from balcony planters. Blooms of oleander—copper-pink- and peach-colored—overwhelm courtyards.

Flowers break up the asphalt, leaving some buildings standing alone in wide-open lots like islands in the weeds.

Everything else looks like a construction site, dusty and crumbled, exposed. The tall buildings are the worst, they stand out like bombed-out monuments to Berlin after the war, or possibly burned-out housing projects from the Bronx in the 1970s—skeletons of broken concrete, exposed girders; giant human hives, denuded and poisoned to remove all life.

The dense death of this place.

It is, Petros thinks, the most terrifying place—it goes on and on. How far like this? Petros fears he will get lost. He is moving as fast as possible, but avoiding the roads. He cuts through alleyways, courtyards, sometimes straight through the middle of abandoned buildings. Inside, the walls are bare, save a stray photograph, a tattered poster, an occasional intact, dusty mirror.

A part of him wants to stop, to explore it all, but he is afraid of pausing—he came here for a reason, he has things to accomplish, goals to achieve. He reminds himself that he has all day in front of him. There is time, he thinks.

Random memorabilia in homes. A long sepia-hued photo in a frame, still hanging on a wall; in it a dashing man with a thick, broad mustache stands next to a young village woman with her head covered. There is no way to guess how old it might be—50, 100 years? He could take it with him, bring it back, see who it belongs to, return a memory, an anchor, a mark of legacy, a gift to a family somewhere over there in free Cyprus. Gently, he wipes the dust from the glass. He is about to take it, but thinks better of the idea. Perhaps whoever owned this house would prefer to find it here when he or she returned.

He exits on the beach side, for he must take a better look at the beach and its buildings, buildings that look so much like skeletons they feel like death.

On the beach: ten-story hotels, shattered glass, giant pigeon roosts, pigeon dung in thick layers on walls and ledges. They were designed so that every room faced a connected balcony at an angle; so that all guests had access to views of the sea. Now the safety railings are broken up, fallen to pieces. A few buildings have lost entire faces. On the far end of the beach, a lone construction crane stands against the skyline, a reminder of how this place was being built when it all came suddenly to an end. Carob rats, citrus groves, sand on the floors. No smell: hotel pools, empty of water that evaporated decades ago. Somewhere along here is the hotel Papa and Michalis owned and ran together.

A few blocks inland, tattered clothing still hangs on clothes lines, the most surprising detail. The fat, fleshy leaves of strange cacti drape themselves over chunks of broken asphalt and concrete as if to protect them as they would protect bare soil from the roasting summer heat with their succulent, water-gorged flesh.

How had he imagined it? Not like this—somehow, he imagined it as an ancient place, a place like the villages he knew in the mountains, not this strange monument to modernity—a modernity that, unlike the ancient ruins that age gently like wine, decays almost instantly. In a generation, he thinks, it will all be gone.

Fig trees, pregnant with fruit, are everywhere. He picks some as he goes along, the meaty, sugary flesh dissolving like sweet water-candy in his mouth. Figs were never his favorite fruit, but at this moment they taste like a precious gift, and he eats too many, wishing he could bring some with him, but there is only so much he can carry. He tries to make a mental note of where the tree is, in case he decides to return to it. He feels no fear of being discovered, maybe because this place is so vast and so empty; two men could wander for days here in different parts of the city, he thinks, and never discover one another.

~~~~

After eating, he drinks, deep quaffs of water—he needs more of it than he expected, but the heat is terrible. He worries that he may run out.
~~~~

How strange, thinks Petros: you can still find street signs and the numbers on houses, at least some of them. He has taken the map out and found the location of his parents' house. The walk is several kilometers—both a tiring distance and surreally close. He realizes that up until that moment, he had not really believed it would be possible to find his home, but with the map and the street signs, the path home unfolds in front of him, almost too easily. Ploutinos Street, Leophoros Evagorou, Leophoros Dhimokratias.

If the marks on the map are correct, Joanna's house is on the way, so he decides to stop there first.

Finding it is too easy. He checks the map, his notes, his memory again, until he is certain. Then he pulls out the old photograph of Joanna, the one of her as a toddler, almost falling off a chair in this very courtyard.

The low wall enclosing the courtyard is still there. Just beyond it, a chipped concrete patio, weeds of all sizes. The dry green leaves of a gnarled olive tree almost shimmer in the stark daylight at the corner. The house itself is flat-roofed, with curved balconies at the corners, held up by concrete columns, protected with intricate wrought-iron balcony rails.

Petros imagines the green wooden shutters swinging out, on a not-too-distant, cool summer morning, as Joanna leans out to call to him.

He steps over the wall and goes inside. The interior is a tumble of splintered wood and shattered glass. Much has clearly been removed, but much also remains. Piles of unrecognizable cloth, linens and bed sheets perhaps, litter the floors, mixed with dust and dung, nests for insects, birds, reptiles and mammals.

Petros tries to take it all in, darkness and light, his eyes adjusting from moment to moment to the stark patches of sunlight and deep shadows. He puts his things down in a corner, relieved to be released of some weight. The water is the heaviest, so he decides to leave most of it—the two plastic liter bottles—along with some of the sealed rations.

The house is in good shape and fairly secure compared to much of what he has already seen, a good temporary base of operations, he thinks. His father and mother's old house is perhaps a few blocks away. The beach, and the family hotel, is further away, but he hasn't decided if he'll venture that far.

He sits and rests, but only for a moment. He is acutely aware of the time. His plan was to drop his things and move on quickly to find his house, but now that he is here he can't resist looking around to see what he can find to bring home to Joanna.

He doesn't find much at first. The kitchen is stripped bare, ransacked, drawers thrown on the ground empty. Even the refrigerator is gone. *Strange,* he thinks, the haphazard looting of this city.

Upstairs, he has more luck. Amidst the piled-up linens and half-collapsed chest of drawers in the front room, he finds delicate old Lefkara lace, a couple of icons and a small metal jewelry box, empty of course.

The whole house smells of sand and dust and other scents he doesn't recognize. As he walks through the hall to a second room, past the top of the stairs again, something moves, fast. He sees it out of the corner of his eye coming from the darkness and steps back, throwing his hand up to protect himself. His foot misses the first step and slips on the dust at the edge of the second and he falls backward down the stairs.

Fortunately he catches himself, grabbing the bannister, which holds, in spite of being rotten. He falls too fast to see whatever moved, but he hears what sounds like wings flapping. A bird, a bat.

He recovers, shaken. He pulls himself back up the stairs, determined to find something worth coming for.

At the top of the stairs he turns toward the back, walks down the hallway toward the room that he knows would have been Joanna's.

The door is shut, locked, but dented, beaten and half off its hinges, as if someone had tried to kick it down once or many times, and given up, not knowing what treasures are inside. Petros kicks it now, with the heel of his boot—once, twice, three times, until it finally comes fully loose and he is able to push it aside.

With the door open, a path for cross-ventilation opens up in the house, and a blast of hot, dry air rushes past his face, blows the hair from his eyes, rustles the dust in the hallway behind him and lets loose a two-decade-old sigh. Somewhere else, another door slams shut and Petros jumps with a start.

Now he moves into the room, and sees with a deep, skin-crawling shudder that he is where he thought he was. Inside the tiny room are two beds, a narrow twin where Joanna's brother would have slept and a crib that had been converted to a toddler bed that would have been Joanna's. *That was my room*, Joanna told Petros.

And then, in the corner, exactly as Joanna had described it, the antique safe.

Petros cannot believe it is still here; of all things for a looter to miss …

He dusts it off with his sleeve. It is black with brown trim, elegant lettering: "Safe and Lock Company/Cincinnati, Ohio." The door is decorated with a small landscape painting, of some far-off place.

And if what Joanna told him is correct he knows the combination is here also, taped to the back of a bookshelf, he tries to remember where.

If he finds the combination, he can open it; but wonders if he should. What secret things lay there inside? And yet, how could he leave it there to the Turks? How many years would go by before Joanna or her mother would have a chance to open it themselves? He resolves to look for the combination and open the safe when he has more time; but first, he wants to see the rest of the house.

The front room belonged to Joanna's mother and father. Without a locked door, very little is left: the room is as messy as the others, full of strange things: broken plates, shards of glass, an ornately painted serving dish.

And then, to his surprise, he finds the most important thing. In a generic wooden frame, a black and white photograph. In it, a father holding a little girl in his arms, standing in front of the very house Petros is in. Both are laughing. The little girl is unmistakably Joanna; if she weren't wearing a different dress, it could have been taken on the same day as the other one Petros had from that time. He smiles at his achievement. He has it: the one thing she asked for. *I can go home,* he thinks.

~~~~
~~~~

He had planned to go from here to see his family's home, and from there to his father's hotel—the hotel, at 15 stories, would be the most visible place to fly the flag if he could tie it to something. That would be the thing to show the Turks.

Now that he has the photograph of Joanna's father though, the idea suddenly seems less relevant. He could tie the flag to the roof of Joanna's house. No one would see it, but he would know it's there; he could tell her it's there. More importantly, he could bring her the photograph of her and her father.

He drinks some water, contemplates the idea, and then dismisses it. He has not come this far to leave without seeing the home of his parents—the home he would have been born in if the Turks hadn't come.

He considers leaving the photograph in the house with the water and rations—undoubtedly this would be safer, but now that he has it, he can't imagine letting it out of his sight, so he takes it as carefully as possible out of its frame, and slips it into the envelope with the map and the other photographs.

It is still the heat of the day when he ventures out again. Not the best time, but he has hopes of reaching his home, and possibly the hotel, before nightfall. Ideally he will return to Joanna's house in time to open the safe, and head back south. He prefers traveling in the city during daylight; nightfall is the time to cross the Green Line.

He leaves the house quietly, in search of his mother and father's home. He doesn't have to go far.

He walks down the block, turns one corner, and then another, and there it is, just where the map had said, again almost too easy. He takes out the photograph the boy's uncle gave him to confirm he is in the right place. He looks at the photo, and then back at the loose bones of the building in front of him. This is their house, or what remains of it.

At first he can't believe he's found it. For some reason, his home has fared even worse than the rest of the city. The ceiling is collapsed; the arms of a young acacia tree reach up through the roof, as if to envelop the house from the inside. Its limbs push through the windows and doorways, as if to say *this is my home now.*

A tree growing through the body of his home—the image strikes Petros with an archetypal resonance. *If I were someone more superstitious, like Elias or Joanna, I would have dreamed of this before I came,* he thinks.

He walks directly to the house facade—the metal fence that had marked the front courtyard was completely gone—and crosses himself, preparing to enter. Not that there is any "inside" to enter into—even the floor tiles are missing. An empty picture frame hangs by one corner on the wall. An archeologist couldn't put this back together, he thinks.

He begins to weep; he feels his heart braking. There really is nothing left. What hope is there of finding anything here, anything that will help his life? He feels weak. Like some vagrant, seeking shelter, he finds a corner amidst the weeds, sinks down, and puts his head against the wall. Well, he thinks, I've seen it—what now?

Chapter Ten

Kadir feels fear. It comes from nowhere—a sudden rush, something he cannot explain, something like a movement from his peripheral vision, like a jolt of electricity, like some kind of crawling, stabbing sensation. He looks suddenly at Emre, as if this sensation had been thrown at him by his fellow solider, but Emre senses nothing. Kadir is about to say something but Emre has made it clear he doesn't want to be disturbed, he is entirely engrossed in reading a letter he received that morning.

Midday approaches, the soldiers have taken refuge from the August heat in the shadow of a shell of a building in abandoned Varosha. Kadir is not entirely clear what they are doing here, but he knows not to ask too many questions; he fears Emre's patronizing glare. Their presence, he gathers, is semi-official, maybe they are supposed to be patrolling, but they are also scouting for treasure—in the waxing and waning of the Turkish military's policy on looting, it seems that they have entered a somewhat permissive phase—and he is hopeful that he might find something of value, that he could sell and send some cash home to his parents. But he is unclear as to the rules, and no one seems to think it worth explaining.

Maybe this is why he is suddenly afraid, he thinks. Or maybe it is just the strangeness of this place, a city in which everyone is gone. Now, some twenty years on, most things of value are gone as well. It seems wrong; not that they have taken it (he imagines the smug Greeks running in fear from the heroic Turkish army, and finds the image satisfying) but because it has been left this way, abandoned, empty, literally ghost-like. If it were up to Kadir, he would have bulldozed the whole thing and built something new, but it is not up to him. What does he know, he is just a farm boy from Anatolia who was lucky or unfortunate enough to land a rotation in Cyprus.

He thinks now of the day before, walking through the narrow streets of Lefkosha, looking at the shops.

"I would look very well in that suit," he says suddenly. He saw it in the window of a tailor shop—pin-striped, dark blue. Classy. Rich. He saw it and he immediately imagined himself wearing it, first here in Cyprus, then maybe in Istanbul, or a foreign city somewhere, and finally back in his village, where he would be the only man to wear such a fancy suit. His mother would smile at him proudly, his father would pat him on the back, his brother would whistle, impressed.

"What suit?" Emre snaps, irritated.

"That suit! The one we looked at yesterday in Lefkosha."

Emre shakes his head. "Why are you obsessed with suits?"

"I'm not obsessed with suits," says Kadir. "But I think I would look good in that one."

"It doesn't matter if you would look good or like a homeless Anatolian beggar," says Emre. "You're not getting it. You can't afford it. You will never be able to afford a suit like that. And even if you did you would have no place to wear it. So why are you still talking about it?"

"I like suits," Kadir says glumly. "I had a suit once. When I was younger. Not that nice. But I wore it all the time. Wherever I went. I wore it even when it got too small and they laughed at me. If I had a nice suit like that I would wear it every day."

Emre grunts.

"If I had a nice suit like that I would wear it all the time. You're fortunate. You're an officer. One day you'll own lots of suits." Kadir takes a long look at Emre and feels both admiration and envy. They are close to the same age, but Emre is not like him—Emre is from Istanbul, is educated, is a junior officer. Emre understands things, without explanation. Whatever happens, Emre seems to know what to do.

Emre is a graduate of officer training school, which he entered when he was fourteen; he was on the fast-track to promotion, to seniority, to a position that every Turk respects, although his career seems to have stalled—another thing Kadir doesn't understand.

~~~~

Emre gives Kadir a sidelong glance, and looks back at the letter —a rambling letter he has received from his brother Burak in Istanbul. "Do you consider yourself to be a man's man?" asks the letter.

Emre, regards the words dispassionately, knowing that while Burak is trying to provoke him, he refers not to Emre but to himself, that he projects his own doubts and insecurities about the path his life has taken onto that piece of paper that he seals and sends, across the Bosphorus, through the heart of Anatolia and the Levant, across the narrow straight to Turkish army headquarters in Cyprus.
~~~~

Two sons of a successful grocer in Istanbul, two poets, of sorts, the older a rebel and a bohemian who whiles away his hours in seedy cafes in the shadow of the Blue Mosque, quoting Nazim Hikmet ("I love my country, I swung in its lofty trees, I lay in its prisons. Nothing relieves my depression like the songs and tobacco of my country") shaming his family and getting beaten up by the police. The other son: a nationalist who believes in the poet Ziya Gökalp's vision that the greatest thing is to become "Turkish, Muslim and modern."

It is a strange letter; a strange way to ask your younger brother for money. Strange too because Emre knows how Burak feels about him; how little he respects his patriotism, how he disdains Emre's military ambitions, how he wishes his brother would come and join him in the movement that might make solidarity and peace real. *Yes, yes*, Emre thinks—and what of Cyprus? What of our enemies, enemies who surround us on every border? Emre used to find their debate in letters and poetry invigorating but by now, he is tired of it. Maybe for him too, it is the sad, strange energy of this place that exhausts him —this place that was once alive, and is now dead; this place that reminds you that no place is ever truly Greek or Turkish, that every place, every land belongs ultimately only to God and to the weeds.

In spite of his Istanbul roots, Emre never really thought much about Greeks before he came to Cyprus. He knows, of course, that the Greeks slaughtered Turks here in Cyprus when they had the chance; that they almost exterminated them in the 1960s, and that they would do so again; that they are crafty strangers, scheming manipulators, infecting minds with their lies. He knows that they are superstitious, susceptible to the manipulations of the cassocked fundamentalist priests, that they are not really Greek anyway, not related to the ancient people who lived here; that they are just pretenders, trying to scratch some glory from the ancients. (Not like the Turks, who are related to the first men. Turkey, after all, is the most ancient culture on earth.) He knows that the Greeks, given half the chance, would march into Istanbul and exterminate the fourteen million Turks who live there, as if they could reverse history.

And he suspects what every good Turk does, that the Greeks are helping the Kurdish terrorists in the east. In that regard, it is personal, because he knows soldiers who have died at the hands of the PKK, and has fought there himself. Turkey, he thinks, has enemies on all sides.

This is what he thinks when he thinks about such things, which is not often. For now, he is thinking only about how to put the letter from his brother out of his mind and what it would take to get old automobile parts out of occupied Famagusta.

"Hey!" Kadir shouts suddenly, the sound of his voice startling them both. Emre jumps off his seat, almost falling to the ground. "Shit!" He reaches out to smack the idiot across the face, but stops short when he sees the boys expression; Kadir is convinced he saw something in the distance.

"Shh!" Kadir points toward a house at the end of the block, the most dilapidated on the street—barely even a house anymore, it has been taken over by a giant tree going through roof—and then, seeing his fellow soldier's disdainful expression shakes his head. "No," he mouths silently. "I am sure. I saw something."

Emre rolls his eyes. So Kadir has seen something; Kadir is always seeing something; he is afraid of his own shadow, always jumping, at something or another. He is the kind of soldier who really believes the propaganda about the importance of this post, about the chance for conflict at any moment; the chance, the hope that something would happen and he would become a real, fighting soldier—no matter how many times Emre told him to forget it, that there is no action in Cyprus.

Here in Varosha especially, it is easy to imagine things. Everything is so still, so silent for so long that the slightest movement—of a dog, a snake, a leftover piece of cloth swinging on a clothesline—can catch your eye and make your mind believe unbelievable things.

"No," says Kadir quietly, his gazed fixed on the house. "It was a person."

Emre shakes his head and looks again where Kadir had been looking. And then he sees it too. "*Kahretsin*!" Movement at the edge of the building at the far end of the street.

Emre motions to Kadir to be silent, and slowly stands up, moving his rifle into firing position. Whatever it is has moved behind the edge of the building, out of sight. Emre pauses to reflect on what to do, which direction to advance from.

Rules of movement in urban areas: advance rapidly, from one position to another. Look around corners on your stomach. Stay below window level. Beware of kill zones: streets, alleys and parks—places that can be easily cut up with stationary machine guns. When moving in buildings—take care not to be silhouetted against the windows. Emre knows these rules and many others as though they are a part of him, and yet he finds himself momentarily helpless to make a decision.

From across the street he thinks that he and Kadir might get a better angle to see around the building's edge, but his training tells him that this could also be an ambush, that he will be open to enemy fire. On the other hand, if it were an enemy intent on ambush, wouldn't they have moved already? Kadir motions to his radio; standard protocol, not to mention wise soldiering, is to call for help immediately, but Emre motions *no.* He is not sure they have seen anything more important than a stray dog, and he has other reasons to hold off on help anyway.

He glances at Kadir as if his fellow soldier will give him an answer, but from his expression, Kadir looks as though he is going to either piss his pants or rush forward toward the building like a berserker. Finally, Emre motions Kadir to keep his gun trained on the corner of the building. Then Emre moves quietly, stepping slowly sideways to cross the street and then along the sidewalk toward the building. He knows he is exposed, but the only other option is to circle all the way around the block, at which point whatever was moving near that building will surely be gone.

As he moves closer, he motions Kadir to push in on the other side of the street; they both advance in a low, steady walk, keeping their bodies level and rifles in shooting position. Half a block closer, Emre is finally able to see around the corner. What does he expect? The most plausible scenario is that it was other Turkish soldiers on their own unsanctioned treasure-hunt. The second most plausible was that it was Greek Cypriot special forces, conducting some kind of reconnaissance, although it would be crazy for them to try such a thing in the middle of day.

What he does not expect is what he sees; a man, leaning face-first against what remains of the building's retaining wall, arm over his face, as if he is weeping. From across the street, Emre cannot tell if it is a Turk or a Greek, but he knows he must take cover before he is seen. He slips into a courtyard and positions himself behind the remains of a cinderblock wall for cover, and aims his gun again. By now Kadir has moved closer on his side of the street; he moves quietly, but Emre can almost smell his fellow soldier's panicked adrenaline and worries that he will blow the element of surprise at any instant, so he decides he must announce himself sooner rather than later.

"Halt!" he shouts, but his voice chokes in his throat, so he tries again: "Halt! Who goes there?" his voice booms across the street, echoing through the hushed alleys and desolate, silent crevices of poor abandoned Varosha.

Startled, the crying man jumps back and looks around wildly in terror. All at once Emre sees that he is not a Turk, that he is a soldier, and that he is armed. In the next split second Emre makes the decision to fire, but it is too late, the soldier spins and runs, the bullets splinter into random walls and the chase is on.

~~~~

Petros hears a sound, something like a scratch, a movement, and almost in slow motion he jumps back as the voice barks out.

For some irrational reason, his first thought is *animal*: that's what it must be, there are animals everywhere here but almost as fast as this thought arrives it is already gone, and he realizes that what is about to happen is something different entirely, something unlike anything he has ever experienced.
~~~~

He can't believe he didn't hear them coming. Later, when he remembers this moment, he will tell himself that he was more surprised by his own stupidity and arrogance than by the presence of soldiers; he will tell himself that he was a fool, who had for a moment given up on his life and therefore almost given it up, but that he decided to live. He will tell himself this story, will imagine that this was what was going through his mind, but of course the truth is more like this: he runs because that is what you do when someone shoots at you.

He has no idea how many soldiers there are; the voice comes from across the street, but he could easily be surrounded. He runs in what he thinks is the opposite direction, no time to think about anything, no time to say goodbye to the home that is not his home, no time to think about the fact that he will never see it again.

It would make sense to run toward a cluster of row homes, to lose himself there, but instead he finds he is sprinting across a wide intersection toward a wild cluster of palm trees, into an empty lot. He ducks behind the chipped concrete wall of some kind of out-building, a garage or shed. He is exposed to the east —there are only a few houses on that side, and then a major boulevard and across from that a wide-open expanse, undeveloped land—but for the moment he thinks they are coming from only one direction—though he can't tell for sure. The thudding of boots stops suddenly, and there is silence; both sides have taken temporary cover, both sides listen intensely for hints of what the other is doing. The choice: wait, ambush and charge them, or retreat as quietly as he can.

Petros drops to his stomach, pulls himself to the corner of the building, and slowly pokes his head around the corner. The sun scorches the earth, and concrete and asphalt; its light is so bright that Petros fears his eyeballs will be sunburned. Sunglasses: not standard issue, but he wishes now that he had them.

Looking around the corner, he sees nothing, but knows his hunters are out there, hiding amidst the abandoned buildings and bushes and the weeds. Time is against him, he thinks; a smart soldier knows when to retreat. Surely they will call for reinforcements, soon he will have the entire Turkish army breathing down his neck. The thought simultaneously fills him with self-satisfaction and dread.

Mentally, he calculates a path away from where he came: crossing the backyard lots, getting to the next street and to the buildings on the other side. He knows he is retreating to the north, but that's the only place of cover. From his location there, he thinks, maybe he can make his way from courtyard to courtyard avoiding the roads. The city is bigger than you would think, there are many buildings and lots, many places for a lone figure to lose himself, but then what? He fears lines of sight less than sounds: it is impossible to move quietly enough here, against the backdrop of so much deadly silence.

He rises and backpedals as quietly as he can, keeping the street in his line of vision, framed between the two homes. He backs past the palm trees and through a grove of citrus. Behind him: another low wall, concrete rubble, another building.

He bumps into the edge, feels a piece of rebar, and stumbles for an instant. Hearing it, a Turkish soldier pops out from behind the wall, firing without aiming. Petros fires back instantly but almost before he pulls the trigger, the Turk has ducked back behind the corner; Petros' burst hits the building and sends sparks and splintered brick into the street.

Now: charge them or run? He turns and runs, leaps over the retaining wall, through the back yard, between the buildings, mustering the will to overcome the dense heat, the brutal August lethargy, one last time.

The Turks give chase—he hears them behind him. He cuts around the little house to the left, back around and behind it, and then sprints across the empty brown lots that make up the backyards of the homes. Without thinking he runs diagonally, northeast. Gunshots—but by now he has made it between two homes, leapt over another iron gate and is darting across the street toward a small, red-shingled, single-family home. He knows he can't run forever, he must get cover, get hidden somehow.

The gunfire stops after the first burst; now he hears only boots scuffing and stomping the ground, an unknown number of feet chasing him. He pounds through the building courtyard, leaps over a wall between porch columns and slams through a broken front door. Inside, the sudden darkness overwhelms his eyesight, his sprint becomes a stumble and then a tumble, he falls and rolls, hard, over his shoulder, the fact the he is holding his rifle saves him, keeps him from catching himself on his hands. Without thinking he springs to his feet and sprints up a flight of stairs, realizing as he does that he is trapping himself on the second floor with no way out.

~~~~

The instant the soldier bolts, Emre fires without thinking, and the chase begins. There is no time to speculate; no time to
~~~~

make up theories, though the most important question obviously is whether the soldier is alone. This thought makes Emre hesitate for a split second, long enough for the boy to get a head start.

The chase begins: Emre follows between the buildings, at each point moving just fast enough to catch glimpses of the fleeing solider as he ducks behind walls and around corners, not long enough to take aim and fire a shot. Kadir is steps behind him, Emre wants to give him orders, tell him to circle around, come from behind, but things are moving too fast.

He hesitates for a moment as the soldier ducks off the street between two buildings—a voice in his head tells him to be cautious, that a cornered man is dangerous. He comes to the edge of the building. Kadir is behind him, he can hear his fellow soldier breathing, huffing like a train, he wants to turn around and curse the fool, but he is afraid to look away. He holds up his hand, makes a signal that he hopes Emre will understand, to circle around to the other side of the street. *And don't shoot me,* he thinks. Kadir runs.

Emre hears a sound, almost like someone stumbling, so he steps around the corner and fires a burst to cover himself; he is stepping back into cover as the soldier returns fire; sparks and chips of concrete fly off the wall like shrapnel—something flies toward his eye, he falls back blinking, and for a moment he fears he has lost an eye. Blinking, crying—the August sun is brighter than ever. A moment later he regains his vision, realizing that if the solider had charged forward at that moment he would be a dead man, but instead he hears steps receding, the sound of the soldier running. The shock of his almost-blindness hits him, but for some reason instead of hesitating he charges forward, his terror exploding as hatred and anger. Maybe Kadir will get lucky, he thinks, and catch the boy when he crosses the far street, but it doesn't happen that way.

Emre crosses through the backyard, following the direction he is sure the soldier took, but when he emerges onto the next street, the boy has disappeared. Emre curses, and then spins around, but there is no one behind him, the boy could be anywhere. A moment later, though, he catches a glimpse of Kadir at the end of the street, moving toward a building opposite, completely open. *Get off the street you idiot!* he thinks, and waves him to the side, but Kadir keeps moving forward toward the building across from them, his rifle raised. He points dramatically at the building, as if Emre is too stupid to understand.

Emre signals for Kadir to go around the back—for all they know, the soldier is already escaping out a back window. Emre moves quickly to a position behind a wall on the other side of the street where he can simultaneously see the front door and Kadir.

A long, slow, torturous pause falls over the dead city; even the wind stops, leaving them with only the cruel, silent beating sun.

Emre glances at Kadir, who is motioning to his radio. Emre shakes his head; Kadir looks confused. For the love of Turks—why not call for help?

Indeed, why not? Emre cannot justify it to himself: here they sit, on an island with 40,000 Turkish soldiers. Protocol, patriotism and common sense suggest they get support. Logic and caution would tell anyone to prepare for the possibility that the Greek has friends, that they are at that moment elsewhere in the city, missing him, looking for him. Wisdom tells him that there is no heroism in going it alone, only foolishness. But he cannot bring himself to call for help.

The problem is that they are not supposed to be here, and he knows it, and while looting has been tolerated, it is frowned upon among the dignified officer corps—where Emre believes he belongs and is desperate to rejoin. The problem is that Emre, while still officially an officer, has been an outcast for over a year, an outcast ever since someone found out that his older brother had become a raging leftist. The problem is that while Emre comes from a good, respectable family, it only takes the faintest taint of suspicion—guilt by association—to derail a soldier's career.

Had they known, had his brother come out as a radical a few years earlier, Emre would never have been admitted to junior officer school. Now that he had put in his years and earned his rank they couldn't exactly shove him aside for actions that were not his own.

He remembers: growing up, the club not too far from his home where only officers or their guests could enter. He remembers them being driven up in their Cadillacs and Mercedes, manly-mustached men with their beautiful wives and girlfriends, the cream of the crop, protectors of the nation, the men whom every man respected. He remembers the pride of his father when he brought the note that he had been accepted to officer's school, the dignity and honor of it. There were rumors—rumors some laughed at—that some recruits would be so moved the first time they saluted the flag that they would tear up and become faint. But those were not rumors for Emre, because he was one of those recruits.

He remembers then, the humiliating grilling the captain's commission put him through when they first heard rumors of his brother: baiting him with leading questions, almost begging him to admit his secret communist/anarchist/socialist sympathies, to give them an excuse to kick him out. But he was resolute and sure—he told them he wished he could kill all the communists, even his brother, if necessary. He was almost afraid that they would take it as a challenge or test; and he was yet more afraid that he would do it with pleasure, that was how much he hated his brother for ruining things.

After eight years, he has earned the right to be one of the elite, one of the exceptional men with the solemn responsibility of protecting the great nation of Turkey—not just the nation, but all the great Turkish people—from their many enemies (Greeks, "Kurds," Armenians, Syrians, Iranians, Islamists, communists, politicians of any stripe). After eight years, he has the *right.* His flag, his uniform: he has *earned it.*

Wisdom and common sense: *call for help*. Dignity and honor: *take the Greek bastard yourself and string him up on your own*. He just imagines the farce of calling for help at this point, the looks they would give him, the sniggers of disgust at how far he has fallen. He was not supposed to be here, looting a long-since looted city like a peasant. But of course, if he and Kadir caught the Greek on their own, well, who could look down at that?

But there are other reasons: in spite of everything, he is an officer after all, and he has a feeling for how the authorities think. The last thing they need is anther international incident, a major military operation that would hand the Greeks another sympathy card from the world. Better to handle things quickly, quietly, if only the idiot Kadir could hold things together.

Of course it is possible that the solider is not inside the building; it is possible that Kadir made a mistake, that he never went in that house, or that he managed to slip out the back before Kadir made it around to cover it. It is possible, but Emre doesn't think so. He has a feeling that the boy is inside, a feeling like you might have when chasing a rat into a corner, and the rat lies very still but you know he is there. Emre has a feeling, a feeling he attributes to officer's intuition, to his years of training, and suddenly he feels bitter again.

He looks at Kadir's face; his fellow soldier can barely stand the tension, he is motioning for them to rush in. *Wait*, Emre mouths silently.

Then: he sees movement, the faintest shift of a shadow in the second-floor window, proof that the boy is inside this very house, that they have him trapped. Suddenly his eagerness vanishes. He doesn't want to be here, doesn't want to do this. It is strange, he thinks, he has never fantasized about actually killing someone. Unlike more than a few soldiers he knew—soldiers who would take pleasure in inflicting pain and death on an enemy—for Emre being a soldier was about authority, status, respect. Yes, protecting his nation. But not this. He feels nauseated. He considers leaving; he considers just walking away. It would be easy to signal Kadir to retreat, or better to simply stroll away, as if the whole thing had never happened. But there would be a witness; Kadir would see him, would demand to know why, would wonder if Emre was a coward, and Emre would have no answers to give him. Perhaps I am a coward, he thinks. Perhaps I am truly not fit to be an officer. The thought infuriates him.

Killing a man teaches you things about yourself, things you can't learn any other way, but he is sorry that this will be Kadir's first experience of it. Killing someone in a firefight and executing someone in cold-blood—both necessary evils—were entirely different experiences that taught you entirely different things about yourself and about your life.

He forces himself to think about the impudence of the boy, and how the boy had shot at him, had almost taken his eye out. He forces himself to think about how the Greeks were in Cyprus, how they planned to exterminate the Turks, how they *were* exterminating the Turks before the 1974 peace operation came. He reminds himself: this boy would kill me if he had a chance.

It's time, he thinks. *It's time to see what Greeks and Turks are made of.*

Chapter Eleven

At that moment, on the other side of Cyprus, Elias sips bitter coffee and plays backgammon under the arched cloister of an ancient monastery in the hills above Paphos. Dozens of terra-cotta planters, overflowing with fragrant green life—dwarf lemon and orange trees, herbs of lavender and basil and oregano, potted palm trees, flowers of all kinds—line the arcade. An old stone bell tower reaches up above deep-pitched cascading rooftops. Here, 700 meters above sea-level, the summer air is somewhat cooler than by the sea.

In spite of the fact that he is usually a defensive backgammon player, Elias finds himself throwing a series of low numbered rolls of the dice, leaving three pieces open. The monk opposite studies the board, throws a double-six and cries a shout of victory. He grabs the pieces, slams them on the wooden board with a loud crack and hits all three of Elias' exposed positions. "I've got you again, my friend!" he says.

Elias punches the air and slaps his forehead, resists cursing. He has always been uncharacteristically competitive with backgammon.

Father Anthimos sits back in his chair and smiles. Elias takes some comfort in the fact that he can still recognize his friend, and yet this too is strange. If anything, now, two years after his tonsure and a year after his ordination, Anthimos seems more himself with his long black beard and long black robes than he had when he was just another hotel owner's kid, an older boy that he knew and played with on the beach.

After that, the game goes quickly, it belongs to Anthimos, no question. "Ah, relax," says Anthimos. "Take a moment, and then we can talk about why you're really here."

A cat rubs itself along the line of planters, marking its territory. Somewhere in the distance a car grinds its gears, winding through a nearby village, but otherwise, all is silent. Elias takes a moment, and thinks about the question.

"I am wondering if you will take my confession."

Earlier, when he arrived, there had been no one there, but the courtyard was open, so he entered. He wasn't surprised to be alone; Elias wasn't sure how many full-time monks lived here, but he knew there were few. After several minutes, he went to the gift store, where he found an old monk with a wispy gray beard sitting in his black cassock behind the counter, counting knots on his prayer rope. The monk greeted Elias and suggested he wait for Father Anthimos in the chapel. After lighting a candle, he crossed himself and went forward to kiss the icons. Inside, a veritable counsel of saints looked down at him from the gilded iconostasis as though they were speaking not only to him but to each other and to all the believers in the world.

"Sometimes I wonder if kissing icons is idolatry," he says.

Father Anthimos gives him a crooked smile as if to say why are you bringing up childish theological debates? "What is idolatry?" asks the monk.

"I don't know," says Elias. "Worshiping graven images?"

The monk shakes his head. "No," he says. "It is worshiping anything that is not God. Why do you think that these are the first of the commandments? It is because it is from idolatry and having other gods before God that all sin springs."

Elias nods his head, but his is unsure what Anthimos is getting at.

"Let me put it this way. I doubt very much that you are here today because you are afraid of kissing icons."

Elias nods again. "I feel as though I am being stalked by death," he says.

"What do you mean?"

"Last year the motorcycle protesters, this year the boy on the Green Line ..."

"And this has to do with you?"

"Look," says Elias. "I want to confess, but I don't know how."

Anthimos smiles and looks around the sunny courtyard. "Does this look like confession?" he asks. "We're just talking. We can do the sacrament later. One thing at a time."

"I don't even know what I believe," says Elias.

"We could talk about that," says Anthimos. "I could take your confession and you could confess your lack of faith. That would be good. But I don't think that is why you are here. You have another reason. Unless you tell me what it is, we won't really solve anything."

Elias shakes his head. "If you knew about my life," he said, "What I've done ... the women ..."

"I don't want to hear about women," says Anthimos.

"Okay," says Elias. "But hear me out. You see, we only have one life to live. Of course people say that. Then other people say, this isn't our real life anyway, all that matters is the next life, when we will be judged." He pauses for a second to see if he can ascertain his friend's reaction to what he has said, but he can't. "I mean, that this life is just a rehearsal for the next one. But I always thought that was crazy. Not just crazy; cowardly. It's not that I don't believe in God—I do believe in God, how can you not believe in God? Have you ever looked at the cliffs near the *Petra tou Romiou?* Have you felt it in your gut when you see a really beautiful woman walking down the street?"

Anthimos slams his fist down on the table. "I don't want to hear about women!" he shouts. "Tell me: why are you really here?"

"I ..."

"I can tell you what I think," says Anthimos. "One possibility. You have come here because you have stopped enjoying it, this, your life. Yes, you get to experience, to taste the beauty that God has created, but you feel it's not enough. You want more, you want another way to reach out and feel God."

Father Anthimos pauses, pours himself another shot of *zivania*, and takes a long, careful sip before continuing. "Another possibility is that there is something else bothering you."

"Okay," says Elias quietly. "Here is the story." He begins.

"I met him last year, the boy. The one who was killed on the Green Line. He approached me to ask me about the *Filiki Eteria*." Fortunately Anthimos has talked to Elias about his grand plans to liberate Cyprus from the Turks before, so there is nothing to explain.

"He wanted to join, he said. He was from Famagusta, or his family was. He was bitter at the world and disillusioned by politics, just like the rest of us.

"At first, I was furious. The *Filiki Eteria* was a secret. Who had told him about it? I wanted to find whoever it was and kill him! Anyway, I told the boy I had no idea what he was talking about, that he should go away.

"But he kept coming back to me, kept telling me he knew about it, knew I was involved, which wasn't even true anymore anyway. At that point I just wanted to be done with the whole idea. This was after the biker protests—what had that accomplished? Our ideas weren't any better. I just wanted to forget about the whole thing but he kept asking me about it.

"So finally I started telling him things. Small things at first. And then I asked him questions. What would you do if you were in the group? He said he didn't know. I asked him for ideas. He went away for a while and didn't come back, and then he did and it was the same conversation all over again. So eventually I told him about our plan to raise the Greek flag in Famagusta.

"I also told him we didn't have a plan to get there. That was a lie by the way—we had a pretty developed plan—but I wanted to see what he would say. I told him he could help us. He was stationed on the line; he could talk to the soldiers on the other side, make friends with them. Find out things. I wanted to see what he would say, what he would do. But he told me no, it was too dangerous. I said, 'you're scared to talk to them across the Green Line but you're thinking about crossing with us all the way to Famagusta?' You have to understand, I thought this would put him off."

"And?" asks the monk.

"And so he went away. I thought *good riddance*. But then he came back. 'There must be something I can do,' he said. I said 'Forget it, if you don't have the courage to do this thing, then you are not one of us.' This made him very sad. I could see it—it looked like I had crushed his spirit.

"I'm telling the truth, the first conversations I really thought I would put him off. But when he kept coming back, I started wanting to see what I could get him to do. It's something about me; I like to see if I can get people to do things. I provoke them, I enjoy it. I can't resist it—it's not always a bad thing. Do you know how many soldiers who were too scared to pick up a foreign tourist girl until I pushed them? But other times, it can be cruel."

Father Anthimos ignores Elias' implication that pushing soldiers to pick up women is a good thing. "So that's the end of it? He talked to the Turks?"

"Not quite," says Elias. "He called me, told me he had made friends with a couple of them on the other side. He told me he was thinking about trading with them, building good will.

"I told him not to. It's crazy, I said. I told him there was no *Filiki Eteria*, that it was all a lie, that I was just messing with him. He got depressed. I thought that would stop him, but it didn't."

"The next thing I heard was a rumor that a soldier was trading with the Turks over the Green Line. I knew it was him—of course it was him. I thought I should call him, try to convince him to stop, but by that point I was angry too. No—more than that: I wanted to see what would happen.

"The next thing I heard was that a soldier had been shot and killed."

Father Anthimos rubs his beard thoughtfully, pondering Elias' story. Silence sits between them for an excruciating moment, and then longer. Elias watches his old friend, remembers when they were both just spoiled hotel boys, with too much money and too much freedom.

Finally, the monk speaks. "You are responsible. You are entirely responsible for the boy's death."

The conclusion hits Elias like a blow to the chest, but he agrees with it; after all, this is what he has been saying. "So what, then," he says hoarsely, "do I do?"

The monk leans back in his chair, and closes his eyes. In his hand he holds a knotted prayer-rope that he runs through his fingers. "Have you talked to the boy's family?" he asks.

"No," says Elias.

"Good," says the monk. "Don't talk to them. You will only bring them more pain. Instead, pray for them. Pray for the salvation of the boy."

Elias nods quietly.

"Come with me," says the monk. They are still talking as he rises and leads Elias into the chapel, and to a small table in the corner with a gilded gospel on it.

"But I would wager that this is still not the only reason you are here."

Elias is taken aback by the monk's rapid dismantling of his defenses. He realizes with a sudden sense of relief that there is no point in hiding anymore. "There is a woman," he says. "And my cousin ..."

He remembers moments, times he and Joanna had together —Elias had of course been with any number of women, but he believes Joanna is the first woman he ever truly loved.

"You have to let her go," says Anthimos.

"But I can't!" A couple of ugly German tourists in tight, high shorts have entered and are watching what is happening as if it is performance art.

"You must," says the monk.

Elias takes a deep breath. And then: "Alright. I surrender."

"Kneel," say the monk.

Elias is on his knees; the monk drapes his stole over his friend's back. The prayers for redemption wash over him. Yes, he thinks, the path to forgiveness, redemption.

Minutes later, he rises, unsure of what to expect. He feels both clean and unresolved. After all this there is more to be said, more to be decided; there is the question of what to do now, but confession is over, and Father Anthimos seems to have moved on. "Come," he says. "Let's sit and get another drink and play some more."

Through the chapel doorway, the open air and bright hot summer beckons. They step through the threshold together, from the gilded shadows spilling out of the chapel into the piercing light of day, and Elias feels his breath catch in his chest.

They sit and drink and play in silence, the taste of heavy-proof alcohol burning in their throats; for a long time, the only sound is the whisper of a faint breeze rising from a ravine below them, and the clicking pieces on the lacquered wood of the backgammon board.

Father Anthimos wins three games a in a row. "We monks have more time on our hands than you soldiers," he says.

Elias, slightly irritated, asks if holiness has anything to do with rolling three double-sixes in a row. Anthimos laughs again and says it is just as likely be a trick of the devil as anything.

"So," says Elias. "What do I do now?"

"What do you want to do?"

"I'm not sure," Elias says.

"What do you think you should do?"

Elias puts his face in his hands.

"Ah," says the monk. "You know the answer. But I will tell you anyway. You must go to them, tell them you have repented, and ask for their forgiveness, as painful as it is. Go and speak to them; repent and trust in the Holy Spirit to guide your voice. Go to them and surrender yourself to Christ's will. Allow this suffering to break open your hardened heart; only in this way will you transcend the self-love that is not true love; only in this way will you finally be open to feel the love of Christ opening and flowing through your heart."

Elias nods. "And what then, of the dead soldier and his mother and father?"

"Pray for them," the monk says simply, "and accept that some things cannot be undone."

Elias leaves, holding a new knotted prayer rope. He knows where Joanna is; he will go to her. He must find Petros as well. He reaches into his pocket and pulls out an unopened envelope addressed to him from his cousin that he picked up from the station in Deryneia just before he left that morning. It was postmarked the day before; it was just luck that Elias got it so soon.

He has put off opening it, he is afraid of what his cousin will say. Petros knows he lied about being with Joanna, he must, and this will be what the letter is about, that much he knows. But what will it say? What kind of spite and pain lies in the ink there?

Now, after his confession, Elias is finally ready to know. He opens his pocket-knife and cuts the envelope open, carefully unfolds the letter, and begins to read it. He is correct about the spite and pain, he feels it through the ink and into the nerves in his fingers, nerves that connect directly to a pool of guilt in his intestines, a pain in his heart.

And then: *I am going home,* says the letter finally. *I am returning to Famagusta.*

Elias curses.

Chapter Twelve

Petros slumps against a wall, hugs his legs to his chest. If he were a more religious boy, he might think that this is a good time to pray; instead he tries to catch his breath and then drinks half a canteen of water. He isn't sure; he has the feeling that one of the soldiers may have seen him enter the house, but there is no sound or movement now. They could have retreated or moved on; they could be looking for him elsewhere, or they could be outside, waiting for him to make his move; or they could be calling for reinforcements.

This is unexpected, he thinks. He can't believe he let them surprise him. It makes him feel sour and uncertain.

The second floor of the home is surprisingly hot, open and exposed. Petros finds a room and closes the door. He should scan his surroundings, think about next steps, but all he can do is catch his breath and bake.

He smells the sea. Under other circumstances, such a home would make him feel happy and alive (he imagines it now, fully furnished, with a late-summer breeze blowing in) but now he wishes only for darkness, a place to be hidden. He understands suddenly the impulse of rodents and snakes; most people fear the darkness for what lurks there, but when you are being hunted, you want to be the thing that lurks. He must find an escape route and a vantage point. It is too late: he hears soft footsteps on the first floor, and then on the flight of stairs.

It takes a moment: and then a pounding hits the door; it splinters, cracks, twists, holding on tenaciously to its rotting hinges. A boot smashes through the center panel, a leg follows, falling through as if surprised, and then pulls back, momentarily stuck. Petros backs away rapidly, reaching for his sidearm, wishing he had pulled it and shot. A voice clatters in Turkish, and then yells "freeze!" in English, but by then Petros has retreated into the adjacent room, another empty bedroom, out of the first door's sightline, but there is no other way out, he feels the summer breeze from the window behind him, realizing he is exposed, backs into the corner, and squats, just as the frustrated Turkish soldier pulls his leg in and begins firing—both at the door and through it, sending splinters of wood and flecks of green paint through the room as bullets slam into the wall opposite. The sound is deafening, each shot startles him, causing his body to jerk involuntarily, his guts twisting and wrenching.

He aims his pistol at the doorway.

The world becomes a tunnel: thank God he can still see the doorway. God? Should he not now be praying to God, to save his life or at least his soul? *There are sins to confess*, he thinks.

Strange that he has so much time to think, and yet this is what he is thinking about. Even as his fingers fumble with the holster, his fingers that suddenly feel as numb and clumsy as little balloons.

Strange, how multiple trains of thought run through his head, multiple voices: one in a low tone saying over and over *think think think think* and just above it, a voice that is laughing at him for his foolishness, that he is about to die for a woman who doesn't love him; and then just above that, a voice wondering what it will feel like to kill a man.

The sidearm rises, finally; he aims at the doorway and remembers to think suddenly that he should be crouching. Shots leap out of the muzzle of his gun, as if it has decided to fire on its own. What is he thinking? He should have waited; waited for one of them to step through to take a good shot; now they are on the other side, waiting for him.

Ringing in his ears; spent shells on the floor. How many Turks are waiting on the other side of that doorway? He can't be sure, he feels his bowels loosening, there is no escape. A warm breeze rises through the window, and Petros remembers that he has a grenade, but isn't sure how to throw it through the doorway and stay out of range of the shrapnel, and just as he thinks this, a lone hand hurls its own grenade through the open doorway into his room. It bounces off the back wall, rolls to the edge.

He stares at it for perhaps less than a second. A breeze blows through the open window. Later, he will think for a long time about that window; he will contemplate the fact that he was on the second floor, that it wouldn't have been hard to jump through it, maybe even without injury; he will contemplate how it might have been possible to escape.

Instead, he stands up and walks briskly through the open doorway into the room where the Turks are, as if he is an irate actor storming off the set in a fit of disgust.

~~~~

Kadir isn't sure what he expected when he pulled the pin and threw the grenade—but this wasn't it. The soldier walks past
~~~~

them without making eye contact, out of the room toward the building's front stairway.

Kadir and Emre stare at him, realizing too late that they should have trained their guns on the doorway. Kadir recovers first, aims his M16 at the figure just as he passes through the doorway toward the building's front stairs. Emre is still shouting "halt!" in Turkish. Emre sees the boy's face: a face not unlike his brother's face; a face not unlike his own. Maybe they had made a mistake, after all.

But by now, Kadir has pulled the trigger and unleashed a burst of automatic rifle fire at the doorway, but it is too late, he is already past, bounding down the stairs, two at a time. The grenade explodes in the other room: all three soldiers jump with a start. The boy trips—they hear him tumbling now, down the stairs, head over heels.

Kadir rushes toward the door, eager not to give up the advantage, but Emre intercepts him, catching him before he can reach it. Wait, he mouths. They squat on either side of the door, not exactly good cover, but neither of them thinks the boy is coming back up the stairs.

Kadir fumbles with his belt, looking for another grenade, but Emre stops him again, hushes him. For a few seconds there was no sound, but now they hear the soldier moving again, as if his is pulling himself up from falling. Kadir starts to move forward —he is prepared to shoot the boy from the top of the stairs, but Emre moves first. He takes the flight in two bounds, hurtles down, raising his rifle over his head and slamming it on the back of the soldier, smashing him to the ground as he tries to rise.

Kadir is behind him, he tries to cover Emre with his rifle, but the stairwell is far too narrow. It doesn't matter anyway, they can both see the boy isn't a threat—not exactly unconscious, he is still moving slowly, more like a damaged insect than a man.

Emre motions for Kadir to come around, to get a clear shot. Then he kicks the boy's pistol away, picks up his rifle and slides it across the room, far from where the soldier could reach it. Both of them exhale suddenly, simultaneously, as if they had both been holding their breath, and can now release it, now that the boy is disarmed. Then Emre kicks the prostrate figure sharply in the ribs. The boy cries out.

So this is what we're doing now, thinks Kadir with a slight smile. He steps forward and swings his foot back.

~~~~

Fuzziness; things move rapidly now. Boots kicking him; ribs, guts, the back of his head, now his face. Gasping for breath; pain, blood. Somehow his weapons are gone, his shirt ripped. Somehow it comes to this. He is cursing himself; he thinks of how he had believed that his life was over when he found out for certain about Joanna and Elias, but he understood nothing. This, this was real death, now in front of him. He feels like a man who has jumped from a bridge only to realize as he falls that life is indeed worth living after all.

Petros: in and out of consciousness, though he feels he has been awake the whole time—but how does that explain the fact that he is suddenly weaponless, his pack strewn across the floor, his shirt ripped? The boots and fists and rifle-butts rain down on him; the blows to his head are the worst, every time it feels both like something is splintering and as if his whole body is being wrung inside a church-bell. Then he thinks, *no,* the blows
~~~~

to his body are the worst; the ones to his back making his torso seize up, the terrible pain in his kidneys, the cracking sensation on his rib, the emptying of breath—he gasps and squeals like a barking seal trying to suck in air, they kick him in the chest again—blood spurts out, around from somewhere, his heart burns, *it could be stopping,* he thinks, *they have stopped my heart, they have killed me.*

~~~~

"Stop, enough!" Emre cries out finally. They look, both of them, at the dog of a Greek; he has been beaten down. They look for craftiness, calculation, but the boy just looks weary. Emre tells Kadir to keep his pistol trained on the soldier, while he retreats to the corner of the room.

In spite of his appearance, Kadir is sure that the soldier is about to make a run for it; it is, after all, what he would do. He trains his pistol at the boy's face: his hand shakes so violently that it looks as though the gun will fire itself.

The soldier gathers himself to his knees and vomits on the floor, shuddering violently. "Please," he chokes in English. "Don't kill me."

Kadir understand this, even though he doesn't speak English. Emre does, but at that moment Emre is on the radio, trying to summon someone, to get someone with some authority to tell them what to do. Emre has realized he is in over his head.

Kadir strains to hear—but Emre's voice is hushed, and the hiss of the radio makes it all but impossible to hear, and anyway his eyes are on the soldier in front of him. Finally, he shouts back to Emre, suggests that they tie the boy up until they figure out what to do.
~~~~

Emre thinks this is a good idea, but they have no rope, so Emre orders Kadir to remove his belt, and tie the boy's hands behind his back. This is a weak solution, and all three of them know it—as tight as they tie it, the leather will eventually loosen—which means that Kadir still has to keep his gun trained on the soldier at every second, with a focus that would have been exhausting in any case, but is worse with the feeling that his pants could fall down at any moment. (He was a skinny boy, you see.)

Then Emre realizes he has zip-ties in his equipment bag—he had forgotten, he was using them for some tent work recently—so he takes over, covering the prisoner, and sends Kadir back to the house where they had left their large packs.

A few minutes later, Kadir returns with the zip-ties, they replace the belt, and Kadir's pants stay up. Nonetheless, he is infuriated and humiliated, and wants to take it out on the prisoner.

"What did they say?" He is referring to the radio, to senior command. Kadir's own voice surprises him—usually low, suddenly he squawks like a bird, like he did when he was 12. This is not what he expected, in no way what he expected. He feels ashamed of himself, ashamed of his shaking hand, ashamed now of his voice. No one told him that it would be like this, that the first moment of violence is always like this, that if he is lucky there will be other chances to prove his courage and manhood, and he might get better at it.

"Quiet," barks Emre. "I have to think." He seems frustrated, which makes Kadir more nervous than ever. For the first time, he is starting to think there is no one in control.

~~~~
~~~~

Emre has just gotten off the radio with command, he wants to smash it. They have told him nothing, just "await further instructions." It is the third conversation he has had with them in the last hour.

The first conversation came after they had dragged Petros from the bottom of the stairs, before they splashed water on his face and started trying to kick the life out of him. Both Emre and Kadir had believed the commander when he said they were sending reinforcements, but now time was passing. Kadir had expected jeeps, perhaps helicopters. He wondered if there were other Greeks around, hiding in the buildings—it makes no sense that the soldier would be alone.

Emre is cursing, a string of violent and disgusting epithets. He does this now every few minutes. "We need to move him," he says.

He glares at the Greek, the Greek who almost took his eye out, now humbled, on his knees, hands behind his back.

"Where are they?" he barks in English.

The boy looks at him in despair. "Who?" he asks.

"The others!" Emre's voice booms. Kadir cannot tell if he truly is this angry or if he is putting on an act to scare the boy. If it is an act, it seems unnecessary; the soldier, bleeding and wheezing, hands tied behind his back, looks as terrified as anyone Kadir has ever seen. "The others!" Emre continues. "The other spies! Do you think I believe that you came here alone?"

"There are no others," says the soldier. "I am not a spy."

Emre laughs. "Why would you come then?"

The boy chokes for a second, and then spits blood on the floor. "I come," he says, "because this is my home."

Emre talks to Petros for a while, and then stops. Every so often Kadir asks him what the boy is saying, but when Emre says "nothing important," he can tell from his expression that he didn't believe it.

Then he asks about the army, when are they coming? Emre is unsure of what to say; he feels sorry for his fellow soldier, too slow and dimwitted to understand the truth, that no help is coming—no help, and no answers. The command—men for whom, until a few hours ago, Emre would have literally killed his own brother—are too cowardly to send help or give a direct order of what to do. Every time he calls them on the radio, their answers are increasingly ambiguous. Emre understands—the last thing they want is another international incident. But he and Kadir are standing face to face with the enemy, and don't have the luxury of such worries.

Kadir, Emre thinks, doesn't understand yet the truth about noble armies—that, however they present themselves, even noble armies are made up of ignoble men, cowards and liars; that all armies are made up of men, men who are incompetent, men who are afraid, just as you are afraid, my brother soldier.

Already Emre knows the truth; he knows what he and Kadir will be called upon to do. They will be called upon to make the problem go away. It is now just a matter of time.

Against his better judgment, he decides to start a conversation with the boy, with a different tone. "Why are you here?"

~~~~

Petros looks up, surprised at being addressed. Everything hurts. Thinking disappears, the only thing left is the experience of his body, its pains, its hunger and thirst, but also a strange,
~~~~

creeping euphoria. Why is he here? A good question, a question without an answer.

"Hey! You!" shouts the Turk furiously. "I asked you question!"

Petros' voice crawls up his throat, comes out his mouth soft, low and hard. "By what right," he says, "Do you ask me that question?" he pauses. "This is my home."

The Turk nods, and then shakes his head. "Not anymore," he says.

Petros coughs; there is blood and phlegm in his mouth. He spits on the ground, but some of it sticks on his lips, runs down his chin, mixes with the slowly congealing blood that ran down his face when Kadir had kicked his head. His shoulders ache—they have wrenched his arms so far back that the muscles in his shoulders feel about to rip.

He looks up at the young Turkish soldier, who has realized that he is getting nowhere with this line of questioning. What happens next, Petros wonders. A voice in his head begins to run down a list, things he knows about the Turkish army and what they are capable of. Stories of torture, rape. Not just from the invasion, but all along, for hundreds of years.

He remembers from the history books how, in 1571, the Turks surrounded the old Venetian walls and laid siege to Famagusta; how they cut off the ears and chopped off the nose and skinned alive the Venetian general, Marco Antonio Bragadino.

The Turk shakes his head again, realizing he is getting nowhere. "What's your name?"

Petros doesn't answer.

"I am Emre," says the Turk with a forced smile. "This is Kadir."

Petros looks at them suspiciously. Does this solider really think he can earn Petros' trust?

"Why are you here?" Emre asks.

"I already told you."

"I don't believe you."

"Why do you think I'm here then?"

"I think you're a spy."

"Not a very good one," says Petros.

"A very bad spy," says Emre.

Part of his mind gropes around for some kind of dignity. There has to be a reason, a justification of the stupid death he is about to experience.

"Why are you here?" Emre asks again.

"Why are *you* here?" asks Petros.

"This is my job. We are here to protect Turkish people."

"You are doing your job." Petros spits on the floor. "I am trying to live my life."

"My job is my life," says Emre. "I am a professional soldier."

"Then you are a sad excuse for a person," says Petros. He is not sure what he is doing, why he is provoking him. He looks at the other soldier—Kadir—to see if the boy understands what they are saying, but he sees only confusion on his face.

"I don't blame you," says Emre. "You are not Turkish. You can't understand."

"I understand that you are all butchers!" Petros is shouting now, or trying to, even though every breath, every word is pain in his side.

"We? What about you? How many Turks have you Greeks killed? You should see the photographs! Do you know about the bathtub murders?" He is referring to an infamous slaughter of Turkish-Cypriot women and children in the back-alley war of 1963.

"They deserved it!" Petros shouts. He is not even sure he believes that Greeks were responsible, but this is no time for forensic arguments. Emre responds with a sharp strike to Petros ear. *Yes,* Petros thinks. *Finish it. End it.*

"You fucker," says Emre. "Now I will make you admit that Cyprus is Turkish." He kicks Petros again. Now he shouts again in Turkish, and hearing this the other boy shouts as well, pumping his shaking fist into the air, and it doesn't take understanding the language to know what they are saying: *Cyprus is Turkish.*

Finish it! Do it! Petros cries in his mind.

But instead, Emre calms down suddenly, gets a cool look on his face, and then he smiles, as if he has just won a victory in refusing to let the Greek boy provoke him. He talks quietly to his fellow soldier.

Petros strains against the ties that keep his hands behind his back, but he can't move. Emre steps forward and grabs the front of what remains of Petros shirt, pulling him toward his face. "Cyprus is Turkish," he growls. "We will kill you all or drive you into the sea!"

Then he leaves the room again, leaving the other soldier to stand guard.

Kadir aims his pistol at Petros again. His hand is still shaking, but less so. "Cyprus Turk," he says.

Time goes by.

Petros looks around the room; they are on the first floor of the house, in a hallway full of doors, a chiaroscuro of light from differing directions illuminating the broken walls. Dust, peeling paint and years of dried animal droppings mix on the floor. At the end of the hall, the shell of an old refrigerator lies on its side as if it had been dragged halfway out and then abandoned. Closer, a lone wooden chair facing one of the inner doors is the only piece of furniture left.

Through the door, both of them can hear Emre on the radio, but the words are inaudible, and for Petros at least, incomprehensible. He tries to tell himself that he is not afraid to die here, now, in his city, but this is not true. The truth is, he is more afraid of living, of what kind of pleasure they will take in hurting him.

His home, his family—the warm body of the girl he felt so briefly against his own—seems many lifetimes distant from him now. *This is my home,* he thinks, but this is no one's home.

After a long time, Emre returns again, a cruel, self-satisfied look on his eyes. He smiles. "Petros," he says. "Very nice to meet you."

Chapter Thirteen

In Ayios Pavlos, a suburb of Nicosia, the elementary school teachers gossip. There is a Greek Cypriot, they say, who gets drunk, crosses the Green Line and pulls down the Turkish flag, while Turkish guards sleep. Then, he runs back through the United Nations-controlled buffer zone waving it and shouting.

They have good reason to take interest in what happens on the line, since it runs no more than 200 yards from the school. From the playground, the children could wave at the Turkish soldiers opposite, if they wanted to.

People in the neighborhood have complained about the sounds of sporadic gunfire from the Turkish side ever since the invasion, but it has gotten worse since the protests. Now, they say, windows are shattered by bullets late at night, as if to remind the Greeks how close they are, how easy it would be to roll over the line and kill them all in their beds.

Joanna has lived not far from here for most of her life, with her older brother and her mother, in a little house built with the help of the government and some kind of foreign aid after the war. Like everyone else, they built it with a veranda facing north, toward the Kyrenia mountains; facing the villages and landscape they could no longer touch. They did it as a kind of remembrance but also defiance.

What is the point? Joanna wonders. So that every day she could wake up and be reminded of what she lost? She looks out now toward the village of Deryneia on the side of the range, where the Turks have painted two enormous Turkish flags, next to a quote from the founder of modern Turkey, Kemal Ataturk, which reads in Turkish, "It's best to be a Turk."

"I can't take it anymore," her mother says as they drink their afternoon coffee. She has been saying this for years, and she even meant it for a while, when all three of them left for Salonica, until it became clear that being even farther away from home wouldn't cure their loneliness.

Everyone felt sorry for Maria, for what she had gone through, and Joanna always suspected there were reasons for this even deeper and older than the invasion and loss of Joanna's father. But why wouldn't she talk about it? Didn't she want to remember the good times, the happy family that they were—even if it was only for a few years? More importantly, didn't she understand that Joanna wanted—needed—to build and hold onto some picture of that time for herself?

But Joanna knows she won't talk about it, and she won't leave, not again, so there is nothing to do but change the subject.

"Anna is moving schools," says Joanna.

"What? Where?"

"Here, to the school in Ayios Pavlos," Joanna says.

This is not shocking news, but Maria looks as though she had been struck. "But ..." she says, "what about you? Are you moving too?"

"No Mama," she says. "Not this year. They only had one position anyway."

"But why her and not you?" she asks. "You are a better teacher than she is, I am sure of it!"

No, thinks Joanna, I'm not. She doesn't tell her mother that she never applied for the position, even though she heard about it first, because she doesn't want to come back from the mountains. Not here, anyway, to this neighborhood. "There will be other opportunities," she says.

They sit quietly for a few moments. Joanna picks up a newspaper. There is another story on the front page about how the Turks are threatening war over the Cyprus government's purchase of a Russian missile system. The system was supposed to provide an air-defense against the long-range American cluster-bomb missiles the Turks had purchased. World leaders were pressuring the Cypriot government to cancel the deal, which all the Greeks in Cyprus thought was outrageous—does a nation not have the right to defend itself, especially when the enemy has already eaten half of it?

Joanna is no longer sure how she feels about such things. Something in her life-long rage and hatred of Turks has shifted in the past few months. At first she ascribed it to weariness—hatred, after all, is exhausting.

But the change really began the day she and Anna went to see a pacifist Turkish Cypriot poet speak at the Famagusta gate—the portal through the old Venetian walls in Nicosia that face the city of Joanna's birth. It was a strange event for her to attend; for most of her life, the idea of reconciliation with Turks was anathema to her.

The poet was a small woman, who seemed at first to recede behind a curtain of black hair that hung in front of her narrow face and dark eyes. But when she spoke, her voice was forceful.

How many Turkish Cypriots were willing to live in Greek Cyprus now? Joanna wondered.

My father said to love my country, the poet read. My country has been divided into two, which half of it shall I love? It is time to end the nationalism and militarism on both sides, she said.

Joanna tries to push the thought aside. She folds the newspaper and picks up the mail. There she sees it: another letter from Petros. Dear God, she thinks, haven't there been enough letters—enough confessions?

She has barely stopped thinking about him in the days since he rode away. She wants to talk to him—in person—and tell him, again, that she hadn't meant for it to happen that way, that she blames herself. She wants to ask him to be patient for her to sort things out. She wants to ask him to start over from the beginning, to see if they could find a way to do things right.

But the moment she thinks these things, she is overwhelmed by the mess she has found herself in—the mess she has caused, the mess thrown upon her by these men. Elias has been calling, twice so far that day. Each time she hears his voice she slams down the receiver, which, she suspects bitterly, just encourages him. And then there is Anna, her best friend. How can she explain to her that she has been carrying on with her little cousin, but that it's over, and now she is thinking about her little brother? My life, Joanna thinks, is like a miserable Greek soap opera.

~~~~

The phone buzzes, and buzzes again. It is the fifth time Elias has tried to call Joanna since he left the monastery, each time as unsuccessful as the last. He keeps trying as he drives back,
~~~~

stopping at the central cafe of every other little village to use their phone as he winds his way through the mountains toward Nicosia.

The first two times he called her from stops on the road from Paphos, from little village cafes where he stopped to use the restroom and drink another *frappe.* Sometime in late afternoon he closed in on the village. By then he already suspected that she wasn't there, but he came by anyway. The little house she and Anna rented seemed strangely dead, no car in the driveway, but he pounded on the door anyway.

He wants to apologize for betraying her and hurting her so many times; he wants to tell her that he knows it is over, that he will leave her alone. But more importantly, he needs to ask her if she knows where Petros is, if she too has received a letter, if what he suspects his idiot cousin of doing is true.

The third time, he called her mother's home from Platres; her mother answered. "Just a moment," Joanna's mother said, "I'll put her on."

A moment later, Joanna: not her voice, exactly, but her heavy breath, before she spoke: *do not call me again.*

"Wait," he said, "You have to listen to me," but she had already hung up.

The next time he called her it was from Kakopetria. Her mother answered again. "Joanna and I were cut off," he told her, "I thought I would try her again. Tell her it's important."

A minute later, he hears Joanna's voice. "Don't call me again," Joanna said. "I am going out. I will not be home, you will not reach me tonight, do not call me," and the line goes dead.

Wait, he said, *You don't know that I have changed my ways, I am calling to make amends.* But she was already off the phone.

Now he calls her from a little cafe out of the foothills, and the phone just buzzes, even her mother is not picking up and he wonders what Joanna has told her.

As the phone rings, he looks up, the cafe television is on, playing the evening news. He thinks how late it is getting and only as an afterthought catches what the report is saying.

The story is about unconfirmed reports of a Cypriot soldier who is missing; one witness says he saw the soldier walking toward the Turkish side near the Famagusta region two nights ago. The same reports say that the soldier might be mentally unstable, and has twice failed to report for duty on time in recent weeks. The army officially denies the report and claims no knowledge of the alleged incident.

Elias' cigarette drops from his mouth and he hangs up the phone. Petros was supposed to meet him for coffee yesterday, and didn't show up. He must call someone, find out if it's correct, what's true. He reaches into his pocket, but is out of change. "Sir!" he shouts. "Please! I must make a phone call, I need some change!"

It is late when he arrives in Nicosia; he stops first at Petros' mother's house, but Petros is of course not there, and his mother has not seen him. It seems as though she hasn't heard the news. Elias smiles, acts casual, "tell him I came by when you see him," he says.

"I never know when I'll see him."

Elias smiles and tries to give her a knowing nod. Then a pause. "I'm also looking for Joanna and Anna," he says.

"Oh," she says, "she and Anna went out. Something down by the Famagusta gate."

The Famagusta Gate: a haunting spot, the historic way in and out of Nicosia. The word gate is almost a misnomer—it is like a giant network of vaulted catacombs. The British used it as a warehouse; since the 1980s it has been a cultural event center, chic centerpiece in the revival of that part of the old town, illuminated by soft lights, and usually filled with cutting-edge art.

It was a place of artists and intellectuals—a place where invariably a communist would be standing outside handing out pamphlets "explaining" that the invasion was just us much the Greek Cypriots' fault as the Turks'.

By the time Elias gets there, however, the event is over. There are still people filtering out, heading down the street. Someone—an attractive young woman—stops him and hands him a flyer, tries to get him to talk about politics, about what it all means. "What do you think?" she asks. He can feel her staring at him, he is wearing his favorite linen jacket and a white shirt, he is aware he looks good, he always looks good.

He is not looking at the girl; his eyes scan the street to see if he can find Anna and Joanna. "I think it's complicated," he says.

"Oh, but that's where you're wrong. It's actually very simple ..." she starts in on a story about how the Turks may be on top now, but it wasn't always that way, how it was *they* who were the victims once, and we who were the oppressors.

Elias waves her away, there is no time for silly debates. He can't wait, he must find Joanna, must find them both, so many reasons now.

He wanders now, away from the gate, inside the walls, down the raw, narrow cobblestone streets of the Taht-el-kale district, streets where Turks and Greeks once lived in some primitive cosmopolitan stew, trading wares and attending each other's funerals. Only Turks, they say, were allowed to ride through the gate on horseback in Ottoman days, but what difference does that make, Elias wonders. Some houses here were restored, their doors sanded and revived with fresh blue paint, while others decay in style, with sultry decadence.

Elias is about to give up when he suddenly remembers a place. A little nightclub, the kind he used to go to in Athens, where people drink themselves to a stupor and dance to *rembetika* music and little gypsy children sell flowers. What makes him think of it? It is not exactly either Joanna or Anna's style.

The place in Nicosia is neither as gritty or subversive as the clubs people go to in Athens; it is, like everything here, Greek, but with a Cypriot character—spirited but polite, uninhibited but well-behaved, wild but not crafty. Cypriots, compared with mainland Greeks, are guileless, and this is the kind of thing Petros and Elias love and hate about them.

Elias had actually taken Joanna to the club once, in spite of her protests; but she had gone, had enjoyed herself, had proven herself to be a lively dancer.

By the time Elias arrives, the club crowd has already overflowed its walls, and is spilling out into the street, clusters of young men and women breaking off into groups, the men still dancing and slapping their feet, the women clapping and singing along to the songs, songs everyone knows, love songs, songs about the *Frangosyriani*, the beautiful girl in Syros, playing the *baglamas* ... But just then, the music pauses, and he takes the opportunity to squeeze through the door past the streaming crowd.

It takes a moment to adjust to the dim light, but then he sees them: Anna, squatting and clapping as Joanna dances the *zebbekiko*—the old *rembetika* dance, the dance that came from somewhere deep in Anatolia, traveling with the refuges of Smyrna after they were forced out of Greece by the Turks in 1922. The *zebbekiko,* an introverted dance of tender-hearted refugees. Unlike other popular Greek folk dances with their fervent and definitive steps, the *zebbekiko* is danced not in a line but in a group of two or three taking turns, with one dancer in the middle and the others squatting and watching, clapping along to keep the strange beat.

Elias watches Joanna dip and sway, strands of her light-brown hair falling over her half-shut eyes as she twists and snaps her fingers, and Elias feels a kind of satisfaction, perhaps he is responsible for this—for breaking the poor girl out of her shell and helping her to see more of life.

Once upon a time it was a man's dance, a dance of warriors, a dance stolen from the Zeybeks, the Turkish irregular militia who moved with their arms out like hawks circling their pray. Now the women dance it too, clapping and howling, standing on chairs and wine-glasses, just as the men do.

Now the band is playing one of Mitropanos' songs: "Roza"—a song about a love that was like a fairytale with nightmares, about a need that became history, and a history that became silence.

Elias claps along as he moves closer to the women; they don't see him, not at first, not until the song ends and Joanna looks up and opens her blue eyes. She is shockingly beautiful, standing there in her red dress, Elias thinks. It is no wonder that Petros is so mad for her, and once again, Elias realizes what a shit he is for taking her away from him, and for ruining her to boot. *People must think I am immune to guilt*, he thinks. Had he never had these thoughts before, or does he just not remember? Was he just that good at ignoring his conscience? And what has changed?

Joanna sees him, a wave of shock and rage crosses her face, a shock and rage that makes her even more stunning, he thinks. *They think I love no women*, he thinks, *but I love all women.*

~~~~

It takes her a second: then she grabs her half-drunk glass of wine and throws it in his face. Red alcohol splashes across his tan jacket and white shirt like blood, but he looks entirely unflustered; he has become the kind of good-looking man who can pull off anything, damn him, she thinks with a faint tremble. He wipes the wine from his face; his thick, sensual lips part for a moment, and he smiles his trademarked smile for a brief instant before his expression turns serious again. She wants to kill him; she tells him not to call; he comes to her house. She tells him to go away and he follows her into the night. One might think he is desperate but his manner is casual, he is always in control. He could grab her and kiss her right now and she would not resist, she wishes he would do it. She has told him to go away again and again and never meant it, not really; God she hates him.

"We need to talk," he says.

Anna, now, is glaring at them both, furious, irritated. *Anna I'm sorry*, thinks Joanna. *I am out of control*, she thinks.
~~~~

The next song is starting. "We need to talk," says Elias.

"No," says Anna, "She is not going anywhere with you."

"All three of us," says Elias.

They look confused.

"Outside."

He turns and walks out, knowing that they will follow. They meet again in the alley outside, where the handsome boys and beautiful girls are laughing and talking.

"How many times do I have to tell you!" She shouts at him, not caring who hears. "I do not want you anymore! Stay away from me!" Her head is buzzing with alcohol, anger, confusion and strange thoughts.

After the event, Joanna and Anna could think of nothing to say to each other, so they came to dance, to clear their minds and reconnect with their souls. So they went to the club and drank too much and tried to close their minds from sad and painful things, and that is when Elias showed up.

"I didn't come to try to win you back," says Elias. "Not this time."

"Then why," hisses Anna, "did you come all this way, call her house a dozen and two times, follow us here to this club on a night when she just wants to be alone?"

Elias bows his head. "I came to say I am sorry and to ask for your forgiveness, though I do not deserve it. But there is something more important: Petros."

~~~~

"What do you mean, you don't know where he is?" Now Anna and Joanna are grilling Elias.

He paces nervously.
~~~~

"We were supposed to meet," Elias says. "He didn't come. I wasn't surprised, he is angry at me." He looks at Joanna. "He sent me a letter."

Joanna puts her hand over mouth. *The letter.* It is in her purse. She had to hide it there quickly when Anna picked her up and Joanna realized it was still sitting out on the kitchen table. She pulls it out, and moves toward the building light so she can read it.

Anna looks confused and irritated. "What are the two of you talking about?"

Elias shakes his head, and Joanna says "I don't know how I became this kind of person." By now they have drifted yards away from the club where the air is calmer and they can talk, but all three of them look back with longing; how nice it would be to be back inside, sweating and dancing until dawn.

"Anna, have you seen him?" Elias asks, his voice now slightly desperate.

Anna shakes her head slowly and with increasing suspicion. Something is going on, but she cannot yet tell if it is just romantic drama—petty jealousies and love triangles that she was tired of overhearing—or if something more serious was happening. "Elias," she says, "What do you know?"

Joanna has opened the letter now, and is reading it.

I am going back for you, it reads. *I am going back to put a flag up for you in our city. I am going back to bring you a memory you can hang on to until you and I can return to our free city together.*

With the letter, a photograph, one Petros has clearly taken of himself, probably with a camera timer. His expression is somehow both stern and relaxed, as if he can't decide to smile at Joanna or to frown at the seriousness of the situation. In the photograph, he stands on the roof of a building; in the background, the distant skyline of Famagusta.

She understands and starts to cry.

At that moment, a passing conversation, a group of boys, talking: "Did you hear? They say another one of us has crossed the Green Line."

Elias reaches out and grabs the boy by the sleeve: *what do you know?* The boy shakes his head—it was in the news, a soldier crossed the Green Line near Famagusta, that is all he knows.

Anna still doesn't know what's going on, or maybe she is still in denial. "Has your mother seen Petros recently?" Elias asks Anna. He doesn't know why. He is still behaving as if there is a chance that Petros hasn't left yet, when he knows this isn't true.

Anna doesn't respond, but instead walks quickly toward the only other open business at that hour, an outdoor cafe. It is less busy and noisy than the club, but still lively, full of young couples and groups of friends drinking coffee and wine, smoking cigarettes, laughing and arguing. A more philosophical crowd, Elias thinks—or a crowd having a more philosophical night. Anna goes straight in to the bar to ask to use the phone. Elias takes the moment to interrupt the conversation of young men to ask them if they have heard anything in the news about a solider who crossed the line. They either haven't heard or plead ignorance.

He can feel Joanna's rising sense of alarm; Petros was just foolish enough to do what they all now suspect. She steps inside, and he follows her. Anna is on the phone, waiting for her mother to answer. There is a television behind the bar, she asks if they will turn it on for her. The bartender shrugs and reaches for the television—an old Greek soap opera is playing. "Would you mind turning on the news?"

Anna gets off the phone and shakes her head.

"He asked me to go with him," Elias says. "I told him to be a man, go by himself."

"He went back for me," Joanna says softly.

Finally, they find what they are looking for. The story: the military is denying reports that a Greek soldier has crossed the Green Line near Famagusta. Then, to his shock, the reporter names the person they suspect is the solider: a young soldier named Petros whose father and uncle had owned the four-star *Golden Aphrodite* hotel.

Anna is pulling her hair, "You are both crazy! All three of you—crazy!!!" She starts crying, leaves for the bathroom.

Elias leaves the cafe, walks out onto the street, he must get some air to think. The night is sultry as usual, and his shirt is damp with perspiration. Joanna runs after him, she is shouting, screaming. "It's your fault!" She is shrieking at Elias ... she looks down at her feet, then pulls off a shoe and hurls it at him, and then the other one.

Shit, he thinks, *she is in love with him*, after all. *What have I done?*

"Don't panic," he says. *I need to make a call.* He leaves Joanna, shoeless, drunk on the cobblestone, crying, and goes back inside, his sense of honor crushed.

It is the fifth time he has tried to reach Stelios, the one person who might know where his cousin is, but every time he reaches an army station, he is transferred somewhere else. This time though, by some miracle, Stelios picks up. "Yes?"

"It's me," Elias says. "I have lost him, my cousin." He remembers then for a split second before Stelios responds, how he and Petros used to play together in the alley behind his house in Strovolos. Elias was older, it was expected he would protect his cousin, and he did, mostly, except for one time …

Stelios confirms it: it is most likely true that a soldier has crossed over, and if so, it is almost certain that solider was Petros. What is the army doing? Elias asks. What do you think they are doing? Stelios responds. Pretending its not happening, that's what.

We have to go and get him.

He returns to Joanna; by then her tears have stopped; her face looks smeared and worn. She is holding her shoes in her hands, looking into the distance, toward the Famagusta gate. Anna is nowhere to be found, probably in the bathroom, he thinks.

"Don't panic," he says. "He found his way there, he can find his way back."

"If he dies," she says, "I will never forgive you."

If he dies, you will never forgive yourself, Elias thinks, and he feels it like a rock in his guts.

"You have to go get him," Joanna says.

"I know," says Elias.

Then Anna returns.

"I'm going go get him," says Elias.

"What?" says Anna.

"You'd better," says Joanna. "And you'd better come back alive. Both of you."

Chapter Fourteen

"How do you know my name?" Petros asks, his voice trembling.

Emre grins. "Now we can be friends," he says.

Petros tries to shuffle away.

"Now I know this," says Emre. "That you came to Famagusta to die."

It takes all Petros' strength not to shake his head. He has shown too much fear already.

Emre moves, but instead of coming for Petros, he goes toward his pack, which, Petros realizes, they still haven't opened. Now they begin dumping the various items out unceremoniously onto the floor. Petros winces when his father's camera hits the ground, but it doesn't appear to break.

While they are distracted by his bag, Petros takes the opportunity to look around the room. His rifle and sidearm lie unloaded and disassembled in the corner, along with the clips and grenades.

He looks back at the Turks; Emre has sprung open the camera and pulled out the film, which he is about to expose by pulling it from the casing. At the last minute he changes his mind and puts the roll in his pocket, to keep as evidence. Then he throws the camera on the floor.

The sight of it makes Petros heart sink, and his guts churn with rage—it was as if these Turks were bent on stealing his memories again, stealing even the possibility of remembering, as their fathers before them had stolen the memories from Joanna and the others.

At the same time he realizes that it was foolish to come as he had—how must it look, a soldier armed to the teeth, with a camera? He could have come as a civilian, he thinks, unarmed, and maybe they would have just let him go, though this was unlikely. Still, at this point the only hope of survival, he thinks, is submission, either feigned or real (which one, he is not sure of yet).

Rations, his night goggles, the first aid kit—now all these come tumbling out of the bag as well. Amidst the jumble, he sees the envelope, the one with the map and the photographs: of Joanna on the beach in Ayia Napa, the old one of her as a toddler and most importantly the one he had picked up from her house, of her with her father.

Emre, picks up the envelope, looks at Petros, and immediately understands that it is important. He opens it with grimy fingers and slides the items out. "Careful," says Petros in a low voice; for a moment, his submission turns to rage.

Emre looks through the small pile. Frustrated, throws the photos and map to the ground in disgust, as if the idea that a solider would risk his life to pick up a few keepsakes in a dead city strikes him as utterly ridiculous.

"Why did you come here?" he shouts.

"I came for a woman," says Petros says quietly.

Emre is not sure he has heard correctly. "A woman?" he laughs. "There are no women here!" He seems to think that

Petros is mocking him, so he walks over and kicks him sharply in the ribs. Petros cries out. "What do you mean?" he asks.

Petros looks at the ground, shakes his head. Tears in his eyes; he feels shame—shame, shame, shame.

"Tell me," says Emre, "Or I kick you again."

Petros nods at the photographs on the ground. "A girl," he says. "My girl. She wanted a picture of her father."

The other soldier interrupts now, his frustration at not understanding the conversation overcoming his deference to the senior soldier. The two of them chatter in Turkish for a moment.

"Tell me," Emre says finally. "Tell me about the girl."

Petros looks up, confused. Are they now taunting him? His expression says "have mercy, end it now, if you are to end it," but he doesn't have the courage to say the words. He has been praying as they talk. Not that he was usually one for prayer, but now, he has found it. At first he begged God for mercy and a chance to escape. Then he bartered, running through things he could offer, amends he could make if only he were given the chance. Now though, the only prayer he whispers is "Thy will be done, Thy will be done, Thy will be done."

He can't tell if the soldiers are laughing at him by asking, or if they are still trying to decide if he is a spy, or if they are just passing the time. Petros resists the urge to tell them at first—what point is there in giving anything to these evil strangers who have his life in their hands? Eventually, though, he relents.

"She loves someone else," he explains. "She loves my cousin, my best friend."

Emre nods sympathetically. For the first time he looks genuinely sorry. He grabs the old wooden chair, turns it toward him and sits, as if settling in for a long haul.

Petros swallows hard. Evening is coming. He can sense where things are going.

He knows that Emre has been communicating with higher-ups, but no reinforcements have come. This means that, for whatever reason, they expect these boys to take care of the situation themselves.

It irritates him; irritates him to come this way and draw so little attention. If I am going to die here, at least let my death cause an incident, make a statement, he thinks.

He starts to get a nervous, sick feeling in his stomach, a feeling that goes beyond the physical pain of the beating he has received. By now he is off his knees; at some point he shuffled over to the wall and slumped against it. The Turks seemed bored of torturing him by then and they could tell he wasn't going anywhere, with his hands still zip-tied behind his back.

He must decide: to live, or to die? To give in to the inevitable or to make at least a final stand, a final attempt to survive?

Is there anything to live for? He thinks again of Joanna, but this time not just of her; he thinks of her and Elias, perhaps together, and he alone, or with another girl, it doesn't matter. He imagines his life going on without her, even if he still loves her. The fact that she is somewhere, he thinks, is maybe the most important thing. If she is alive, then being alive is worth it, no matter what is happening.

He thinks then of his mother, and how she will cry; his sister, on the verge of happiness. He thinks of Yiorgos and Eleni

Zenios, like a second mother and father, who understand him better than anyone, who he knows believe in him.

He begins to feel like a fool again, but stops himself; there will be plenty of time to live with regret if somehow he escapes.

He looks at the two Turks; the younger one, who is nevertheless the superior officer, pulls out a cigarette and lights it. "Can I have one?" Petros asks.

Emre looks quizzical, and then shrugs. He walks over and offers Petros a drag from his own cigarette, which is the most he can offer and, quite frankly, all Petros can accept, after all, the boy's arms are tied behind his back. Petros coughs then, violently and with excruciating pain; he coughs up blood and wonders if they broke a rib.

Then he asks, "where are you from?" He wonders what is to be gained from talking about his life, but also can see that the Turk softens a bit.

In spite of the fact that Emre speaks English, Petros has a sense that he is actually the crueler of the two; he exudes a kind of brutal professionalism, an odor of arrogance. The other soldier, Petros thinks, is little more than a boy, despite his older age, a village farm boy, and Petros knows plenty of them.

He asks Emre to translate what he is saying to Kadir. Emre is instantly suspicious. "Why?"

Petros sees the apprehension on Kadir's face. Kadir has realized, he thinks, that they will have to kill Petros. He decides to provoke the question, and asks why, finally reinforcements haven't come. Emre doesn't answer.

Petros turns his head then, and looks straight at Kadir. "I know you can understand me," he says. "I only ask, if you're going to do it, do it quickly." Emre responds by kicking him.

For a long time, no one speaks; Emre sits in the lone wooden chair and smokes; Kadir paces nervously, and Petros wonders what they are thinking. He is not sure if he should speak, if words could help them see his humanity and show mercy, or if words will just enrage them.

Day creeps into twilight. Petros pretends to be asleep or unconscious. At some point, Emre gives Kadir instructions to watch Petros and leaves the building, probably to relieve himself.

The minute he leaves, Petros senses a chance. "Hey," he says. "Can you give me the photograph?" he nods toward the place in the dust where Emre has thrown Petros' only photograph of Joanna.

Kadir walks over to it, and bends down to pick it up and studies it for a moment; then he brings it to Petros and shoves it into his front shirt pocket. "I like girl too," says Kadir.

He backs up. "Wait," says Petros. "Water. Please." Petros nods toward his canteen, which lies tossed aside on the floor next to the backpack. Kadir looks toward the front door, as if to see if Emre is returning. When he sees that he isn't, he moves forward, picks up the canteen and walks over to give Petros a drink.

Petros looks up into the soldier's eyes and then lets the less-than-cool water wash the painful dust from his throat. He returns his gaze to Kadir; he says thanks, and then nods his head. Kadir suddenly looks alarmed, as if he had caught himself unaware.

Late afternoon light pierces the room, as the sun sinks over the Mesaoria plain. An offshore breeze blows dust and the smell of oleander through the windows. This—his last sunset. Perhaps, he thinks, he should have asked them to let him see it.

The air cools, and Petros feels a hint of giddy strength rise in his body; suddenly he can feel pain in places where he had not felt it before; pain, he thinks, means life, he feels as though he is at last alive. He begins quietly working on the zip ties again, but his shoulders feel frozen, they have tied him so tightly. He wonders if he can bargain for his life; promise them riches from the other side, or cigarettes and beer at least. Why not, he wonders, what does he have to lose? He takes some comfort in the thought that he has given headaches to the Turkish command, but he is still surprised; he would have thought that the Turkish military had efficient methods set up—on-call death squads or something—to deal with problems like him. He has a cartoonish idea of the enemy that he doesn't want to let go.

Emre returns a few moments later, carrying a battery-powered lantern, illuminating the room with a sick-green light, casting bizarre and malformed shadows of men and objects into the dusty, dung-filled corners of the room. He says something more to Kadir in Turkish, and then motions to Petros' pack. Kadir retrieves it, and starts picking things up to put them inside.

"Almost time to go," Emre says to Petros.

Petros realizes that the moment has arrived. None of them believes any longer that reinforcements are coming. So, what were they waiting for? Nightfall. It will be at night when they finally kill him.

Just as he is about to start shoving things back in, Kadir looks into the bottom of the pack and spots something. He reaches the bottom, feels around, and then, almost in slow motion, pulls out the white and blue stripes of the Greek flag—the flag that belonged to the soldier who had died, the flag that Petros had promised to raise in Famagusta.

"*Sikeyim*!" Kadir shouts with surprise. And then he turns toward Petros, wrath in his eyes. "*Ata Sikeyim*!"

Chapter Fifteen

In 1941, they say, when the Nazis rolled into Athens, they ordered one of the Greek Evzonas to climb to the top of the Acropolis and pull down the Greek flag. The guard did as he was told, pulling down the Greek flag; but instead of raising the swastika as he had been ordered, he wrapped the blue and white around his body and hurtled himself off the rock to his death.

He must have died instantly, Petros thinks, and he cannot help feeling envious, as the kicks from Kadir's boots slam again and again into his side and back and stomach. He tries to protect his head, twisting his body to keep his legs between them and it works for the most part, at the expense of his extremities and his back. Blows to the kidney and groin send arcs of pain shooting through his whole body. He gasps, can't breath, black spots float in front of his eyes.

Time passes. He is not exactly unconscious. Emre splashes some water on his face. He looks up and sees the flag in a pile in the center of the room. Kadir has unzipped his pants, is preparing to piss on it, but Emre stops him with a shout. Kadir looks furious, but then Emre explains something to him in Turkish, and the boy relaxes, and then smiles. Emre shoves the flag back in the pack.

No one speaks; it is only once the shadows fall fully upon them that Emre finally throws his last cigarette on the floor and rises from the chair. "Time to go," he says quietly.

"Where are you taking me?" Petros asks automatically because he needs to know, not because he expects an answer.

"You'll see," says Emre.

The soldiers are almost gentle now, as they march him out into the Famagusta night. The smell of the sea reminds him of places nearby, beaches barely a few kilometers away where you could get drunk and make love to foreign girls and fall asleep in the sand and wake up without a care more serious than a headache and the question of where to go for breakfast.

"You came here to die." Emre asks, or says—it's not clear. On the one hand, it sounds like a question—they have been trying to figure him out since he arrived, why anyone who was not a spy would take such a risk, and it mystifies them, even after Petros tells them what must seem like a preposterous story about his best friend and the girl he loves.

They walk forward in silence, marching the stumbling Greek along. The houses in this part of the city are far apart, separated by large, empty lots, a reminder that this part of Famagusta wasn't finished, that it had been erupting in growth and the promise of prosperity before it was all snatched away.

Emre guides them in a route toward a Turkish military jeep—undoubtedly the one the two soldiers had arrived in. Petros expects that they will shove him in the back, but instead Emre instructs Kadir to hold Petros while he retrieves something from the back, a jerry-can full of some liquid that sloshes as he picks it up. Emre motions for them to continue. Kadir shoves Petros forward.

Petros stumbles; with his hands behind him he can't catch himself or even regain his balance, so Kadir is forced to grab his arm and bring him upright.

Kadir says something in Turkish to Emre; Emre responds with a one-word answer.

Petros glances back at them; even though he cannot understand what they are saying, he knows that if he is to survive he must put himself in their shoes—try to understand what they are thinking.

Emre pushes Petros a few steps in front of him to move him out of their line of sight, and then points to the hotels by the beach. Petros glances back to see Emre pointing. Whatever they have in mind, it will happen down there, at the beachfront by the hotels.

Why, he wonders, when they could just shoot him in an empty lot and let him rot? You came here to die. Of course they would want to make it look like a suicide. He looks again at the silhouette of fifteen- and twenty-story hotels; all at once he realizes what they have planned.

The houses on the walk to the beach are spread at some distance apart. Between them hard-pan, undeveloped lots are covered in weeds and shrub and occasional trees, illuminated now by moonlight. It is terrifying out there in the unknown blackness, but not as terrifying as his current situation.

He decides to bolt; he tears off toward cover, praying that they either shoot and kill him now, or that they let him go. The awkwardness of running with his hands bound behind him slows him more than he expects. For the first few steps he feels as though he is moving through jello, his legs rubbery and as sore as the rest of his body. His thighs burn as he plunges headlong into the dust brush.

"Halt!" one of the Turks shouts behind him, and then Petros hears the crack of a shot; he thinks they are firing into the air, which he doesn't understand. Why not just kill him and be done with it?

Of course the plan is ill-conceived, he can't run with his body in the shape it is in, and not with his hands bound behind him. They don't even have to give chase; a few dozen yards in he trips and falls into the dirt, and before he can find his way to his feet again, they are upon him.

This time it is the other boy who hits him, a hard punch to the back of his head. Both of them seem even angrier than before at the impudence of this Greek, who is not making life easy for them. Who knows, thinks Petros, by now they probably expected to be back at their basecamp, relaxing after dinner, watching a little television, drinking *raki*.

They pull him to his feet and begin the march with him again. At the beginning, he had to decide every few steps, over and over again that he really wanted to live, but now something both more primal and calculating takes hold. He stops stumbling; earlier he kept falling to his knees as both a sign of protest at his impending fate and an opportunity to catch his breath and rest, but each time one or the other Turk would hit him, and he realized that he was losing more strength by getting hit than he was gaining from resting. That protest and resistance only made sense if he had given up on leaving Famagusta alive, and he most certainly has not given up. The longer he focuses on living, the stronger the determination becomes. Now the decision is certain, all that remains is the means to do it.

They turn right on Espiridon Street (he can make out the street sign) and walk south toward a road that leads to the beach where the hotels are. It is still twilight. Petros speculates on their plans: they will take him to one of the tall buildings, upstairs, and when nightfall finally comes they will release his hands and throw him from the top.

Petros wonders how they will choose the building in which he will die. Emre seems strangely confident, as if he has done this before, and Petros suddenly wonders how many Greeks he has thrown from buildings.

They arrive at an almost classically bombed-out hotel, a half-destroyed building in the style of Dresden, Berlin, or London during the Blitz, except that unlike those images—images of rainy, cloud-covered cities from old black and white photographs and films cloaked in gray and sepia—this hotel is bathed in the luminous colors of the Mediterranean at dusk, its exposed and broken red brick outer walls almost glowing against the pinks and oranges and rapidly deepening blue of a post-sunset sky.

Ten stories tall; Petros counts. About a quarter of the building's backside is missing, as if it had been shaved off; twisted arms of rebar reach out and turn back in like exposed entrails. The image of it takes Petros' breath away, and he feels tears of love and conviction and fury swell in his eyes.

Only then can he read the weathered sign with the name of the hotel: *The Golden Aphrodite.* His father's hotel, the one that he and Uncle Michalis had built together so many years ago. He falls to his knees suddenly as he realizes that this is where they are taking him. "No," he says.

"You came here to die." Emre's voice is almost horse, like a whisper.

"No," says Petros. The meaning of what is happening is gradually dawning on him. They know his name. They know who he is, where he comes from, who his father was. How they know scarcely matters; all that matters is this is where they will end his life.

There is a part of him that is grateful, as if the decision to execute him in a place that has meaning for him were an act of kindness. If he must die, let it be here. How will they do it? The simplest thing would be to shoot him in the lobby, but the more logical path would be to throw him from the rooftop, and then he understands the story. He—an unstable, lovesick (now they know this too) Greek has come back to his father's hotel to kill himself. He wonders just how much they know about his life.

They brought the flag with them. Maybe they will let him wrap himself in it, as the brave soldier had in 1941. Maybe they will let him die as if he were a hero, a symbol, not realizing what such a gesture means to the Greeks. The thought makes him feel sick as soon as he thinks it, because he knows that he is not a hero.

Before they enter the hotel, the Turks take him along a path toward the beach, and then Emre orders Kadir to take a loop to secure the perimeter. From the beach side, the hotel rooms —stacked concrete blocks with balconies—seem intact; Petros can almost imagine them filled with young families and tourists and honeymooners, each fully engaged in the small dramas of their lives, where to eat, which beach to visit tomorrow, whether to take a shower before dinner or before bed.

It is time to go inside, he thinks, but instead they take him up an outdoor staircase, to a second-floor attached patio where the hotel's outdoor restaurant must have been. Then they make him kneel. He closes his eyes. *This is it,* he thinks, and he wishes that his life were flashing before his eyes, that he was thinking of all that was important to him, but it isn't, all he can think of are random absurd words, apple, peach, plum, airplane, smoke. Then he smells gasoline.

"Open your eyes!" Emre screams.

Petros opens his eyes. The soldiers' faces glow bizarrely in the light of Emre's lantern, like ghouls.

They have put the pack down and pulled the flag out, piled it in the middle to the patio; Kadir is pouring gasoline on it. *They mean to burn me alive*, Petros thinks. It is, he thinks numbly, a rather cruel way to get rid of him.

Instead, he watches as Emre lights a match and flings it onto the flag—the dead soldier's Greek flag, the one Petros had promised to raise in Famagusta. He watches as the blue and white lights up in blue and orange and yellow flames, rises into dark gray smoke and spreads into the ever-darkening sky. The flag is gone; Petros suddenly feels a great weight lifting from his shoulders. The flag is gone, and with it any hope that his death will be meaningful; the only thing that matters now is his life. *Joanna,* he thinks, *I am coming for you.*

"Cyprus is Turkish," Kadir says.

Chapter Sixteen

Ancient amphitheaters, medieval castles and drawbridges, fortresses and minarets and Cypress trees.

In Limassol, a no-longer-young restaurant owner prepares to close up for the evening. He knows he should be unhappy to have had such a slow night, but he is happy, he is happy when it is slow, and this is why he will never be rich he thinks, but does that matter?

The incident with the soldiers is still fresh in his mind. It was one thing to expect such behavior from the British troops from the bases—they were all low-class hoodlums—but from our own boys? The thought makes him click his tongue and shake his head. He should get out of the business, but what is a man to do at his age?

He pulls out his paperwork, throws it down on one of his empty tables, and calls for the waiter to bring him a beer. Bills, notices, unopened mail, all would be more tolerable if he had a better place, maybe some place closer to the beach, with more air …

Bills, notices … he sees a strange letter, a hand-addressed envelope, not something he expects to see (he has no children abroad, and can think of no one else who would write him a personal letter).

He opens it, begins unfolding the letter when a number of large bills falls out—nearly 200 Cyprus pounds. He grabs the money, squeezing it in his hand. There must be some mistake, he thinks. He continues unfolding the letter.

Dear Sir, it begins, *I write to ask for your forgiveness at my shameful behavior several weeks ago.*

The letter goes on. The man realizes to his amazement that it comes from one of the boys who tore up his place. The boy has sent him cash from his own savings that he hopes will make up for the damage he has done, he apologizes that he doesn't have more, offers to work it off if he makes it back. *If he makes it back?*

He sees then that the letter had enclosed a photograph that the boy had taken, with the skyline of Famagusta in the background. Confused the cafe owner reads on.

He reaches the last line, and puts his hand over his mouth. "Yiannos!" he shouts. "Get me the phone!"

~~~~

Elias sits on the parked Vespa, smokes a cigarette and feels the sun droop low in the sky. A slight breeze rustles the leaves of the olive trees that line the street and populate the courtyards of Strovolos. The smell of fruit—apricots and plums—crawls over the walls, mixes with the ripe exhaust of the odd bus and motorbike, filling the air with a quality that could only be felt, Elias thought, right there at that very moment.

From across the street, the plaintive sound of a violin comes through a window, as if to put the finest point on an already utterly distinctive moment. The first song is classical, Elias does not recognize it, but then comes the other songs: old tunes of Cyprus and Greece, wedding songs, the beautiful moan of old
~~~~

Aeolian melodies. Elias knows that it is Yiorgos Zenios who is playing, for this is his house, and anyway it is only Yiorgos who can play the violin that way.

The sound of the music moves him, but it is not Yiorgos the violinist he is looking for; it is Yiorgos the curator, Yiorgos the map collector, Yiorgos the man who knows everyone and everything that is going on here on the little island of Cyprus. It is past time for Elias to finish his cigarette, knock on the door and announce himself, but he is still mustering courage and trying to imagine how he will ask for what needs to be asked for, so he begins to pace, back and forth. It is time to get some answers; it is time to ask the right questions.

But before he can get up and come inside, the door opens and Eleni Zenios appears. "Elia," she says, "Come join us at long last." How long has she known that he was outside?

He tries to shrug casually, but he enters eagerly. He feels like a schoolboy on his way to confession for the first time, anxious and full of questions he doesn't know how to put into words. Yiorgos and Eleni have already eaten dinner, but there is fresh-cut watermelon and strawberries and plums and apricots for desert. Elias sits with Eleni and eats; the violin plays in the background. "He will be in soon," she says.

Elias feels his face turn, his expression sour. He knows how Eleni and Yiorgos feel about his father; God only knows how they feel about him. He has always respected them though, felt both close and distant from them, especially Yiorgos, who, Elias knows, was a hero of EOKA, even though he talks only rarely about it. A few minutes later, Yiorgos joins them.

You were patriots, heroes, Elias thinks. He looks at Yiorgos' expression, which seems to contradict him. *What does it mean to be a patriot?*

Finally, Eleni asks: what brings you to us?

"I…" Elias pauses; a long time passes. "I need to know some things. Things—perhaps—you might be able to answer … have you seen the news?"

Eleni shakes her head, Yiorgos nods. "Petros," he says. "He is the boy who has gone over." Elias watches as Eleni's face goes white; this is clearly the first she has heard of it. Yiorgos, by contrast seems disconcertingly calm about it.

"They're reporting his name," says Elias. "Idiots. We have to stop them." His implication is clear. Yiorgos, in spite of his humble house and bearing, knows everyone on this island.

What do you expect me to do? Yiorgos' expression seems to say. But then he responds, "I have already made some calls. They won't mention his name again."

"Do you know, then, if the army will get him back?"

Yiorgos shakes his head. "I have called people about this too," he says. "There is no way they will go. They don't want to start a war. Why are you boys bent on starting a war?"

"Then I have to go and get him," says Elias. "I need your help."

Eleni looks shocked. "You think he's going to Famagusta with you?"

Elias smiles. It is a testament to how the world looked at Yiorgos—the tough old rebel—that she would imagine this was what Elias meant. He shakes his head. "I need a way to get there. Myself, and another soldier."

Both Yiorgos and Eleni shake their heads at this.

Elias reaches into his back pocket and pulls out a folded map. It is the one that he and the boys of the *Filiki Eteria* had acquired a year earlier. "I already know a lot." He has photographs as well, accumulated from various places.

"This is Famagusta," says Yiorgos. "Where did you get these?"

"It doesn't matter," says Elias.

Yiorgos looks at the marked map. "How do you know where these houses are? How long have you been researching this?"

Elias doesn't answer, but looks up at Eleni, wondering how much she knows about revolutionary activity, whether she should be part of this conversation. She reads his expression and returns it with a look that answers his question.

"I need a better map," says Elias. "And an approach. We have a way—a couple of ways we've been researching. But I know that you also must have a way in."

Yiorgos raises an eyebrow, but Elias doesn't hesitate. It is inconceivable that these old revolutionaries have not made plans for future wars. The Turks have 40,000 troops on the island and the most modern, vicious weaponry in the world. The Greek Cypriots have men like Yiorgos Zenios.

"Yes of course," says Yiorgos. "I have an old map somewhere…" He is legendary for his maps; he collected them, not just from Cyprus but from everywhere he had been, Greece, Russia, the Holy Land. He loves the ancient ones, the ones with ornate script and browned edges, but is content to pick up the cheap tourist ones, too, multiple copies in foreign languages, replicas of the old distorted maps from the times when the far corners of the world were as distant and inscrutable as heaven or hell, filled with monsters and leviathans.

Yiorgos returns with a stack of accordion envelopes and begins to go through them. Finally, he finds what he is looking for, a folder labeled "Enslaved Territory: Maps." He opens it up and pulls them out, maps of Kyrenia and Morphou and Famagusta and all the other little places of occupied Cyprus.

Yiorgos' maps are more detailed; one has street names, another geographic features with contour lines. Yiorgos opens it and scans the streets for a long moment.

"Can I take this?" Elias asks. "I will bring it back."

Yiorgos studies the boy carefully. Then he folds up the map. Eleni speaks first. "Yiorgo," she says, "Do not give him the map." There is an icy chill in her voice.

Suddenly, the voice of a child intervenes, crying out—a little girl of three or four runs into the room. "*Yiayia!*" she says, and runs into Eleni's arms. The child had been sleeping; Eleni's voice had no doubt awoken her. Eleni takes the girl back to bed, and Elias wonders if it is time to seize his chance.

Yiorgos folds the map, and leaves it between them on the table. "What you are planning is suicide," he says.

"I have to go," Elias says quietly.

Eleni returns. "You must be careful," she says.

Yiorgos quietly picks up the map and puts it with the others, back in the accordion folder. Elias rises cautiously. *The map,* he thinks.

Yiorgos shakes his head. Elias follows Yiorgos down the hallway, trying to look casual. The house is small; there are not many places to hide things. In Yiorgos' case, accordion folders are kept in a plain-looking filing cabinet in a corner of the living room.

Elias turns to leave, his heart pounding. He has noticed that they keep their keys on a rack next to the kitchen; he asks to go to the bathroom. On his way, he slips three keychains off the rack, praying that no one notices and that at least one of them will open the front door.

They say their goodnights, and he walks out into a still-lit evening.

~~~~

Elias leaves; he waits, out of sight at a cafe a few blocks away. Patience is a strain, the clock is ticking on his cousin's life.

He looks at his watch, gets up, asks the cafe owner to make a call. He reaches the base; they patch him through. Stelios is expecting his call.

"*Nai.*"

"It's me."

"Go ahead."

"Is the line secure?"

Stelios laughs. "Does it matter?"

He has a point, Elias thinks. "What have you found out?"

"Not much," says Stelios. "What did you get from Mr. Zenios."

"Not much," says Elias. "He's already called his friends at *Antenna* and the papers. He seems to think that will work."

"I hear they are taking care of it on my end," says Stelios. "What about the map?"

"He has a good map, but he doesn't want to give it to me. Or maybe his wife—"
~~~~

"His wife? How many people have you talked to? And you're worried about a non-secure line?"

"She is trustworthy," says Elias, who knows for a fact that in her life Eleni has been trusted with more important secrets than this. "She's just worried. I'm waiting until later, to go back."

"Forget it," says Stelios. "We can do it without the map. Things are ready."

"Give me another hour," says Elias. "I can get it."

"He might not have an hour."

"Give me an hour," says Elias.

"Something else," says Stelios. He tells Elias how the army base had received a mysterious call from a cafe owner in Limassol. The owner had received a letter, a letter that could only be from Petros. The owner had called the base with information for Elias. The letter said that if Elias wasn't available, to give the information to Stelios.

"What did he say?"

"He said to deliver this message: 'The Lover of the People Speaks from the Heavens after midnight.' What the hell does that mean?"

"It means we need to get to Deryneia and watch the horizon," says Elias.

~~~~

It is at least his fifth cup of coffee; by the time he returns to Yiorgos and Eleni's house, Elias' arms are shaking as if he has a fever.

He slips the key in the door, and tries to turn it quietly, but these magnetic locks with buzzers are impossible—it clacks loudly, and Elias freezes, listens. The evening August air is cooler now; a breeze blows past him through the open
~~~~

doorway. The lights inside are all out, but the moon cuts through the open window shutter slats, illuminating the far walls and corners of the room in long strips of sepia-colored light. Elias waits, and then slips inside. He need only be here a minute, the cabinet with the maps is but ten paces away from the entrance; he moves quickly and as silently as he knows how.

The filing cabinet door squeaks like an old cat as he slides it open, and he curses it in his mind, but there is the folder, should he take the whole thing? He must: there is no time and these old Cypriots are no fools, they will have heard him, he is sure of it.

He moves now toward the door; home free, but at the last second, a voice behind him hisses with deep authority ("Hsssst!") and Elias stops in his tracks, turns slowly around. There is Yiorgos: standing there behind his thick old mustache, a shadow over half his face, his arms to his sides but his hands open, exuding a kind of silent, dangerous energy; his presence filling the room like Kolokotronis himself, and Elias would not be surprised if the old man were holding a gun. Elias grits his teeth.

"I am not sure," says Yiorgos, "If you are a brave man or a fool."

"The map," Elias says quietly.

"Take it then," says Yiorgos quietly. "Take them all. Take them all, and know that Eleni and I will pray for you, but that our prayers mean nothing."

"Thank you," says Elias, and he takes his leave.

Chapter Seventeen

The Turks take Petros inside through the dark and ruined lobby, kicking aside the shards of broken glass, stepping over the rebar-filled concrete rubble. The Turkish soldiers argue for a moment, and then Kadir goes outside again and brings Petros' pack back inside. Kadir is grumbling, Emre snaps at him and Kadir blows up, screaming at his fellow soldier, a cluster of alien words wrapped in rage and fear. Emre gives up, waves his hand, shouts something and Kadir drops the pack on the floor, relieved to not carry it anymore.

They walk Petros toward the stairwell, confirming his fears again. Petros suddenly stops walking and drops to his knees, looks down at the floor as if to prostrate himself before them. "Don't kill me," he whispers.

He must appear as defeated, as crushed as possible. He has already tried to escape and been beaten; he has already run and failed. It is time to beg for his life, he thinks, because this is what men in his situation do. He must convince them that he has no hope left, that he has exhausted his capacity for resistance. He must make them believe he is defeated, get them to drop their guards. He feels a hint of life returning, a spark of hope.

They lift him to his feet. "Don't resist," says Emre. "You resist, we hurt you and you go anyway."

"I can give you information," says Petros. "I am a spy. There are others here."

Emre laughs, clearly no longer believing that Petros could have anyone with him.

Kadir on the other hand seems increasingly distraught. *What's the matter*, thinks Petros, *is this not what you imagined being a soldier was like?*

They enter the stairwell and Petros pauses, gasping for breath. They take him up, up up. By now night has fallen almost completely, and the stairwell grows darker by the minute. Some kind of creature runs in front of them, and Petros wonders what kind of life there is to be found here.

Emre makes them stop, curses Kadir, something in Turkish. Kadir pushes the muzzle of his M-16 to the back of Petros' head; Petros can feel it trembling as Kadir trembles—do they mean, then, to kill him here, now? He wishes he had managed to free his hands, his arms ache, hope seeps from him again, but he is determined at least to not go quietly. He must resist, must try, he wants to send out loving thoughts to the world, prayers across space and time if only he believed in such things, he wonders if he believes in God. He prayed earlier—first for deliverance, and then for strength, and then for dignity; but at the moment all of those prayers seem foolishly small, not selfish exactly but at the wrong scale. If he is to die, he thinks, the only possible prayer is acceptance, not really a prayer at all.

~~~~

In the stairwell, Emre fumbles with the light—his flashlight, which should attach to the base of the gun. It is just for a
~~~~

moment, but Petros feels it, a tiny window; he smiles. He has decided to survive.

He turns his head and torso abruptly to knock the muzzle of Kadir's assault rifle aside; with his hands still bound behind his back, for an instant it seems as though he just stumbled, but then he brings his foot up and kicks backward like a donkey, with as much force as he can muster. The boot hits flesh and bone, something cracks and Kadir spills backward into Emre; the light flies up into the air, spins and bounces, hard metal clanging against metal, light itself bouncing and flickering in rapid dots on all the walls and on the ceiling above them.

Had they been on a flat surface it would have been hard for Petros to get up, but because they are on an incline with stairs, he is able to push himself to the side, brace his shoulder against the wall and begin pushing himself up the stairs, sliding at first and then stumbling to his feet—stumbling, he is almost running up the stairs now trying to move his feet fast enough to keep them under him, he reaches a landing and bounces into the walls, using his sore and bloody shoulders, one side and then another, like a pinball, up another flight.

It takes a moment, but then he hears them behind him, recovered and coming for him; he must get out of the cursed ties. Around him everything is black, he is facing death in the dead body of a building in a town that many called home but was home to no one. For a moment he feels utterly exhilarated, as if a part of his soul is determined to find joy in this moment, the first moment in hours in which death no longer feels like a certainty, just one path among many.

Above him he sees light, and for a second he believes it is another flashlight, it's not possible: how have they gotten ahead of him? But then he realizes it is starlight and the diffuse glow of the moon; an opening in the stairwell leading to a hotel floor that in turn is open to the sky beyond.

He pushes himself up and onto the landing, and out into the stark-black hallway. He runs down it—most of the doors are closed to him, but somewhere halfway down, one of them is open and there is light, beautiful, amazing starlight. He wants it so badly, wants to *see* it so badly. He passes by.

He can't go through the first open door; they will find him in a heartbeat—he runs at a good clip now, through the darkness, sure that at any moment he will slam his head into a wall, but his eyes are better than that, they have adjusted quickly, aided by the faint celestial glow. He slows and turns his body, as if by some hidden sense, in time for his shoulder to clip into the wall; then he turns around, as quietly as he can to see which direction he can go in.

The Turks are not quiet: he hears them shouting and cursing at each other as they pound up the stairs. He waits and tries to hold his breath, until they have passed on, up to another floor.

Now he realizes he can move by sliding along, his back to the wall, moving to the left. Where to go? Move toward the light, or away from it? Stay hidden, silent, use the dark—or seek the light?

Two-thirds of the way down, he feels a strong breeze, getting stronger; it comes from another open door, this one to a room that has lost most of its outside wall and half its floor. It surprises him with a sudden vertigo: instead of a wall he is looking at a wide open firmament of stars, constellations of the gods, a howling, breathtaking expanse of speckled light.

He has thrust himself into the room so fast that he almost runs off the edge, hurling himself to the ground ten stories below, but he falls to the floor just in time, sliding almost to the edge. His face is exposed to the wind, he smells the salt, the sand, the sea—the ever-placid sea. The sea that sways and swells to its own rhythm, always, always whispering that the world, the universe is bigger than you are, that there are a million things that have been here before you, and a million things that will survive you. He longs for it, the dizzying, black sea; he wishes now, with his face bleeding and his ribs broken and his life in ruins, that he could reach out for it and embrace it, but those damn Turks have tied his hands …

Noticing that sensation—the sensation of his bound hands—brings his mind back to the moment at hand. He begins by wriggling his body backward, away from the edge: a more difficult task than it should be, but with his hands tied he worries that it would be all too easy to wriggle himself into an even more immobile position and accidentally roll off the side.

He is breathing heavily. He hears movement in the hallway. At least one of them is coming. Can they hear him breathing? If he can hear them, they can hear him. He must get his hands in front of him; he twists his bound hands underneath his thighs, feeling the wrenching and pulling in his shoulder, his rib—bruised or broken, who can tell?—screams at him and he grunts involuntarily in response, maybe the effort of pulling his hand underneath him will break the zip tie but instead he just feels it cutting more deeply into his wrists, a sharp, excruciating pain. A cluster of different kinds of pains—cutting, pinching, biting, aching, nausea, frustration, despair—and now his hands are behind his knees. He is on is back in a fetal position, and now this is the hardest part. He tries to ignore the Turks in the hallway, it is only by the Grace of God that they haven't found him yet, he thinks. Finally, his wedges the heels of his boot on the band and pushes, he will either break it or break his own arms off, it hardly matters at this point.

One leg through; he grabs his other leg and pulls it toward his chest, and he can hear one of them at least in the hallway; from the corner of his eye he sees the glow of a flashlight through the doorway, coming closer. His heart is now racing so fast; it feels as though it is trying to crush his lungs from within, he is panicked, gasping for breath, he will not make it.

Close your eyes and think; think of other places and other times and other people who have faced humiliation and death. He pulls his foot toward his face, and slides the ties around his knee, and under his boot, and suddenly, his hands are in front of him. He doesn't wait, he stands up, brings his arms high over his head then thrusts them down as if throwing a large rock at the ground; at the last second he brings his elbows back and flares them out—the tie snaps, his hands are free.

He takes a huge gulp of air and then stops breathing, and squats in the corner of the room, on the door side, just as a blinding beam of light sweeps into the floor. Whoever is holding it pauses just outside the doorframe, and sweeps the room slowly again.

Petros realizes his advantage in the dark; if they use their flashlights, he can see them coming but he must stay out of the moonlight coming in through the broken roof. He feels around on the floor for a weapon, notices his fingers are bleeding; his head is crusty with blood. He finds a chunk of broken concrete, too small to do any damage and then, stroke of good fortune, a loose piece of rebar. His clothing is dark, but his face is surely visible, he has nothing to cover it. He feels the concrete, wonders if he can hurl this at one of them, doubts he can hit anything reliably.

A flash of an idea. Petros throws the rock overhand, hard, toward the opposite side of the door. It hits the far corner of the room with a loud bang and almost without hesitation Emre springs into the room, spins toward the corner and fires a long, panicked burst toward that corner; a long muzzle-flash lights up the darkness, bullets chew up the wall.

For a brief instant, Emre's back is to Petros, and Petros lunges forward, swinging the rebar like a baseball bat. It cuts the air with a whistle, cracking into the back of Emre's head, hard enough to kill a man, Petros thinks. But somehow it doesn't, Emre stumbles forward and begins to turn toward him. Petros rushes forward to close the gap, get inside the end of the muzzle; he catches the rifle with his left hand to keep the end away from his body and raises his right arm to hit Emre again with the bar.

To his surprise, Emre lets go of the gun with his left hand and brings it up quickly, blocking the blow with his forearm and grabbing Petros' wrist. They struggle, one hand each on the rifle, the other hand struggling to control the rebar; Petros pushes Emre back against the wall, and they are stuck in a momentary stalemate—both unsure of what to do, neither willing to release control of either weapon to try for the upper hand. Petros is both stronger and weaker than Emre, stronger from months and years of self-punishing calisthenics, weaker from hours of abuse. He is taken aback by Emre's resilience, why can't anything be easy? *But of course,* he thinks, *it has all been too easy.*

Then Emre snaps his head forward in a brutal head-butt at almost exactly the same instant that Petros thinks of doing it; his forehead hits Petros straight on the upper lip, splitting it with a gash, and then Petros is pushed backward, quickly at an angle toward the edge of the room—toward the abyss.

Petros is caught off guard but catches himself, even though he is slipping and stumbling toward the edge, and he feels himself almost falling already toward the yawning expanse; no, he thinks, I will not go. And if I do go, you will come with me, we will die together Greek and Turk in the Famagusta sand.

He lets go of the gun now and grabs Emre's shirt instead, pulling him forward, both of them stumbling toward the edge. Petros twists to use Emre's momentum to throw him over. Emre falls, but they are not quite there; both fall to the ground, the rifle clatters to the side and they struggle, dragging and pushing each other over the brink, Emre now on top, frantically searching for a foothold, some leverage to force Petros off into the darkness; Petros slides, feels his shoulder slip over the side, another push and he will tumble over. He is punching Emre with his left hand but the blows land weakly, he can get no purchase so he shoves his thumb toward Emre's eye; Emre is still holding the wrist of his right hand to keep the rebar away as he tries to send Petros over the side, *don't you see,* thinks Petros, *if I go over, I am taking you with me.*

Emre leans back for an instant to avoid the gouge, grabs at Petros' other wrist and then Petros pulls, rocks the Turkish soldier over his body into the air and he thinks it is over, but there is an edge of wall and Emre grabs it, Petros is now backing toward the center of the room. Emre drags himself up against the wall and grabs his rifle, but this time Petros is faster, closer. He pulls Emre toward him, flips the boy over his hip and jabs the end of the bar into Emre's chest.

Time stops. The flashlight, attached to the bottom of the rifle, held across Emre's stomach, gives just enough light to illuminate the details on the boys' faces.

Emre's mouth opens in protest as Petros grunts and wails, shoving the metal bar down with all his weight through the cracking ribs. Emre's mouth opens; his eyes look up in terror and bitterness, and Petros cries out wailing as he twists and drives the metal in. Tears in his eyes; he looks at his enemy, a boy who could just as well have been his friend, and mouths the words, *I'm sorry*, but it is then impossible to know what Emre sees; his breath roars suddenly from his chest as his body shudders with a terrifying violence; it takes a moment, but the shuddering subsides, life dissipates and death crawls in.

He is dead, Petros thinks numbly. Then Uncle Michalis' words: "Strictly speaking, the Turk was doing his duty." His duty: his dishonorable duty done honorably, perhaps. Maybe Emre was only doing his duty, but what was Petros doing here? "I have a right!" he cries suddenly. "I have a right to be in my own country, my own city, my own home!" But of course the now utterly dead expression of the boy can answer nothing in return.

Petros hears another cry, and footsteps running down the hall, Kadir's voice: "Emre!" he shouts. "Emre!"

Emre's warm body still grips his gun tenaciously; the flashlight, still attached to its underside, casts a circle of light on the wall and then spills out into the hallway as Petros wrestles with him to free it, pull it, pry it somehow from the boy's hands. But the gun won't come loose and Kadir's footsteps thunder down the hall—how much time has gone by? The two soldiers must have split up to find Petros when he ran.

Realizing that he will not get the gun loose in time, Petros moves to pull Emre's sidearm from his holster. He gets it up, aims at the door and fumbles with the safety. Later he will wonder if it was honor, cowardice or stupidity that prevented him from killing Kadir—he can hear the eager desperation in the boy's voice, the same desperation he has shown all along, and from this he knows that the boy will charge blindly through the door to reach his friend; he knows this because he knows what it means for a young man to look up to and rely on a friend; he knows—can feel in his own heart—the panic. Kadir runs down the hallway to find Emre the way a drowning man claws desperately, unconsciously at a would-be rescuer.

Petros knows all of this in a fraction of a second's calculation, and he knows because of this that Kadir will charge through the door, straight into Petros' line of fire: he knows that he can end this now.

Instead, he pulls the trigger, shoots at the doorway a half-second before Kadir reaches it. Kadir skids to a stop, slips, stumbles and backpedals before he reaches the entrance. Petros charges the door, firing as he runs; Kadir gets to his feet and runs back down the hall. Petros empties the clip into the darkness. Its muzzle flashes like a strobe light, and he sees Kadir's retreating form captured in momentary stills. The gun empties; he retreats to Emre to find more ammunition.

His boots squish as he steps into a rapidly expanding pool of blood. He realizes now his hands are sticky with it as well; the glow of the flashlight and the moonlight and the stars illuminates grisly death on the face of the first man Petros has brought it to. He wants to run from the room; he feels now an unholy terror in the presence of real death. The smells—an indescribable mix of terrible body odors—overwhelm him and he wretches, thank God he hasn't eaten. He wants to run from the room but he must rearm, at any moment Kadir will realize he actually has the upper hand.

Petros digs through the many now blood-soaked camouflage pockets of the Turkish soldier, unsure of where to find extra magazines for the automatic pistol, the ones in the front are for the rifle, and he can't bear to try to pry it loose again. In Emre's sleeve pocket he finds something small and cylindrical: the roll of film they pulled out of the camera. Finding it almost makes him choke up—his only record of this place, he thought it was lost forever. It is now caked with blood like everything else in the room—in training they told him to prepare for more blood than you can imagine, but nothing can prepare you, he thinks.

In the third pocket he finds another flashlight—this will be useful, he slips it into a pocket—but there is no second magazine for the pistol he can find. He comes across a canteen of water and in spite of the blood and stench he pulls it off the boy's belt, opens it and takes long, heavy gulps, he tells himself he should stop but the water has the strangest taste. Tasteless like all drinking water, and yet it tastes somehow alive to him, like it is filling him with life. *Water,* he thinks, as if to begin a sentence in his mind, but there is nothing else to think.

He drinks, but there is no ammunition for him; he is unarmed, unarmed and facing an angry soldier whose friend he has killed; unarmed and soon to be facing the entire Turkish army. He leaves the room with the pistol pointed in front of him, slides down the hallway with his shoulder pressed against the wall, moving as low as possible. The pain, all the pain of the day, sharp and aching, all the sadness and soreness is suddenly and mysteriously gone. *More pushups,* he thinks, *just like doing a few more pushups.*

He reaches the corner without incident, sinks low to the ground and quickly looks around the corner toward the stairwell, the only escape route, but Kadir has been waiting, guarding the way out; somehow he hears Petros' movement and at that moment the Turkish soldier flicks on his own rifle-mounted light.

Petros ducks behind the wall again. Kadir doesn't shoot; Petros is not sure if the boy has seen him, but then he hears footsteps moving closer.

"Stop!" he shouts. "I don't want to kill you!" realizing that his enemy doesn't speak his language.

Still, the footsteps stop. They face a momentary, illusory stalemate, one that will be over the moment Kadir realizes that Petros has no working weapon or ammunition.

Kadir shouts something in Turkish, his voice quivering.

Here again, no way out, Petros thinks. He should just surrender, he thinks, he doesn't have enough life in him to run again, but it's not the running, he thinks, its the thinking, its the terrible *effort,* like playing a mental chess game while running a marathon, without knowing the rules.

Don't be an idiot, he thinks, both to himself and to Kadir. *Leave me here, go and call for help, you know that is what you want to do.* But instead Kadir moves forward, his footsteps almost silent if not for one squeaky floorboard.

At that moment, Petros comes up with the only other solution: the exposed elevator shaft at the far end of the other hallway. But there is no way to get there without passing Kadir's position, so he turns suddenly, and runs back toward the open room. Kadir comes around the corner, uses the flashlight to get Petros in his sights, but he is too slow, Petros is back in the room with the open wall, with still-dead Emre.

He leaps over the body, and rushes toward the open balcony; he grabs the railing and swings himself over the side. The breeze and salt air rushes over him, he feels as if his body is spinning in the moonlight. He has jumped without thinking, and now a surreal rush of euphoria washes over him; he is finally free—or he could be if he just let go, but he doesn't want to let go.

He swings down, momentum carrying him back in toward the building, his weight wrenching the balcony railing from his arm and he falls, just close enough to catch the railing of the balcony on the floor below, he opens his arms as if to embrace a lover. He catches it all at once, both arms and one leg grasping it; it punches him in the face and chest, kicking his bad rib, knocking the wind out of him as if it is trying to break his grasp, and he mentally curses the inert railing. All he has to do is get himself over the side and there is a chance he can escape. He looks over the edge and sees the sandy ground calling for him, but he rejects it—up, up up, and over.

Just then he hears the wail of shock from above him: Kadir has discovered Emre; Petros feels his breath catch in his chest, feels the sensation of having crossed from a world that makes sense into a world of chaos, a world in which he is responsible for the life and death of strangers.

There is no time to reflect, reflection will have to wait. There is only life and death and at any second Kadir will recover from his shock, will look over the edge and realize the Petros has not leapt to his death but is alive, so Petros stands up, wobbles to his feet.

The glass sliding door on this floor is intact; he is locked out of a room on an eighth floor balcony in a dead hotel in a dead city as a dead body bleeds on a floor above him. He kicks at the tempered glass, weakly, and then pounds at it with the butt of his empty pistol; finally, a crack. He leans against the glass now and listens, but can hear nothing, even the breeze is quiet now. *Again*, he thinks, and hits the glass again as hard as he can; this time it shatters, splitting, alarmingly, into a million pieces, and Petros is through, stumbling through the darkness. For some reason this room has retained its furniture, but he doesn't see the bed as he charges in and so he trips, flopping down onto the ancient tousled sheets and a mattress that hasn't felt a body in twenty years. God, he just wants to be in a safe bed somewhere, sleeping, waiting for the sun to come up before dawn, if only there weren't shattered glass under his chest and the blood of a dead man on his hands.

Up, get out of the room now, run down the hall, listen, listen, listen and hear. Listen for the sound of your enemy running the halls above you, coming down the stairwell. Be surprised; you have not expected him to be so courageous. Turn now then, and run toward the bombed-out elevator shaft you saw when you arrived, its cables hanging out like vines; run, don't stop, hear him now, behind you, reach the end of the hall, give thanks that the elevator door is open, leap out catch the cable, grab it and swing, slide down from where the elevator shaft is still undamaged and enclosed—slide down and out into the open air, slide and look at the darkened city, the black sea, the silent sand; look north also, where you can see the lights on the Turkish side, so nearby, just past the cyclone fencing, a city lives.

Keep sliding, grip the cable with your sleeves and pants as much as you can, it will still burn the palms of your hands and the inside of your thighs. Ignore the Turk who is now shooting down at you; remember that it is more difficult for a man to hit a man in war or peace than you think, especially when the target is swinging in space five stories below, especially when the other man has just seen his best friend split open with a piece of rebar, and finds himself in the midst of a story that is unlike any story he has ever thought about, prepared for or imagined.

The cable would have lead Petros all the way to the rubble-strewn basement, leaving him once again trapped, if he hadn't had the sense to slow his descent, kick his legs and swing side to side until he could release it and land on the low lobby above the rooftop.

He doesn't wait but runs across the rooftop, runs and limps, drags his lame and beaten soul toward the edge where he can jump off into the yard. It is only a single story down, compared to the long slide it is nothing but as he falls it feels surprisingly far. He hits a cluster of rogue landscaping, a thick-limbed, bushy mix of naturalized plants that should not have survived without human attention.

He starts to move toward the nearest building but it occurs to him that he is just leading himself into another trap, and anyway he has no more heart in him to run, so he pushes himself into the shrubbery and tries to find a position where he can see the hotel—see if and when Kadir comes out looking for him—without being seen.

He doesn't have to wait long; Kadir bursts out from the lobby, stumbles into the ancient parking lot that hasn't held a parked car in so many weedy decades. Kadir stumbles out, a broken man. He is crying, wailing, and Petros can feel the waves of hatred coming toward him, but the Turk is no longer a man on the hunt, he is for the moment broken and lost. Petros wonders that the boy is not afraid of him, if Petros had more ammunition he could have lain in ambush, but Kadir doesn't seem to consider the possibility; instead he wanders west, stumbling like a drunken man back toward the residential area.

Petros takes a long breath, and then another, and a third; suddenly he cannot stop taking deep, long, choking breaths, they come over him like sighs. He sighs in terror and mourning and in gratitude for his life, he gulps air as if he can drink the spirit of life itself, he gulps air the way a drowning man gulps air, the way a man dying of thirst in the desert gulps water.

The gasping and sighing continues for a long time, past the point of reason, but he can't stop himself, and meanwhile he must find a place to wash the blood off his hands, he just wants to wash it off, wash it all off, to take his clothes off and burn them and plunge himself into a river, to wash himself and be clean again. But this he cannot do, so he wanders toward the beach, stumbles into the thick deep sand that is so hard to walk through, toward the sea.

Something moves on the beach, and then something else. It startles him until he realizes what he is seeing is not human. More and more shapes appear—large, dark blobs, sliding, creeping through the sand, each one the size of a man or a small table, and this is the strangest end to a dream, he thinks.

It is only when he sees the long neck of one moving in the moonlight, sees its head turn toward him that he realizes that they are giant sea turtles, nesting, and that they are everywhere on the beach; dozens of them, he thinks, maybe more, though it is of course impossible to tell. The turtles come to nest in Cyprus, but they are shy. Here, they have found a wonderful place where they can be ignored—they were probably not expecting gunfights and chases, Petros thinks, and he apologizes to each of them in his mind as he tries to step past their bodies to reach the water.

At the water's edge he collapses into the damp sand, plunges his hands deeply into it, as if the earth could absorb the dark, sticky feeling. Then the water rolls up and he starts to scrub his hands in it, each rolling wave another chance for clean water. The abrasions on his hands and wrists—from the zip ties, from sliding down the cable, from who knows what else—burn furiously in the salt. But he keeps washing, embracing the pain—a burning, cleansing pain that suggests if he just washes long enough he can burn off some of the bloody sin he has incurred.

He thinks he can wash his hands over and over, but he has limits as well, so eventually, sooner rather than later, he lies the rest of his body on the beach to see if the water will continue to wash him, after he passes into what can only conventionally be called sleep. *Tomorrow*, he thinks, *tomorrow, tomorrow, tomorrow.*

Chapter Eighteen

Some time later, he is awake, at first drifting in and out of consciousness. He is lying on his back, the water is running patterns around his body, his body is sinking into the sand, he has the sensation of sliding into the sea.

Sliding into the sea; the sea, the sea beacons, a large wave now comes over him and splatters water into his mouth, he spits it out, feels the saltiness on his tongue. It would be easy, to stay here, to wait for whatever will happen next, but waiting is a decision in and of itself. He must decide to decide. He must decide to live: this is the first step, the only step. Concerns about honor and purpose have receded, he understands now why militaries indoctrinate order and routine and discipline with such ferocious commitment, because at the moment of life and death it is order and routine and purpose that vanish first, all that is left is either the will to live or the resignation to die.

He knows he doesn't have much time. Before daybreak, or earlier, Kadir will have called in reinforcements, and there will be no way to escape. The Turks will not make the mistake of leaving him to one or two soldiers; he will feel the full force of the Turkish army come down on him now.

Finally, he pulls himself to his feet. In the time he has rested, the sea turtles have crept away, giving him a wide berth. He sees their dark, half-spherical bodies now yards away. He is thirsty. He decides to fill the empty canteen with seawater, murky thoughts suggesting that he will find a way to distill it later.

He needs to move away from the hotel, but he has one more thing to do there, so he goes back toward it and imagines, for a moment, what it was like; and what it could have been like.

He tries to move quickly. He needs to reach the roof, but the roof is very far above him, and he can barely walk. Fifteen stories, one at a time, the urgency in his mind fighting with the blisters and cuts and bruises and wrenched muscles and splitting headache that slow him to barely a shuffle.

Passing the floor with Emre's body is the worst. Even in the stairwell he can smell it, the fresh stench of death, a combination of blood and rank body-fluids. *Try not to think about it.* There will be time later to contemplate life and death if he lives.

Once he has passed Emre's floor, each floor he reaches gets a little easier, the cross-breeze through the open walls gets stronger. At long last, he reaches the roof of the hotel, and emerges into the open night. The onshore breeze is much stronger now.

There's no time to enjoy the view. He takes a quick look to the north to see if the Turks are moving yet but he doesn't see any signs of it. To the south he peers into the empty sky at the lights of Derenyia. He raises Emre's flashlight and points it into the distance.

He realizes that the odds of his plan working are small. It had seemed like a clever idea when he wrote it in the letter to the cafe owner; a trail of breadcrumbs that would take long enough to unravel that he would be back home before Elias figured it out—unless something went wrong.

The two of them had hatched the plan in the early days of the *Filiki Eteria.* At that time the idea was to raise the Greek flag on the roof of their fathers' hotel—the hotel that would have been their own one day. Then they would use a flashlight to signal their victory to free Cyprus. Their friends would be watching on the border.

Of course there was no way to be sure that even a simple message of victory would be seen, even with the timing perfectly coordinated. Who knew, even if they had gotten and understood his message, if they would be there to hear Petros' message now?

He starts with a simple SOS, and then he stops. What does he want to say? Is he asking them to come and rescue him from his own foolishness and stupidity? And for what? He looks over the edge of the building to the rooftop deck nine stories below, but he can't even see the remnants of the burnt flag. He decides to try another message. *Coming back,* he flashes. *Wait for me.*

~~~~

Back on the ground, he moves toward the darkened city. His arms and legs ache, his back, his wrists, his head, his ribs. And yet, movement is less excruciating than one might think; there is still a gap, a small space in which he can operate before his body reaches its absolute limit. Maybe, he thinks, the gap is bigger than he thinks, maybe the body and the spirit have secret reserves that no one can imagine.

Finally he reaches the street, feels relief that his feet are finally on solid ground. So far, he hears no movement, but that will change in an instant—he must get inland. The Turks will
~~~~

set up a perimeter, that will be the first thing they do, so he must get outside it. It's a small city, but even a small city is huge with no people in it.

It will be simple, if not easy, to find his way back, he thinks. His plan: head back south, through Ayios Memnon and occupied Deryneia; make his way back from there. He has lost all his equipment, his food, his camera, his weapons; all that he has now is a canteen filled with seawater, a small, blood-caked roll of film, a flashlight and an empty sidearm. And also: the map, which he has been carrying in an inside pocket that the soldiers had neglected to search.

The flashlight he cannot use, he must do nothing to draw attention to himself. He is thankful for the purple glow of the almost full moon; it bathes the buildings in haunting gold and stark, deep shadows, illuminating more than one might expect. The city now is nothing but strange shapes, silhouettes and empty spaces, but it is enough.

Petros crosses John F. Kennedy street, the main road that runs along the beach, and cuts through a yard between two buildings. Another street, and then he goes between two more buildings and moves diagonally across another large empty lot—he is surprised by how many empty lots there are.

The further he gets from the beach, the more morose he feels. He cannot wash the image of the dead Turk from his eyes, a pointless death; he cannot believe the absurd and pointless adventure he has just undergone, an adventure that could still end with him dead in a well. Even the photographs he took are probably ruined, which means that he will go to his grave without even a record of what has happened, without being able to speak of these pointless moments.

And what of returning? How many years would it be before Famagusta was open to him again, before he could walk its streets as a free citizen, with pride? How long would it be and what would remain by then, if anything?

And what of Joanna? What would he say to her? That he traveled to her home town and killed a Turk, saw her house, found the safe she once spoke of but didn't take a small moment to open it and find out what lay inside?

He crosses out of the lot and reaches an intersection. He can read the signs in the moonlight; Jules Verne and Esperidhon streets, and suddenly he stops. He was on this very road earlier; from here he is not far from either his own family's house or from Joanna's.

He had planned to turn south at the road, but instead he continues, across another wide cluster of undeveloped space and then one block up, to where he found Joanna's house. He turns right; he remembers from the marked map that it is the fourth house in, on the left side. The moonlight is startlingly bright.

He cannot believe what he is doing. He has been given back his life, he has the chance to escape. There will be nothing there, he tells himself, nothing worth finding.

Still, he goes. He realizes that he is no longer trying to win Joanna back, or to prove something to spite her; all he wants is an instant, a smile on her face. All he wants is to give her back a small piece of memory.

He flicks on Kadir's flashlight. It is a risk, but so far he hears nothing, no mobilization, Varosha is shrouded in silent emptiness, as it has been for twenty-odd years.

Now he walks down the street, one house, two houses, three. He reads the numbers: here is her house. He shines the flashlight over it, the beam moving over the iron fence, the dusty veranda, the unbroken windows.

He cannot believe he is here; finding her house in the darkness is almost the most unbelievable thing so far. Nevertheless, he hesitates now; there is no knowing what he will find in the place, it is more terrifying than his own house, with everything gone and the tree growing from the center. No; this house is like a tomb, he thinks, anything he finds here can only bring sadness, it is time to go, time to return to his mother and sister, aunts and uncles and cousins, return to the people who, he realizes now, would truly miss him. Time to return, he thinks.

But instead he walks through the open gate, up to the door, opens it and goes inside.

~~~~

Here he is, then, back in her childhood home, in the middle of a night that refuses to be illuminated. For the first time since he came here, he forgets where he is, reaches out absentmindedly to flick on a light-switch, a light-switch that is on the wall where you would expect. It even makes a satisfying click but of course no light comes on.

He casts the beam of the flashlight down the hallway. Things scurry away. *How many rats and snakes live in this city*, he wonders.

As he moves through the rooms, this time in darkness, he stumbles over pieces of furniture and broken objects that he cannot name. Even in the darkness he catches glimpses of many things that beg more exploration, and he is filled with a sinking feeling. Now he faces the real choice—somehow he had
~~~~

supposed that he would find the house quickly and take his leave quickly, that he would creep back across the border before dawn, but unless he can see the house by light of day it will be as though he hasn't seen it at all.

He retrieves the supplies he left before, and then finds a spot in the pitch black entrance hall to sit against a wall and eat and drink, after which he feels alive again.

He takes the water first and drinks in deep, long gulps, as if he is drinking life itself. Almost instantly he feels his body reviving, enough to fill him with a terrible exhaustion. He wants to sleep, but he knows also that he is starving. The bread and the cheese and all the good fresh food is long gone, so he opens a can of sardines and spoons the salty fish into his mouth with his bare hands. *Careful,* he thinks, *don't cut your finger on the can*, as if a tiny cut like that matters now.

It will take them a while, he thinks, to find him, time to bring in troops and figure out a strategy to go door to door. After all, from their perspective, he could be anywhere—before the war this city was home to 40,000 people and thirty-six multi-story hotels; there is a lot of ground for them to cover.

He tells himself this as he eats; as soon as he is done, he finds a bedroom and collapses on a bed, which, in spite of the fact that it has held no person for decades, seems strangely human and welcoming; he falls then, into a deep, soulful sleep.

Chapter Nineteen

He wakes up in Joanna's house; it is daylight. There is still blood under his fingernails.

The condition of this place becomes clear. Dilapidated doesn't describe it: the house is mere rubble, strewn about as if it had been hit by a tornado.

In the middle of the night the bed frame had cracked and splintered under Petros' weight and dumped him onto the floor: he woke with a violent start. After that he pulled the mattress off the frame onto the ground and fell sleep on it again trying to think about what kind of creatures might be joining him in the shadows. Now in light of day, he sees that the bedframe was barely held together at all; the mattress, stripped of it sheets, could barely be called that—half of the stuffing had been pulled out buy many generations of animals over the years. He gets up; disgusted, he brushes off the raisin-sized animal droppings from his clothes.

A piercing pain shoots through his neck, combines with a nasty sense of vertigo, a vertigo almost worse than what he felt in the hotel room. He thanks God that he has some water to drink and some rations left.

Already in the predawn morning he was awakened by the sound of army trucks grinding by and the clomping of boots.

This is a relief in a way—the more movement they made, the harder it would be for them to zero in on his particular tracks, which left them searching door to door, a large task. Nevertheless, he feels a terrible urgency.

After he has eaten, he begins to explore again. There is so little left; there is so much left. In spite of decades of damage, there is something still here; unlike his own home, there is a spirit of what was once present. *He imagines Joanna and her brother here, as small children, running from room to room. He imagines her mother, not sad, but smiling and cooking dinner; and then they all walk down to the water to run in the surf for a few minutes before the sun disappears for the evening.* He imagines these things and more, and it makes him smile.

He starts his exploration. Fierce morning light pours into the main hallway through the open front doors and the arched fanlight window above, spreading out in comfortable squares, radiating summer warmth. There are random piles of rubble, chipped wood, animal nests, bricks, dust. Petros lets his eyes adjust—not to the light or the darkness, but to the interplay between them, that peculiar quality of light, a stark contrast specific to the old homes in Mediterranean countries, buildings that were built for both shade and illumination.

His eyes adjust, and he sees something face down on the ground—a three-picture frame. He rushes forward and picks it up, but the pictures once inside are long gone. Why, he wonders. Who, wandering in this godforsaken city would stop by a stranger's house and steal a photograph? Impossible, he thinks, blame it on the animals or the elements, anything non-human.

Now he moves through the house quickly. Much furniture is gone, but some things remain—a rotted, moldy couch, a broken dresser, drawers smashed and strewn through a bedroom. A lone wooden chair sits quietly in the kitchen, staring out the open back door at the quiet courtyard behind the house as if waiting for something or someone.

In the kitchen he finds a single old pot; good fortune, he thinks, or maybe someone is praying for him, maybe it is as the priests and old ladies say, that we each have been assigned a guardian angel to look after us, because what else could explain this, this and every other close escape of the past three days? *He remembers suddenly the look of Emre's face … he shudders and cries and wipes his eyes and pretends to continue as he had.*

He constructs a small solar distiller by cutting the bottom off the plastic bottle and placing it in the pot—a survival trick a soldier had taught him in the army, because this is Cyprus after all, you never know when you may find yourself facing the sea with no water to drink. He surreptitiously slides it into the sunlight in the back of the house, and takes a moment to listen. If one is really quiet, there are sounds, a low rumble as from a distant city—sounds, he thinks, from the part of the city outside the fences where the Turks live as if everything is normal.

A *bang!* makes him jump—a truck has gone over something loud, driving fast. He drops to the ground in a panic as he hears it tear by, hearing the shouts of soldiers coming off it. He can feel their terrible fury; if they find him there will be no mercy, no waiting this time. *I am a dead man.*

He has resolved not to move from her house before nightfall, but there is still no time to waste. *Why am I here?* Something, he must find something to bring back to Joanna. His mind goes back to her words, her stories.

He is about to give up, not because he has searched everything, but because he senses he is out of time, even though he knows he cannot leave until dusk, he cannot leave for hours and hours, but he must hide, something.

He returns at last to the bedroom shared by Joanna and her brother. In the corner, he sees it again, dusty but dignified: the safe.

Chapter Twenty

THERE WERE TIMES WHEN JOANNA'S father Andreas used to sit at that little safe and stare at it. Usually, it was after he and Maria had a fight. How can you keep this? he would ask, knowing the answer. Of course he knew the answer, he had known it from the day he married her, from before that day, when he knocked on her door ...

Petros absentmindedly brushes it off, and then tries to lift it, but it's impossibly heavy. This is why it wasn't taken, of course, but Petros cannot help thinking that it is nevertheless a miracle that it is still here.

She inherited the safe after the EOKA war. It came from a great uncle, a patriot, who used it to keep important documents for the cause. He, in turn, had acquired it from a British official years earlier, who moved back to Britain in a hurry and in mourning after his wife died suddenly. Except for the war documents, no one in the family ever used it for much, so after her tragedy when Maria asked for it—for keepsakes and memories—of course the uncle said yes.

She kept it in the spare bedroom, the bedroom that would one day become her son Yiannis' bedroom, later shared with Joanna after she was born. This was the worst insult, Andreas thought, that she would insist on keeping it even after their children were born, keeping it in that room with his own children. But where would he have her keep it then?

On days after her parents fought, Joanna would find her father here, on the edge of her bed, staring at the safe, drinking something and smelling like what she thought of as a combination of communion wine and rubbing alcohol.

"What is it Papa?" she would ask. "What's in the safe?"

"Nothing, my love." He said.

Of course it had been years that he had sat in that room, staring at that safe, and before, when they lived at the old house. He would drink and look at it, and think of all he had hoped for in his life; he would remember the rare moments when he touched his wife and somehow, things worked between them.

"The funny thing," Joanna told Petros later, "Is that they kept the combination taped to the back of the side of the bookshelf—so that anyone could get in at any time."

"How do you know?" asked Petros.

"My brother told me once," she said. "He told me like it was a secret, but it was right there."

"Papa," she asked her father, "Why don't we open it?"

"There are things in the world that we do not touch," he told her.

The bookshelf. Petros finds it, in a broken heap on the other side of the room. Is it possible? He rushes over. Surprisingly, some books remain, even in good shape. He skims the covers as he pushes them aside.

"Why," said Andreas. "Why do you keep it?" At the end it was a question only asked at the bitter end of one or another of their terrible, sad fights, but of course, in the end, all of those other fights were about this. People told him to let go; told him that if he just let his wife have her memories, if he respected her and didn't push things, that she would eventually come around, that she would get over things on her own. Other people—his friends at the cafe—told him to just have it removed. "Be a

man," they said, "throw it in the ocean and be done with it once and for all."

And then, Petros finds it: a small scrap of paper with three numbers.

What they didn't realize was how much his bitterness came from true love, a love that would never let him hurt her that way. And yet, when she nagged him or screamed at him or shouted at him to get out of the house, in those moments when he realized how much she hated him, how much she resented being married to him (though she would never say it)—in those moments when he was pushed to the brink he would shout at her: "what is in your precious safe anyway?"

And she would cry, cry, and he would say I'm sorry, I know, I know, and she would let him hold her, and he would feel a momentary sense of relief to be followed by the realization that he was being cuckolded by a dead man.

Finally, one year, one particularly terrible fight, months before their first child was born (the delay was not her doing, but his—he had thought at first that she was too fragile to have children and then there were the years when they didn't even sleep in the same bed, much less do the things that people must do to make children …) she pulled out a sheet of paper, and wrote three numbers on it with her perfect penmanship, and taped it the side of the bookcase. "There!" she said. "Now you can open that safe any time you want! Take a look, see what you want to see!"

Petros turns the knob, 27, 33—after the second number, there is a small click—and then 7. The final click, the door opens with a creak; opens for the first time in two decades, maybe longer.

But of course he didn't look, he would never violate her that way, but that didn't stop him from sitting at the foot of the bed with a drink in his hand, staring at it, even after the children were born. He would take them to bed and tuck them in, and sit for a time, looking at it.

"Mama," Joanna asked. "What was in that safe?" she was a teenager the first time she asked her mother that question; the first time, her mother ignored her. The second time she asked, her mother shook her head, said, "I don't know what you're talking about." The third time her mother screamed at her: "Why are you asking after such things? Why can't you accept that the past is in the past?"

"What could possibly have been in there?" she asked Petros on that night they lay naked together, flesh to flesh. "What could it possibly have meant?"

Nothing much, he thinks. A pile of papers, newspaper clippings, photographs, a leather-bound notebook. Petros runs his fingers over these; the paper crinkles, makes a soft, soothing, gentle sound, a sound that makes the old documents seem strangely alive.

The newspaper clippings, he sees, were all from the 1950s—reports of the revolution, in Greek and in English, in no particular order. He unfolds the yellowed paper carefully and begins to read. There is a story here, he thinks, a story beyond just the story of the fight against colonial oppressors. Loose sheets of paper are mixed in—fliers, mostly, from *Digenes Akritas,* the *nom de plume* of General Grivas, calling for resistance by the Greeks against the British.

Petros gravitates to the black, leather-bound notebook. Just inside the front cover: an old, sepia-yellow photograph. A man and a woman, smiling. Her face startles him: it is Joanna—the spitting image, only, if anything, more beautiful. A strange feeling comes over him. How is there a picture of her, a grown woman here, in a place she's not come to in twenty years?

Involuntarily he looks around, as if someone has played a trick on him.

It all takes less than a second. Of course it is not her, the woman in the picture is shorter, fuller-figured; this is without a doubt Maria, Joanna's mother. She is wearing a wedding dress; the man next to her is in old-fashioned Khaki military fatigues. He smiles broadly, a sparkling joy in his eyes, reaching out to Petros across the decades. Even though his bushy, 1950s-style mustache makes him look older, he is just a boy, Petros thinks; at most 19, the age of the recruits Petros and the other "old soldiers" harass. It is possible that this is Joanna's father? He thinks not: from what Joanna said, her parents had not married until years later, in the mid 1960s. Who, then, is he?

The woman's eyes are bright too, but slightly sad. It surprises him that in spite of the formality of the photograph he can feel their emotions so strongly across the decades and lifetimes that stand between them.

He turns the photograph over. Someone has dated it, Palehori, August, 1957. He is now certain this is Joanna's mother, and she is getting married. He realizes he knows little about her family, even though his own mother and father were good friends with them in Famagusta, and Yiorgos and Eleni Zenios as well.

Inside the book, he reads the broad-looped, strong handwriting on the inner cover—a man's handwriting, he thinks—on the brittle, cracked and yellowing pages.

`August, 1956.`

```
I omit my name from this account to
protect myself and our organization. Last
night, I swore my oath to EOKA.

It is my intention to tell the story of
my adventures in the Ethniki Organosie
Kypriakou Agonsitou (EOKA) which has been
formed to liberate Cyprus and the Cypriot
people from the tyranny of the British
yoke. As Greeks, it is not merely our
right but our duty to fight for our
freedom as a people. We are confident
that God is on our side.
```

Petros hears the sounds of trucks going by again, and then shouts and voices. He puts the journal down and moves toward the front of the house, as quietly as possible, empty pistol in his hand, thinking as he pulls it out that it is a foolish thing to do—worse to have an empty threat in hand, to give them yet another excuse to kill him, and yet this is what he does.

A floorboard moans, and he stops short, catching his breath. The voices have stopped; he listens as hard as he can, straining as if listening were a muscle, trying to determine whether the silence means that they have heard him or if it is just a normal pause in the conversation.

After a moment, he hears them talking again, low, careful voices. He takes another step forward. From the living room, he crouches and looks out the main window, sees two soldiers stationed at the street corner a few buildings away, looking at once casual and alert. They stand back to back and scan the buildings around them. Petros breathes a quiet sigh of relief that they don't know where he is, but also feels—yet again, once again—a sinking sense of terror in his guts. If there were any question that he would have to wait until nightfall to escape, this has squelched it.

He returns to Joanna's bedroom, puts his back against the wall, slides down to the floor and picks up the journal again.

> Writing this at all is, in fact, an affront to the courage of the soldiers who bear their burdens in silence and peace. I am surrounded by men so self-possessed and assured that they need speak to no one about their pain or adventure. I am not one of them.
>
> Even from my childhood I used to write my thoughts. I couldn't live without it.
>
> I have often thought of joining the cause, but I was afraid. I was afraid of suffering and death, yes, but also that in the mountains there are no books! And no one to tell my problems to. In my childish heart I told myself that I wasn't ready, that I didn't know how to live that way.
>
> I remember the day when my sister-in-law gave me this journal (a gift for my birthday); I felt a rush of joy. The leaves outside the window had changed color, and I saw in the blank pages of this book enough stories to fill up a life . . . a real life, a life that meant something.
>
> It has been months now that I have run around the streets with my friends, spray-painting the English street-signs, but by the daylight we still sat in our

classrooms while the struggle continued without us, in the mountains, with real guns . . . enough, I thought. I was waiting to finish the year, my last year, but with every day that we went on strike from classes, or on a protest march, I felt a pull like nothing else. I was learning nothing but better ways to hate our "masters." Better to die uneducated and free than to live as a learned slave.

But there are other reasons I joined; reasons I cannot go into here.

Petros closes the book and runs his fingers along its spine, smells the leather—a scent, he thinks, that has been there for decades. The pages are in surprising shape; he thumbs through them, just to feel them under his fingers.

Petros begins running his mind through the names of soldiers who fought in the EOKA times. He knows many of them. The ones who gave their lives are famous, or known, at least. Of the ones who lived, most are still around. He has been thinking about them, wishing he were one of them, for most of his life.

It has now been three weeks since I joined, and nothing significant has happened, we have been hiding in three different villages since that time, in the houses of our helpers. The word from our leader is that we aren't ready for any real missions yet. He is moving us around for our training; we walk a lot at night. Now that we're away and hiding in the mountains, I spend my days doing pull-ups on a tree-branch here . . . I still don't feel strong enough to be a soldier.

```
It is the middle of the day, and I am
looking out the window at a girl; she is
carrying a basket which looks like it has
bread in it. Like all the women in the
village, her head is covered by a scarf,
but I can still see her face. She is
smiling.

Her beauty reminds me of my own beauty,
the girl who I left in the city; Maria.
Maria! The girl who lived down the
street. Maria! Maybe you will read this
one day and know how much I love you.
```

Petros now closes the book, his suspicions confirmed; the woman in the photograph was Joanna's mother, married to another man, years ago. An EOKA solider—a hero as well. A slow, realization dawns on him; Maria was married to someone else, someone who served in EOKA, someone who must have been killed in the struggle, someone whose memory she insisted upon keeping alive, no matter how much it hurt the other man, the man she eventually married, the man who would be Joanna's father. Petros suddenly sees the streak of cruelty in the heart of the poor sad woman; and yet, he understands, he can feel it, the inability to let go of someone. People will tell you to let go, but the more they insist on it (for your own good), the more cruel and unjust and unforgivable and inevitable the loss becomes, the more tenaciously the injured heart clings. Is it possible that Joanna doesn't know about any of this?

Suddenly, the idyllic family that Joanna remembers—the memories she is constantly building and rebuilding—seem hollow, and he knows at that instant that there is no way he can bring this back to her, bring any of it back.

He thinks of Maria again: how terrible, that she then must lose another man to war; this war even more futile than the last.

But who was this soldier of EOKA? Petros opens the book and starts flipping through the pages more quickly, knowing that he will have to leave all these secrets here at the end of the day. This isn't exactly true; he could take it all, of course, bring it home and never tell anyone about it; take it all and go over it at his leisure when he was safely at home in his mother's house. *And if you don't survive this?* he asks himself. *Then it makes no difference either way, does it?*

Nevertheless, he flips through the pages quickly now, seeking clues.

He entertains the thought that the soldier was his own uncle, Panos; that, he thinks, would make sense, both Panos and Maria were from this part of Cyprus, they would have known each other …

> Being shot at is strange; not as frightening as one might think. It happened to me for the first time last night. The British were chasing us, and we were almost eaten by their machine gun fire.
>
> One of my comrades laughed though. It would have been worse if the bullets had come close. He said that he urinated in his pants the last time he was shot at, when he could feel the air of the bullets on his face.

But I try not to think about that. For now I enjoy the feeling of being courageous.

The details don't add up, though. The writer of the journal speaks of Maria as "the girl from the sea" and how he longs to go there with her; it is clear that he is a mountain-village boy who had gone to high school in the city.

The woman of the house put a feast in front of us . . . they even killed a chicken. We had *halloumi*, fresh bread, *pastitsio*, and a glass of wine. I don't think I ever drank a better glass . . .

Then she heated up some water for us to wash ourselves off with, and took us into the back room where there were two beds made for us. It was the first time we had eaten in days, the first time we had bathed in weeks.

The story continues, Petros reads on. At some point, he looks up, realizing that an hour must have passed at least. He is parched, his throat hurts, the heat of the day has entered the building again. He checks the contraption he built; almost a cup of water has condensed in the plastic well. He pulls it out and drinks it eagerly; it is of course not enough, he could drink a liter, but it will do. He reassembles the contraption and prays to get more clear water by nightfall.

He returns to Joanna's room, to the safe, to the journal; he enters the story again. It's like a great puzzle, full of references to famous events and people and places that Petros knows, interspersed with the smallest details and personal thoughts. Petros leafs through faster until he hits a revealing detail.

I have taken my brother's place.

Yiorgos words: "My brother took my place."

This is Athos Zenios' journal.

The entry continues; it is unusually angry and incoherent. The soldiers it seemed, had been hiding in the mountains for days after their battle, with no food and little water. They finally found refuge, only to be betrayed and discovered by the British; they escaped again. When they were finally in a safe location, Athos sent word to find out what was happening with his family, and with his beloved Maria.

No word! No word from my beloved—no word of her either! I am sure—as sure as I am of my faith in God—that if she knew where I was, she would send me a note of hope and encouragement. So what then? This can only mean that she is prevented from communicating with me or worse that she knows nothing of my whereabouts!

The ink on the next page is smeared—*by tears? Petros wonders. Is it too sentimental to think so?*

I must be courageous! I must understand! Any communication puts us all at risk. These other men here, who fight without thought of their families ... [the words are smeared and unreadable] ...

Petros closes the book, and looks again at the photograph. There is no question: it is Maria, it is a wedding dress, Joanna's mother was married before, and not to just anyone, but to the brother of Yiorgos Zenios. She was married to the brother of Yiorgos, the brother who took his place in the struggle; the brother who was martyred by the British. Her love was murdered by the British, and she never forgot, she kept his memories locked in a safe in a back room for years and years while she built another family, until the next war came and the Turks ruined it all for her again.

And what then, does it mean? Petros wonders. He begins tearing through the piles of papers, desperate for the one thing he actually had come looking for, a photograph of Joanna's father, but he knows he will not find it, the safe was for hiding memories from him, not for keeping them of him.

The realization sinks in: he has nothing to bring back to Joanna. The envelope with the map, the pictures of her, and most importantly, the photograph of her father—he has left these back at the hotel, with his pack. He curses himself. He could have picked up the folder after he flashed the signal to Elias.

The realization sinks in: he has come all this way, has killed a man, has come within inches of death only to discover things that should have been left undiscovered. He curses again under his breath and punches the wall, forgetting for a moment the need to be quiet. His fist cracks the wood; droplets of blood appear on his knuckles. The pain sobers him a little. It is time to go, and yet there are hours left in the day, he cannot leave.

There is nothing left to do but sit and read more of the leather-bound tragedy; anyway, he can't look away.

He reads more, reads through many dull details, half-finished descriptions, repetitions. This, of course, was life as a guerrilla; 95 percent waiting and boredom. He finds himself scanning, looking for references to events and places and people who he knows of. There are a few. Mentions of the "leader"—mentions of other famous heroes. References to battles Petros knew of: Maheras, Spilia. Petros devours the sparse details like a starving ascetic sucking nourishment from bitter weeds. And then, the author refers to his friends, one of whom Petros is sure is his uncle Panos.

Panos: another person about whom Petros knows little, other than that he too was killed in the EOKA struggle. He remembers photographs, his mother pointing to him in a group of patriotic, serious poses of guerrillas in their vaguely military sweaters and their fatigues and their rifles.

> One of my best friends was killed as well. He was an intellectual like me, but a better poet. He and another soldier were killed carrying out an ambush last week.
>
> He was a boy from the seaside. We talked for a long time, into the night, just two weeks ago. He told me about troubles with his family, reminded me that we all have bitterness in our families. His father had just died, and his brothers and sisters were furious that he didn't come to the funeral. Imagine! To expect a soldier to risk his life and everyone else's to come to a funeral? There are those who don't understand. They say we have abandoned our families. How can they not see that Greece is our mother?
>
> Only a few weeks later he got another letter: his sister begging him to return, that their brother was trying to steal all the inheritance for himself, that he must return, that he was the only one who could set things right.

Do you know what he said to me? "I am ashamed to be one of them," he said. "Here I am fighting to free Cyprus from slavery, to unite us to our brothers, our blood, and this is all they care about?"

Petros closes the book, stands up and paces the room. *I knew it,* he thinks. Michalis—and by extension Elias—have stolen everything. Everything, stolen! He thinks of his poor aunt Xanthe, married to the simple potato farmer (of course a bitter woman who seems to hate everyone—not someone he is inclined to have much sympathy for).

He is thirsty, evening is finally coming. He returns to his improvised water purifier, and manages to sip another half a cup of good water. It is time to begin making a plan, to steel himself for the long crawl home, but before that, he has another few pages left to read of Athos' journal. He sits and starts again.

I kissed my bride tonight, held her in my arms. She cried and held me with such tightness, as if she could fasten me to her body, cleave me to her, and felt illuminated and light and free. "We will be together soon," I told her, and she cried again. I wanted to reassure her, to promise her, the way men promise their women, but the words wouldn't come.

"It's okay," she said, and she touched my face. "Whatever happens, whatever happens from now on for the rest of my life, I will have this. I will have this one moment, and no matter what happens, the joy of this moment will be with me forever. Go, then, and be a hero for our country, unite us to our mother Greece. I will be waiting for you forever." And then she kissed me again and I left before dawn.

Trembling, Petros lowers the diary, staring at the words for a long time, and then suddenly he slams it shut and stuffs it in his shirt-coat pocket.

Joanna, Petros thinks, *I am coming for you.*

CHAPTER TWENTY-ONE

ISN'T IT NOW TIME TO return to the land of the living? he wonders.

His mind runs through the options; but there are no options. In truth, if he decides to return now, he is already defeated, whether they catch him or not; he returns with nothing, no keepsakes to reveal (the notebook can be seen by no one), and nothing else to offer, nothing to justify winning the woman back. If goes back now—if he is not killed on the way—he returns only to quizzical looks and pointless humiliation, to court-martial and scorn at his foolish vanity. Everyone will see him not as a hero, but as a fool.

The final option—one last effort. Go back to the hotel, his father's hotel, where Emre lies dead, retrieve the photo of Joanna and her father, and see if he can find something—some evidence that at least proves that he and his sister deserve something more than what they have been given.

As he sits against the wall, waiting for nightfall, another fantasy unfolds in his mind, in which he returns to Joanna with a photograph of her father, and then takes her in his arms, and says, "everything is different now."

And then he goes to his uncle and throws down a stack of papers (a map? a title deed? he isn't sure...) that proves that uncle Michalis' land does not belong to him; he demands then, his rightful inheritance, he gets a piece of land and builds a restaurant and a hotel, and he and Joanna live there, getting rich and staring at sunsets over Paralimni windmills; and when the Turks finally give Famagusta back, they are the first ones there, finding the old houses and rebuilding them or building something new.

But he has no documents, no proof to show his uncle or anyone else, he has nothing more than idle speculation. If there were any proof to be had in this lonely city it was back in the hotel, where he left the pack and the folder and the photograph.

He leaps now to his feet, the decision made. Time to move before he loses light completely.

His thoughts are interrupted by the sounds of military trucks moving again, in the distance; and closer by, footsteps. He looks again at his fingernails, still blackened with Turkish blood.

A dog barks and Petros feels a rush of alarm.

He creeps forward again, to the front window, looks out toward the street corner, where the soldiers had been stationed all day. They have been joined by two others; the four of them talk in low voices, their eyes scanning their surroundings casually. Wherever the dog was, it is nowhere to be seen, but two more soldiers are now standing in the middle of the street, pretending to talk casually. Petros is certain they cannot see him, but he can feel them, almost leaning in his direction; it seems as though they are actually avoiding looking at the house.

He glances further down the street; another two soldiers have stopped there, looking casual as well, while at the far end of the block, a truck pulls up to the corner; it is fitted with a machine gun. He creeps back inside, feeling a growing sense of panic; they are quietly surrounding the house. The dog—the dog he heard must have caught his scent, and led them to the house. They will move in before nightfall—he is sure of that, they have let him slip through their fingers one too many times.

He slips back, to the rear of the house, looks out at the courtyard, another broken stone wall and the backyard of the house the next street over. Palm trees and acacias grow wild; even the weeds are thick, nearly chest height.

He takes a breath and decides to go, slipping into the brush behind the house, moving as low as possible, keeping the wild grasses over his head. He pauses against the crumbing wall and waits, and then out of the corner of his eye, he sees movement, four Turkish special forces moving into position behind the house; they come through the access alley and the rear gate. Petros has never seen soldiers move so quietly; so quietly that he feels as though he is watching a movie with the sound off. They scan the back yard but don't see him huddling in the weeds and shadows; they seem to assume that he is still inside the house. *Glory be to God*, he thinks, and yet if he moves, tries to leap the short wall or slip along it toward the other side of the house, he will surely be seen.

A moment later, however, he gets his opportunity—the soldiers fire tear gas into the house. A terrifying series of bangs, smoke pours out of the window; three out of four of the soldiers in the back rush the building, while the last drops to one knee behind a tree and takes aim to shoot any survivor. They have made a lucky mistake in thinking Petros is still inside—as they rush in, he takes a chance and vaults over the wall into the next yard, darts through the buildings toward the next street over.

Petros hears a shout behind him. One of the soldiers, probably the one who was left outside, has heard his movement and seen him jump and run, and is calling after him, but he can also hear shouts that sound like confusion amidst the smoke and gunshots. Maybe they will kill each other and leave me alone, he thinks.

They have stationed a couple of soldiers on the next street over. Petros sees them at the last second as he is about to dart out from between the houses; he catches himself, pulls back, sees one of them catch a glimpse of his movement and raise his gun to fire, so he moves to the left, running low, trying to stay between the houses and crumbling low walls of the verandas.

His side screams out again in pain, but he is in better shape than he should be. By the time they take aim to shoot he has gone around the corner back toward the open lots between the houses. He pauses to look around the corner to see if the first soldier has seen him, but for the moment he is on the other side of the house, so Petros sprints across the lot, looking diagonally to his left. Smoke is pouring out of the windows of Joanna's house. He continues running, out from between the houses across another street—this one to the south—into another large empty lot, covered in a young, wild, riparian forest.

One or two of the Turks try to give chase, but they are slow at jumping over gates and squeezing between walls with their rifles and body armor; by the time the rest have organized themselves and reconvened with their new information, night is falling, and Petros has already disappeared again into the wild suburban jungle of this once-famous town.

~~~~

Now he sits again in the twilight. The blue sky grows pink, and then blue again, but deeper, and the familiar specks appear as though someone is slowly poking holes in the sky to reveal the luminous heavens above. He watches it unfold through the branches of the trees that whisper and sway; whisper and sway in the evening sea-breeze.

Now he sits again, in the shadows, this time in the middle of a grove of trees that cover a large block in the middle of the city. He senses creeping things all around him; but worse, he senses the poisonous hatred of the Turks, the seething and unjustified rage; rage like a force of nature. They will kill him, he thinks, but not without making sure he suffers; they will flay him for what he has done, as they flayed Bragadino.

From where he is, he looks south through the trees, thinks he can see the lights of Protaras and Fig Tree Bay, where tourists and hotel owners are even now finishing their *kalamari* and chips, drinking their chilled Carlsberg beers, feeling sated and thinking about ice cream and the beach in the morning, trying to decide if they are too stuffed and drunk to make love to their wives and girlfriends tonight.

So close, Petros thinks. He knows the route back; if he can make his way across the fields before Ayios Memnon. Of course they will be looking for him, but they are also confused, and now that they think they have him pinned down it is his best chance.

He rises and starts again; the long walk to the beach.

~~~~

Now he moves between the groves of trees, slides down the alleys of the buildings, darts across the narrow streets—streets that are barely streets anymore, streets that are covered in wildflowers swaying in the dusk light.

There, then, finally, is John F. Kennedy Boulevard, the wide road that went along the beachfront, separating the city proper from the high-rise hotels. From a building corner he looks down the boulevard, and sees the Golden Aphrodite—the hotel that his father and Uncle Michalis had owned, the hotel they made their fortunes on, the hotel they lost.

In the dusk, the Turks have bathed it in light—halogen spotlights. Petros can hear the rumbling of the generator from all the way down the street. At the sight of it he almost changes his mind as the impossibility of approaching, much less of getting inside, sinks in. What was he thinking? The Turks would of course be keeping their sights on the hotel.

Nevertheless, he moves closer by cutting through courtyards behind the buildings again, feeling exposed. When he is almost directly across from the hotel, he moves again along the edge of a building facing the street and peers around the corner. It turns out that in spite of the lights, the building is now poorly guarded; he only sees one soldier standing listless in front of the main entrance, gazing out into the darkness, his eyes no doubt blinded by the lights shining on the building.

From where he stands, Petros thinks it looks like Kadir—a shocking cruelty, he thinks, unless of course Kadir has asked to guard the death-place of his friend. Petros considers both thoughts simultaneously even as he remembers the look on Emre's face in death once again, and feels another sickening twist of nausea in his gut, the worst one yet. Maybe, he thinks, he does not deserve to live. Maybe the most noble thing at this moment is to sacrifice himself to the Turks, to give them the blood they hungered for and to make a statement at the same time. He tells himself that this is irrational guilt; he was in his hometown when he killed Emre, in his own father's hotel, defending his own life in a war that never ended.

One soldier standing guard—undoubtedly they don't expect Petros to return to the hotel. Still, he can't just walk up to the main entrance. The only other option is to retreat and find a way in from the beach side. This means moving far enough away that he won't be seen as he darts across the wide avenue—an easier task than it might seem, given the bright lights blinding the lone guard and the almost total darkness in the rest of this ghost town.

He retreats, and listens. He can hear a truck moving, but far away. As far as he knows, the sound could be distant traffic further north, outside the fence. He wonders if they're on the lookout for him there too—if the thought of a Greek soldier creeping through the streets frightens the Turkish civilians as much as the thought that there were Turkish spies in their midst would frighten the Greeks, but he doubts it.

He retreats, about 200 yards, and then darts madly across the boulevard and the sidewalk into the open door of yet another abandoned hotel. He takes gulping breaths; his fear waxes and wanes. It's better when he is being chased and there's no opportunity to think, worse when he has time, like now, to reflect on his choices. He knows he can still retreat, like a coward, and no one would ever know but him. No one would know but him, and that knowledge would haunt him for rest of his life.

For an instant he thinks he hears a child, wailing in the distance; a little, ghostly voice, perhaps carried from somewhere beyond the barbed wire.

Inside the hotel it is pitch black, so he turns on Emre's flashlight, panning the room quickly to get a feeling for it, and then covering the beam with his hand to lessen the chance of being seen.

He decides to traverse the distance to his father's hotel on the beach side, moving from building to building, entering each one if he can and moving across them lengthwise. It turns out to be more difficult than he anticipated, full of unexpected dead-ends and reversals.

Even with the flashlight he stumbles frequently, catching his feet on random rubble, furniture and broken memories. His left arm has begun to ache, more than any other injury, though he can't remember at what point he hurt it. Moving along in the darkness, with only a muffled flashlight beam to follow, he begins to feel as if he is moving through some kind of dream; it must be a dream or he has lost his mind. Only a madman would walk straight back into the enemy's lair.

Nonetheless, he continues, like a madman; like a mad dog after a bone.

Finally, he reaches the hotel adjacent to—directly south of—the Golden Aphrodite. He turns off the flashlight now for fear of being seen through an unexpected window, and tries to move through the building instead by sliding his hands along the walls. This works for long enough for him to find the lobby. Moonlight and starlight glow faintly in the distance on his left and right, the street- and beach-side entrances.

He sees no exit to the north, so he moves toward the beach side; he must decide whether to grope forward upright or drop to his knees and crawl, so as to avoid stumbling. He decides to walk upright, like a man, damn the obstacles.

Now he walks quickly, kicking and sweeping his feet in front of him to push aside random debris, until the light from outside becomes strong enough that he can finally see at least the shadows of where he is stepping.

He finds a spot then, where he can look out, through the broken remains of sliding glass doors to a patio.

He pokes his head through and looks north. He is taken by surprise by an intense light—they have placed another spotlight on the hotel, beach side—so he pulls back inside, to let his eyes adjust.

He looks again; there is another soldier on guard, on the back side of the building, but instead of blocking the entrance from the beach level, he is standing on the second-floor patio, the concrete rooftop that covered the hotel's outdoor restaurant where Kadir and Emre had burned the flag.

As with the one stationed in the front, there is no way for this soldier to see him against the glare of the floodlights, and he is amazed at their arrogance; even after he has killed one of their own, they are more interested in a show of force, a spectacle, even one they are putting on only for themselves. But of course they are right; they are the predators, he is but a rat to them, albeit one that bites when cornered.

Of course, they expect him to run and hide, not to return.

Can he enter the building? Again, it is easier than he thought. The soldier on the beach side seems intent on only staring past the blinding floodlights at the sea. What does he expect, Petros wonders. A waterborne rescue? Here?

The sound of the diesel generators for the floodlights is not quite deafening, but it is loud enough to cover the sound of Petros' movement. He takes a deep breath, waits until he is sure the guard is turned away, and moves as quickly as he can to the covered part of the building under where the guard is standing and creeps through another broken glass door to enter the hotel.

~~~~

Now that he is inside, he turns on the flashlight and moves boldly, at once conscious of how little time he has. He tries to convince himself that he is now in the one place they are least likely to suspect.

He finds the pack in the middle of the lobby floor where they tossed it. He reaches inside, finds the precious envelope and opens it. Everything is there, the map and the photographs, including the one of Joanna and her father. He breathes a sigh of relief as he slips it into his pocket next to Athos Zenios' diary.

It doesn't take him long to find the office—through the double doors behind reception. The door squeaks as he closes it, but he does so anyway, hoping—convincing himself—that no one can hear him that far inside the building.

His biggest concern is the flashlight, because he knows from an initial scan that it may take some time to find what he is looking for, and he can't risk someone catching sight of the light from under the door if they happen to enter; so he takes off his jacket, rolls it up and shoves it under the door crack.

The room is a disheveled mess. Someone, perhaps many people, have been here over the years and dug through things,
~~~~

emptied the filing cabinets onto the floor, but, finding nothing of value, they seem to have abandoned most of it as useless paper. Much of what they left is already brittle, the edges chewed and gnawed at by generations of mice and rats and God knows what other creatures. Still, much remains for Petros to dig through.

In spite of everything that has already happened, he feels a wave of shock when he reads first his uncle's name and then his father's on a bill receipt. They were here, he thinks; this is where they built their lives, together. They were close; closer than he and Elias, even at their closest. The thought fills him with newfound rage at his uncle—at the betrayal, at his uncle's ability to rebuild his empire and leave his brother's family in the weeds.

Payroll, old receipts, tax records, useless. Perhaps it would be interesting, he thinks, if there were time to reflect on each scrap and understand its significance, but there isn't time. He gathers a few brief facts; that the hotel was making good money, but that it had major expenses …

But this is not what he needs—he needs evidence, not about the hotel but about the land in Protaras upon which his uncle built his second empire. As he shuffles through the paper though, he slowly realizes the futility of his search; why would the hotel have records of other properties? If such a thing were anywhere, it would be kept at home; and he had already seen that there was nothing left at his own house, and he had never thought to locate the place where Elias' family had lived.

He turns off the flashlight now, and sits down amidst the papers, in the deep blackness in the heart of the dead building, a building that bore little resemblance to what it once was.

He has moved beyond despair now to numbness. He lies down; it would be so easy to just wait here to be discovered, or die of dehydration—to give up, to stop resisting. The idea that he could change the course of his life by coming to this place—if that was even his thought—was always a desperate one, and now he has failed, it is time to admit this and accept the consequences. He doesn't have the heart to come up with a new plan; he doesn't have the courage to return to free Cyprus and face the consequences with so little to show for his efforts. He would feel foolish if he weren't so exhausted, but the splitting pain in his head pushes shame aside and focuses his mind on a present, irredeemable moment.

A long time passes; hours, he thinks, though time itself is something that has slowly lost its meaning for him.

And then—he moves, for what reason, he is not sure. Perhaps he hears a noise amidst the deathly silence of the closed black room, or perhaps some part of his mind, the part of his mind that still refuses to give up, the part of his mind that wants him to survive, the part of his brain that still believes in him, in his cause, his insane, grand cause—perhaps this part of his mind fabricates a sound to make him sit up. A still, small voice: *don't give up*.

So he continues, this time more methodically; he clears an area on the floor, and then piles the papers into stacks with the intention of leafing through them again, when he finds an old-fashioned accordion folder, tied shut with a string. He puts it aside for a moment, committed to his plan of moving in a methodical way; and then something, some impulse, compels him to open the folder.

Inside the folder, Petros finds records, bills of sale regarding land, clipped to a series of maps. The first packet of maps is dated 1957 and has marked plots of land in different places—Varosha, Paralimini and near Fig Tree Bay in Protaras—but in a strange array of shapes, big blocks attached to slender rectangles, little slivers, odd-looking tetrahedrons, each one with the name of one of the three brothers or Xanthe on it.

Then, there is another pile of maps, from 1960; in this one, the same areas are marked, but under each parcel that belonged to the now dead Panos, someone had written the name of one of the other three, except for a few, where they had put in question marks. Petros sees this and understands suddenly and completely—this was, of course, the source of contention between the surviving siblings. Surely their father—Petros' grandfather—hadn't thought to consider the death of one of his children when he willed them his scattershot parcels.

What kind of machinations, then, had uncle Michalis pulled to secure the land in Protaras? But then he looks more closely at the maps, and is startled, confused.

It says very clearly that the large piece of land near Protaras, along with two other parcels near Paralimni, was being given to his aunt Xanthe and her husband, along with 500 British pounds, in exchange for the beach front parcel where they were. The land belonged to both Michalis and Solomos.

In other words, by 1960 the land near Protaras—in fact, all family parcels south of Varosha—was marked as belonging to Xanthe's family. Petros' father, Solomos, had no title in that area at all, and neither did Michalis.

Of course, there is no way for Petros to know details; he is just guessing at how things must have played out, but whatever had actually happened, two things were clear: the first was that if anyone had been wronged it was his aunt Xanthe. The second was that his father—and by extension now he—indeed had no claim to uncle Michalis' empire. If his goal had been to right the wrongs of his family and lay claim to some piece of something—something he could build a life from to win Joanna away from his richer, better-looking, smarter and soon-to-be more successful cousin Elias—then his terrible tour of Varosha had not only been a failure, it had been a hellish waste.

Chapter Twenty-Two

Now what? Petros wonders, for he has truly reached the end of the line. It's a relief; there is nothing left for him to discover in this place and nothing more left to do; nothing left to do but return home or die.

He still believes he has the advantage of being in the one place the Turks are least likely to look for him; the guards who watch the building have not found out that he is inside, they are looking out, which means, in theory, he has the possibility of surprising one of them from behind.

The other option: to wait. If he is careful, bides his time, he can wait and choose to move at the moment when their attention is at its lowest—at a moment when they think that he has already escaped.

The problem with this plan is his own stamina. He knows he cannot survive for more than a few hours in the daytime without water—not in August in Cyprus. His stomach is rumbling with hunger now as well.

He reminds himself also of the dog; by daybreak they will bring more dogs, they will catch his scent, this is how they will find him. The sobering thought shifts his thinking; it is time to go, now.

He looks instinctively at his watch, forgetting that it is pitch black inside. He points the flashlight at it only to remember, seeing his naked wrist, that they took his watch with everything else.

He tries to estimate: he has been reading papers in the darkness for a long time; he thinks he even has slept, but he can't be sure. He returns then to the closed office door. No light is visible underneath it, but he can feel a whisper of fresh air, and this reminds him of how hot and stuffy the room is, and suddenly he is suffocating, gasping for breath, his clothes soaked with sweat. He jerks the door open too quickly, hearing it squeal desperately like a wounded animal, but he doesn't care, he stumbles out of the little tomb and gulps the air of the lobby. It too is stale, thick and hot, but fresh enough to provide a small gasp of relief; fresh enough to give him hope for even fresher air, for the true breath of life outside the rotting concrete walls of this terrible place.

He wasn't able to see it from inside, but now hints of morning light are visible—the faintest, pink-purple glow—coming from the street-side entrance, to the east; morning must be further along than he thought, because they have turned off the generators and the floodlights.

He ducks below the check-in desk just in time to see the front door swing open, and a soldier walk through, rifle and flashlight raised. The soldier calls something out in Turkish—something like who's there?—and moves in Petros' direction.

As quietly as possible, Petros draws his empty pistol.

He is hiding in the only place a person could hide in this room, which makes his discovery inevitable. Even if the solider thinks that he just imagined the sound, he will certainly shine the light behind the counter, just to be sure. The footsteps draw closer; Petros sees the beam of the soldier's light moving against the back wall, over his head.

Strangely, his thoughts are clearer than they were the first time death scraped at his door three days ago. It is as if he is getting used to it. Contempt for death, as the Spartans used to say, is a skill that can be rapidly learned, but only under precise conditions. Fortunately, once acquired, it opens up possibilities of thought and action that fear would ordinarily shut down.

So it is with this new skill that he contemplates his options. Everything depends on where exactly along the counter the soldier is when he finally looks over its edge. If he happens to be close enough, Petros will be able to leap up, grab the rifle and, with the element of surprise, possibly subdue the soldier. But if he comes around at the other end, his only hope will be to leap over the counter and sprint for the front door and be shot in the back.

But even if he can wrestle the gun away, the noise will surely attract the other guard, the one in the back guarding the building on the beach side. *Contempt for death*, he thinks.

Then he hears it—a slight creak of the floorboard—and places it in his mind, a few meters from the counter, at the far end. Petros sees the beam of light turn on again, and this time he does not hesitate, he leaps up, vaults the counter and rushes the soldier. There is possibly three meters between them, enough time for the soldier to turn and fire on him if he were fast enough, but he is not.

Petros has the element of surprise, and that is all that matters. Surprise and the power of conviction; he sees on the soldiers' face that he never believed that there was really someone there, which means that no matter how careful he thought he was being, when he actually saw Petros running toward him he was taken by surprise.

Petros shoves the muzzle of the gun aside and throws his full weight into the soldier with his shoulder, and they both tumble backward to the ground. It is only then that Petros realizes to his shock that it is Kadir.

Hitting the floor, Kadir cries out in rage and frustration; but unlike Emre, he doesn't make the mistake of trying to retain control of his rifle; instead he hurls it aside and begins to pound his fists back at Petros' face; for the moment neither one of them is on top; they scramble both to their knees, pushing against each other as if to climb over one another. Petros strikes again and again with his pistol alternating hammering with the butt of the gun and whipping the muzzle to strike his face, but he fails to connect strongly and now Kadir has him by the throat. If the pistol were loaded the fight would be over.

Petros sees hatred and disgust in Kadir's eyes—a kind of hatred he has never seen in another human being. He has killed the boy's friend; this is the result and Petros understands.

In the middle of the struggle, he hears the thump of boots on the second floor, and remembers that the soldier on the beach side was above them—the soldier will be emerging from the stairwell, time is against him.

He releases Kadir and steps back suddenly as if to run, and then darts for the rifle on the floor, scoops it up as Kadir tackles him, grabbing at his legs; Petros tries to pound the butt of the rifle into Kadir's head but for some reason he can't get any leverage, and Kadir is warding off the blows with his hands, now Kadir has his hands on the rifle.

Petros shifts his weight suddenly, turning Kadir over and landing a strong blow with his right hand. He sees the empty pistol next to them both, he grabs it and shoves the muzzle under Kadir's chin, "stop!" he hisses, first in Greek, then in English.

Kadir freezes, the hatred and misery in his eyes crosses with terror. Petros doesn't wait, he rolls the boy onto his stomach, shoves the muzzle into the back of his head, grabs the strap of the assault rifle with his left hand, and swings it onto his back. "On your feet," he says, and then he pulls Kadir to his feet.

Only then does he hear the shouts from the stairwell. He spins Kadir around to keep him between them; he expects the other soldier to emerge firing, but the soldier doesn't, he just calls out again.

"Don't say anything!" he hisses again into Kadir's ear, and though they do not speak the same language he is sure Kadir understands, and the boy says nothing. Petros backs them both now toward the hotel entrance—the second time in two days that he has had to escape from his father's hotel.

He backs quickly away from the stairwell, dragging Kadir with him; the other soldier is still calling out, confused, but afraid to step through the doorway. Again a choice: he has a weapon now, he could kill Kadir and fire on the stairwell; he could try to shoot his way out, but he does not; instead, he continues to back away pulling Kadir along, with the muzzle of the gun to his head.

"Truck," he says again. "*Fortigo. Auto truck*! *Camion*!"

Kadir nods; he seems to understand the French.

They leave the building by the front, and Petros hurries him around the corner. The sun is rising; light is beginning to suffuse the corners of the dead city again. There are no other soldiers in sight, but Petros can hear the sound of trucks on adjacent streets; there is no doubt that the other soldier has called for reinforcements, that they will arrive at any moment.

Kadir leads Petros down the street, stumbling as he goes; Petros pushes him harder, shoving the gun into his head. Kadir is choking sobs of pure rage and hatred and frustration. It makes Petros feel sick to his stomach; how strange. He has hungered for so long for a moment like this—to make the Turks understand how it feels but in the end inflicting the misery is worse than unsatisfying. He realizes now that for a moment he himself has become the Turk, the hated one, the oppressor, the villain. He has accomplished nothing, has moved his cause not an inch forward; and now it seems certain he will not even survive to say goodbye to the people he loves.

There is a good chance that Kadir is leading him into a trap as well—in the same situation this is what Petros would do with a dangerous enemy who had killed his fellow soldier—but he can't think of any other options at the moment.

Kadir leads him to a truck—a military 4-seater Jeep with a framed, tarp-covered bed. Perfect, Petros thinks. "Get in," he says. "Drive."

Kadir sits in the driver's seat while Petros slips behind him, shoving the rifle muzzle into the back of the seat, pushing it hard enough for Kadir to feel it in his back, while he crouches down, uncomfortably, to avoid being seen. The twisting catches his bruised rib and he cries out in pain—it is amazing that it is not worse, and once again he is surprised to be alive.

It occurs to him that there might be useful equipment in the back, weapons or rations or something but there is no way to investigate and anyway the truck is moving. Kadir is pulling out into the boulevard, still choking and sobbing, a stew of hatred, rage, frustration and humiliation. Petros points his hand to signal turning right to get them on the main road, and then left, south, toward Ayios Memnon.

The truck rolls along quietly, and then begins to accelerate. "Slow down," Petros says, but the truck goes even faster, and in a minute it is racing down the street at 60 or 70 kilometers per hour. "Slow down!" Petros shouts. *Kill him!* a voice cries in his head, but he does not want to kill him, and anyway Kadir now has the upper hand, if Petros shoots they will crash for sure.

"Calm down," Petros says in as soothing a voice as he can muster, "I don't want to kill you, I just want to get away." Of course Kadir doesn't understand. "I didn't want to kill him!" Petros shouts suddenly. "Don't you see!"

They are both crying now, snot running down their faces like enraged babies, Petros thinks, enraged babies who hold the power of life and death.

Kadir accelerates; the truck grinds along faster, bouncing them both up and down—at first angrily, then furiously—on the thin, cracked asphalt. Petros takes his finger off the trigger, he is sure that at any moment a bump will cause the rifle to fire. Buildings rush by now, on the left the long line of hotel high-rises, on the right the low-rise homes of the suburban city; and then another large empty lot; buildings spread out along the long block, the truck tears through what was once an intersection and continues, racing toward a building at the end of the street.

"Stop!" Petros shouts, but Kadir is now committed to killing them both. Behind the building at the end of the street: another empty lot. Petros makes a split-second decision; just before it cross the street to smash into the building, he drops the rifle and lunges over the seat, grabbing the wheel to angle the car to the left, bouncing it over the curb into the empty dirt and weeds. The jeep bumps twice, hard, bouncing Petros and Kadir against the ceiling, and slows abruptly; Petros feels his body floating for a second, he turns his head, flying over the seat, his whole body smashing against the dashboard. He hears —and sees, from the corner of his eye—Kadir's body smash against the steering wheel, his arms and legs flailing in the air as if he were a rag doll. Without control of the wheel, the truck turns abruptly as it slows, skidding and rising onto two wheels before thudding down to a stop.

Petros can scarcely think before he hears shouting, and his brain cries out to his body to move—without looking at Kadir he reaches to open the passenger door but it is stuck, so he kicks at the window. Kadir makes a noise—it sounds like gargling, and Petros almost laughs at the absurdity, the glass shatters then, he has to kick out the corners; he must squeeze through, hoping the cuts are superficial.

He reaches the ground again; the sun is cresting the horizon, a morning breeze washes over him, and for a moment he feels he can smell home, only a few kilometers away. Then: the roar of vehicles, the screeching of tires, the barking orders of soldiers, and Petros runs.

Chapter Twenty-Three

He has left the city now—abruptly, he is in village territory, Ayios Memnon he thinks, but isn't sure. He is still inside the barbed wire, but it feels like a different place; a cluster of buildings in the distance makes up the village heart; a few other structures lie scattered like lone soldiers guarding individual fields.

For some reason there are far fewer trees here as well; the landscape is bare, dusty, barren. If he had time to think, he would wonder why—it's not as though there are more people in the city or more water. He starts by running straight, toward the abandoned hamlet in the distance, but changes his mind, decides to stay close to the road, there is more cover there, scattered trees and buildings.

He half-runs, half shuffles toward the village center, this time staying on the road. He has blotted whatever remains of his injuries from his mind as best he can, but he is nevertheless hungry and exhausted; his legs wobble at moments, and for the first time since he came to this place he fears that they may give out entirely.

He is surprised the Turkish soldiers haven't caught him yet. If he were to bet, he would bet on the Turks at this point. When he crashed, he felt as though they were right behind him, but now the voices and noises and truck sounds seem to fade in the distance. And then he sees it, across the plain to the south—the unmistakable profile of Deryneia, sitting there in the distance, like a mirage. So strange to see it from the north, the way the Turks look at it.

He drags himself along, parallel to the road, in the field next to it, passing behind a few houses and outbuildings. He considers finding one to hide in but he doesn't have the heart to do so—not now, not again—he knows now that hiding is harder than either running or fighting, and in the end the result is the same.

The streets form a triangle, south past the village, southeast through what was once its main square. He wants to continue directly south, toward what looks like home, but there are soldiers there, he sees them in the distance, though they do not see him. He turns toward the village square, perhaps he thinks there is some cover there, but he knows this is incorrect thinking: already he is outside of the dense area where it might be possible for a man to hide for a time in a hundred or two hundred buildings. Here there were at most ten or fifteen, old village houses abutting what used to be fields and a life that followed the cycle of the seasons.

Still he continues—as with everything in life, the story lies in making it to the next turning point.

Now he hears traffic behind him, shouting, soldiers on foot, running behind them, but he refuses to turn around, there is nothing to see there, he thinks, *let them shoot me in the back if that's what they want to do.*

He makes it almost all the way to the cluster of buildings—what once were shops and other places of village business. He makes it almost that far, and almost has time to wonder once again about the buildings, about who lived and worked there, about what their lives were like in the days and months and years before they vanished when the airplanes and the bombs and the soldiers in fatigues came.

He makes it almost that far before he hears the cracking sound of rifles and feels the strangely slow breeze of bullets on his face as they pass his head, the chipping sound as other bullets drill into what remains of the asphalt; the puffs as others thump like drumbeats into the dry dirt of the roadbed. He continues anyway, even though he now sees that his way is blocked by a truck that is rushing toward him from the southeast; on both sides of the road that feeds in from the north, a spread of as many as ten commandos, rifles raised, moving quickly in that strange-looking, terrifying military half-run that allows you to keep your gun steady to shoot.

Petros reaches the crossroads of Ayios Memnon now, turns and looks again at the small skyline of Deryneia, imagining that he can see past it now, all the way past the quiet creaking windmills of Paralimni to the naked beaches of Ayia Napa where countless pretty girls from far-off lands are waiting for him, if he only had the courage to walk up and introduce himself—and then he drops to his knees, the shouts become more audible, the bullets more deliberate. Almost half-heartedly, he puts his hands on his head and feels the damp sweat and dried blood of surrender.

Chapter Twenty-Four

He is on his knees; the final surrender. He feels it in his muscles and bones, the relief and the terror.

The soldiers move in closer, slowly but quickly, professionally terrifying. He takes small satisfaction in the thought that they view him as dangerous, and then he realizes that he is dangerous. He has penetrated their defenses and killed one (possibly more than one—he is not sure about Kadir) of their own. He takes satisfaction in this—only because he thinks he is about to die.

He prays, quietly—not for death or life, but for mercy. He hopes, however, that if this is how it must be, that they will kill him now, shoot him in the back of the head and let him die here, in his own city, on his own land. But of course they won't; now that he has forced their hands, they will be compelled to make a spectacle of him, interrogate him, cause an international incident perhaps. Or maybe just make him disappear, this time more effectively.

The line has drawn closer, three soldiers from the truck now form a semicircle around him, one of them is bellowing at him in Turkish. The troops in the field are further away; but they are drawing closer.

Then: a rifle cracks, not the lighter, airier snip-snip of the Turkish M-16 but a sudden, harder, bullwhip crack of an AK rifle; one shot, then another. The first one drives through the torso of a Turkish soldier in the middle of the line with a hiss; surreally, he keeps walking forward for one step, two, before realizing he has been shot and falling to the ground.

The other soldiers almost react faster, but without more awareness; one of them drops to the ground, others dart in different directions, trying to reach cover, but not knowing where the shot came from.

It takes Petros, however, less than a second to realize that he is alive, that he can live. He jumps up and starts toward the buildings in as close to a sprint as he can manage. As he begins to run, he hears the sound of his name called out from a small grove of trees on the far side of the building: "Petro!" and he runs madly in that direction; a hundred meters away now, he sees Elias, standing and waving his hand, pointing him in the direction of the asphalt of the schoolyard; Petros changes direction, moving toward the cover of the yard, behind the L-shape as Elias raises his gun again and shoots at the Turks, who are now trying to reconvene.

He looks up to see Elias shooting again, loud, careful cracks from his rifle as he turns the corner behind the edge of the long-abandoned school. Then, the terrifying sound of a machine gun roars to life, laying down a line of fire somewhere behind him.

He can barely think; it must be the Turks, he thinks, except that Elias doesn't take cover. On the contrary, he seems emboldened, moving from where he was lying on the ground into a better position. "Quick, quick!" he shouts.

Petros is moving as fast as he can; but he decides not to cross the open asphalt of the old play-yard, instead he runs along the other edge of the L-shape, as close as possible to the building, finally reaching Elias' position. As he gets close, Elias waves him backward toward the small grove. Petros turns to look through the gap between the buildings to see what has become of the Turks; they seem to have scattered, save the one lying prone on the dirt.

Then the machine gun comes to life again, this time its terrifying roar making a distinctive chip/splintering sound, the shattering of glass, a hissing of punctured tires.

Elias turns to Petros, takes a moment, looks as if he is about to say something but instead just smiles.

"*Re Malaka*!" says Petros. His voice is full of reluctant relief. "What the …"

Before he can finish his sentence he looks up and sees a large figure on the flat roof of another building, the one adjacent to the school, with a heavy machine gun strapped to his back. Reaching the edge of the roof, the figure turns and leaps backward off the edge; Petros' heart catches in his throat for an instant before he realizes that the soldier is attached to a line, half-rappelling, half-bouncing down the blank wall of the two-story building. (Not well—the soldier's weight is a strike against him, along with the heavy weapon.) He twists in the heavy air, smashes his shoulder into the wall, and with a loud grunt drops the remaining three meters to the ground.

Petros leaps up to run to him but Elias grabs his shoulder to stop him; there's a long pause, and then the soldier is on his feet, running toward them. Petros sees that it is Stelios—the last person he would expect to come to his rescue, much less carry heavy weaponry.

"How many are you?" Petros asks, and then chokes, the dust catching his breath. Elias signals him to be silent, puts his finger to his mouth and then hands Petros a blessed flask of water. Petros doesn't wait, he drinks and drinks, even as they backpedal further into the grove of trees, Elias keeping the rifle raised, aiming at the space between the buildings.

"We took them by surprise," Stelios says in a low voice, "it will take a minute but they will recover soon and then we're fucked." The desperate content of the sentence is at odds with his calm demeanor. What is the meaning of this? Petros wonders. A very strange rescue if indeed that is what it is. He looks quizzically at them both.

"Just the two of us," says Elias.

"And now you," says Stelios.

"I can't believe you're here," says Petros.

"We can't believe it either," huffs Stelios. Resentment—or else fatigue—catches his breath.

"There's no time to talk," says Elias. "We have to move."

In the distance, Petros sees something above the horizon, growing rapidly larger. A moment later, he hears the sound—a deep, aggressive whumping sound that he recognizes. Not a troop carrier or a reconnaissance ship but an attack helicopter of some kind, probably an Apache, he thinks, fully equipped with gatling guns and missiles. Behind it, another.

He glances over at Stelios, whose mouth has dropped open. "You motherfucker," says Elias, "have you started another invasion?"

We'll never know, thinks Petros.

The helicopters move fast now in their direction. "This is good," says Stelios calmly. "It means the others will wait—will take cover until the helicopters get here. But we have to move fast."

Running again; so much running, Petros thinks.

Once again, they follow the road, but on the other side of the buildings, keeping to groves of trees and shrubs where possible. Once again the tall weeds are friends; thick growth envelops them, transforms their movement into quiet shadow. The sunlight is now bright, piercing, fully illuminating; so they stay on the west side of the homes, hugging whatever shadows they can find.

Elias takes the lead; Stelios follows, with difficulty, the weight of the machine gun clearly slowing him, though Petros cannot help being impressed, stunned even—only a few weeks ago Stelios was the butt of their jokes, even more so after having returned from Special Forces training without, apparently, having lost any weight.

"Take cover here!" he shouts suddenly. They stop, push themselves against the wall. The first helicopter comes in low—so low that Petros has the feeling he could reach up and touch its belly—kicking up huge dust plumes and gravel, whipping it into the soldiers' faces. *We are done for*, Petros thinks, but the helicopter seems to pass without detecting them.

"We have to take cover," says Elias. "Until nightfall at least."

The thought makes Petros sick; another day here?

"Where?" asks Stelios. "We have nowhere to go."

Petros gets up and circles the building on the south side, toward the East; the glow of the morning light shines on the stark blue sea, in the distance the curve of Cape Greco is visible, or so he thinks. Elias and Stelios walk up behind him. "It is so beautiful," he says with a whisper. Strange, his mind; but a minute earlier he couldn't bear the thought of staying another day, now he cannot stand the thought of leaving this place, this corpse of a city that, somehow, is his home.

He is grateful that Stelios and Elias say nothing now, in spite of having risked everything to rescue him. A long moment; and then reality comes home again. "What is the plan to get back?" Petros asks.

"We came by water," says Stelios. "That's how we get back."

Petros looks surprised. "With all this equipment?"

"We had a raft," says Elias. "We pushed it. No time to explain. We need a plan now, to get back to the beach."

Petros takes a moment, looks out across the landscape again, casts his mind back to the map. "We took the wrong road," he says. "We should have taken the other fork—over there," he points East. "There's a road at the end of it that leads toward the water."

They can all see it. From where they are, the two roads diverge in a wide V, one going southwest to lower Deryneia, the other southeast, ending at a L-intersection that goes straight toward the beach. A cluster of low buildings is visible, along with a taller one, perhaps another hotel. The distance to them looks to be perhaps a half-kilometer away, but across wide open scrub. It would make more sense to forget the roads and go straight east, Petros thinks. "What do we do, then?"

"We need to get cover until nightfall," says Stelios. "We can choose one of these houses." He points to the scattered buildings of the road they are on.

"The Turks will peel us out of here in five minutes," says Petros. There are too few buildings; if they could find him in the thick of Varosha, it would be even easier here.

"We need to get to one of the tall buildings," says Elias. "We can hide on one of the floors, cover the entrances, make it hard for them to get us."

"There's still no escape route," says Petros. "If they surround us, there's no way out. We need buildings that are close enough that we can escape from one to the next."

"So we go back north?" Elias asks. The idea is not appealing to any of them.

The helicopter makes a large arc, turns toward the sea, making a wide loop, running north along the beach. They will find us at any moment, Petros thinks. He wonders what the chances of shooting down a helicopter might be.

"They know where we are," says Stelios, "or close, anyway. One way or another we have to move."

Petros looks around the corner again toward the beach, and sees another cluster of buildings that he remembers from his way in. Unlike the hotels further north, this was a resort with clusters of three- or four-story buildings built in wide U shapes facing the water. Enough buildings taking enough space that it would be harder to surround, thinks Petros; maybe there would be a way out.

"There," he says. "We have to reach those buildings."

"How?" asks Elias. The beach is at least a kilometer away in a straight shot, but this area is also exposed, open ground.

"We don't have a choice," says Stelios. "We move to clusters of buildings when we can, groves of trees when we can't. We can stop at the tall buildings as we go." He points to two multi-story structures standing alone in wide-open fields.

The helicopter moves up the beach; they take the opportunity. "Now, run," says Stelios.

They go as fast as they can across the open field, keeping their bodies low through tall grasses. They are fortunate—the field is dotted with trees and shrubs, so they dart, bouncing from one to another like slow-moving pinballs. They are heading back in the direction of the crash, which makes Petros unhappy, but Stelios is right, they have no choice.

Finally, they reach the other road and a four-story building that must have been some kind of office center, Petros thinks. They duck inside, and move up the stairwell to the second floor. A corner office provides views to both the north and northeast. Stelios goes immediately to set up the machine gun in the north window, while Elias stations himself to the east.

Petros collapses against the back of the room, sinking to the ground.

"Fucking *malaka,*" says Elias. "You had everyone shitting themselves."

"I didn't ask you to come for me," Petros spits. He feels bad, terrible, ungrateful as he says it.

"We got your SOS."

"I said I was coming," says Petros.

"Whatever," says Elias. "I guess it's no time to argue."

"It's the perfect time to argue," says Stelios coolly. "We're not going anywhere for a while."

"What do you mean?" asks Petros. "I thought we were just stopping here for a break, moving to the beach."

"I just told you that to get you to move," says Stelios. "We needed to find cover of some sort. Its not safe to move during the day. You know that."

Petros feels the bile rise in his throat. Who was this little shit to speak to him this way? Who is the one, after all, who has survived here in this city—chased, beaten, captured, escaped—for days now? Who knows better how to survive? He wants to say something, to tell them what has happened to him—what he has done. But where would he begin? And in any case, he knows that Stelios is right.

The day creeps on; no one speaks for a while. To his amazement, Petros drifts off, his exhaustion finally overcoming him.

~~~~

When he wakes up, his mouth is dry, his throat sore, but he keeps his eyes shut. Elias and Stelios are talking.

"What now?" asks Elias

"We wait."

"You know there will be consequences for all this."

"I don't think it will be as bad you think," says Stelios.

"How can you be so casual?"

Stelios takes a minute before answering. "There comes a point in a man's life when anything they do to him can't be worse than what they've already done. Well, I came to that point a while ago. Not that I lived an unhappy life exactly." He pauses again, thoughtful. "Anyway, right now we have to concentrate on surviving. Anything else is just details."

Petros opens his eyes. It is now mid-day and it feels as though they are being baked alive in this building. "Water?" he croaks, sounding like a whining child.
~~~~

Stelios slides him a flask.

"What has happened?"

"Nothing," says Stelios. "It seems as though they're mobilizing, but for what, we don't know."

"They don't know how many of us there are," says Elias, "So they have no idea how to look for us. We took them by surprise. According to the news reports—before we left—it was only you here. I don't think they expected us to attempt a rescue."

"I didn't." says Petros. "Did the army send you?" He feels a moment of pride—not for himself, but for his country's army, that it would send a rescue.

Elias laughs. "Don't be ridiculous. We're here on our own. Just like you."

Petros gets up, goes to the window, looks out at the beach and the sea. The hotel resort he'd had in mind cannot be more than a fifth of a kilometer away now, but there are soldiers stationed along JFK Boulevard.

"We took shelter too close," he says finally. "They have established a perimeter. They're going to close in on us now, like a noose."

He says these words provocatively in the hopes that Stelios—or perhaps Elias—will have a reasoned response for him, but they just look distressed, and he realizes that they had been just trying to comfort him; he was right, they should have kept moving.

"Now we have taken one of them down," says Stelios, casting a glance at Elias. "They won't give up. What I don't understand is why they were so determined to catch you—by the time you reached us they had half an army chasing you. They mobilized a lot of men to catch you—why so many?"

"The one you dropped was not the first one," says Petros, "I killed one of their own, two nights ago." More quietly: "I didn't mean to." The somber weight of it strikes him in the chest; he has poked a snake den. He did not go to Famagusta to start another invasion, but he may have done so anyway.

Stelios says he is going up to see if he can catch a better view of what the Turks are preparing. Elias thinks this is a bad idea, and they argue for a moment, but Stelios wins, and goes upstairs, leaving Elias and Petros alone.

A somber silence hangs between them; then Petros looks out the window again. Elias starts to hand him a cigarette, but Petros declines—strangely, he feels no need for it, even though he has been yearning to smoke for days.

"I didn't ask you to come for me," says Petros.

"Not true." Elias replies. "What do you think 'SOS' means?"

Petros doesn't have a good response for this. "I said I was coming home."

"Why did you go?"

"You know why. Why did you come for me?"

"I couldn't leave you here."

"I wish you had."

"No, you don't," says Elias.

"Yes I do. The thought of you coming for me makes me sick." Petros doesn't elaborate. *Especially you,* he thinks.

"I came for you because she asked me to."

"Who?"

"You know who."

"So … she knows too? Of course she does," Petros says. "I sent her a letter." A long pause. He reflects on all the other things he could say to Elias, but in the end he just says, "She is yours."

Elias laughs; not a small laugh, but a big one, a roar from somewhere deep in his gut, as though he had never heard anything funnier, and then he shakes his head. "She was always yours. She loves you."

Petros snorts. "She told you this?"

"She doesn't have to tell me."

"That sounds like the kind of thing you tell a man who is about to jump off a bridge to get him to come down," says Petros. "But I'm not standing on a bridge."

"You already jumped off the bridge," said Elias. "We're just trying to pull you out of the water."

"Are you sorry?"

"For what?"

"For taking the one thing that mattered to me for yourself? Even if she would never have me … did it have to be her?" Petros asks.

"I am sorry for that. I'm sorry for a lot of things," says Elias. "More important things than that."

As they talk, Petros has been scanning what he can see from the window, and notices something. "Look," Petros says, "Look there. Do you see that road?" He points to an overgrown depression leading from the building toward the beach—one of Varosha's many overgrown roads, roads that have been swallowed in weeds, creating the effect that the whole city is sinking, and that the buildings, once connected by human throughways, are now all alone.

Nonetheless, it is visible; once noticed, it is obvious, from the line of trees that go down it for some reason; by now he has seen this pattern enough to speculate that runoff from the road favors them there, along the roadsides, like mini-riparian buffers. Another fifty years, he thinks, and maybe the ancient forests of Cyprus would begin to regenerate themselves in this place.

Just then Stelios returns. Petros points to the furrow. "Can we move along there?" he asks. "If there were an opening..." he points to a place on JFK Boulevard, "and we could cross over, we could make it to those buildings. A better spot to wait for nightfall, don't you think?"

Elias shakes his head, but Stelios is nodding. They all know the chance of it working are slim, but the risk they are taking by staying where they are is worse.

They wait until the helicopter has passed, and the soldiers on JFK have moved down the street. Then they move, quickly, along the edge of the overgrown street, along the trees, past the buildings, finally reaching JFK Boulevard. They stop and wait, but only for a moment; Petros can feel the thick, disciplined animosity of the Turkish army permeating the air around him. "Let's go," he says. They sprint across the boulevard, and down another overgrown alley toward the sea.

Chapter Twenty-Five

Now, the long wait until night. The advantage of the abandoned resort is that it has hundreds of rooms; it will take the Turks a long time to find them going door to door, even if they track them to the resort. Of course, they could always just bomb the building—or bomb all of Varosha, resolve to wipe this headache from the face of the earth.

So the three soldiers sit again and wait; they share food and water, they break bread together and talk in hushed tones about what has happened and will yet happen. Petros eats ravenously, drinks like a dying man, feels his strength returning. Stelios gives him painkillers, too, and what is left of a flask of coffee, and the pain and murkiness in his head starts to fade. He feels, then, as if he is slowly rising from the bottom of the sea, the surface now close.

Petros expresses, once again, his gratitude. You have saved me, he mutters, and then says it louder: "You have saved me." None of the three of them is quite sure if this is true; for one thing, they have not yet escaped, and it is not clear that the three of them will have an easier time returning than Petros would have had by himself.

"Ah, but they would have killed me," says Petros. Even this might or might not be true, though it is likely.

Sitting with his friends now—one of his best friends, and his cousin, his *koumbaros*, the man who could be his brother—Petros feels more alone than ever. As the day creeps on, their agitation grows, while Petros feels at home, acclimated to hiding in the corpses of old buildings. *This is my home,* he thinks, his home in spite of the constant threat of death and ghosts of so many things past.

Long bursts of silence; then more conversation. "Stelio," Petros says, "Why did you come?"

"A soldier never abandons his comrades."

"If that were true, the whole army would be here," Petros says.

"Most of them would have come," says Stelios, "If it weren't in violation of direct orders to do so."

"So why are you here then? Is your loyalty to me more important than your loyalty to country and the chain of command?"

"Isn't that obvious?" asks Stelios. "Anyway, I took an oath—you did too, if you remember—to serve the *Filiki Eteria.* I don't know how serious the rest of you were, but that wasn't a joke to me, you know. There was no way I would leave you behind."

"And what if I just wanted to die out here without bringing you all into it?"

"Then you should have done a better job of that," says Stelios.

~~~~

Night falls. They must get back to the beach, and swim out. Elias and Stelios have hidden a raft somewhere there for their gear. Petros starts thinking about what they can abandon.
~~~~

Petros unsnaps the inner button of his army jacket, and pulls out the leather-bound notebook; inside he has placed the folded title deed and the last known picture of Joanna's father. He is lucky; the hotel still has some scattered bed sheets; he wraps them in one carefully, and then ties his jacket around it; there is nothing to do but hope that the raft will keep it dry.

They wait as long as they can stand, until all hints of daylight have faded from the horizon. Thankfully the moon is less bright than even a few days earlier; but the stars seem more luminous than ever.

They trudge now along the beach, away from Varosha, their eyes growing accustomed to the night, their weary boots dragging through the sand, soft slow waves lapping their leather soles. Eventually, they abandon the boots, and make their way along in their blistered bare feet, feet punished moment to moment by the salt and sand. Soon, they must abandon the machine gun as well, though it makes Stelios cry to leave it, there on the beach for anyone to find.

"Almost there," Elias says. They trudge through the sand along the shore for kilometers; they have left Varosha, Famagusta—its abandoned boutiques, its mulit-story hotels, its lonely courtyards—behind.

Petros looks down the tessellated curves of the coastline—a single coastline that runs all the way to Protaras and beyond, to Cape Greco, where the sheer-face cliffs remind you of eternity and the sunsets make you cry.

They pull the tiny raft out from the tall grasses, pile their things into it—everything that remains, including their clothes —and drag it toward the water; they are down to their underwear now. The breeze washes over them with a sigh, washing off the hours and days of damp discomfort.

"They don't watch this place," says Stelios, "but they may be watching tonight. We have to take it out far before we come back in." The idea is to move down the coastline and swim back on the other side of the Green Line.

The water is surprisingly warm, but salty—days of abrasions and sores spit pain through Petros' legs, arms and torso; now the gentle sea reminds him of every insult.

They wade out into the soft-crashing surf, until the water is above their heads, and then they push off the sandy sea floor and paddle out, out away from shore. Elias takes the lead, swimming on his side, pulling the raft behind him, while Petros and Stelios push from the back, using the raft to support themselves.

The bruise on his rib suddenly kicks him again, and he feels his breath tighten, and then a piercing cramp grabs his leg. He groans loudly, chokes in mouthfuls of thick, salty water as the raft suddenly pulls away from him, and the abyss of Mediterranean threatens to swallow him. "Help," he tries to cry out, just chokes in more water, and he is going under when he feels Stelios' hand grabbing his wrist, pulling him back up to hold onto the raft.

"Slowly," says Stelios. "Take it slowly. There is no sense in rushing now."

Petros pulls himself up, trying to prop himself on the edge of the raft as he coughs himself back to life. He wishes he could pull himself on and ride, but the raft is not meant for passengers, and anyway, he can see that Stelios is not doing so much better at swimming than he is.

They continue, far out, far past the point where Petros would have looped back. "We have to get real distance," Stelios says. "Take no more chances."

Finally, they turn the raft; Petros looks up and down the coastline of his beloved island, from the lights of Turkish Famagusta north of Varosha, past the darkened towers of the city, to the south, where the new resorts of Protaras are illuminated.

"How far are we?" Petros asks. They have been so focused on getting away from the shoreline that he can't tell if they've moved south much, though the darkened towers of Varosha seem to be receding.

"Far enough," says Elias. "I can see Trinity Beach."

Petros cranes his head around the side of the raft and scans the shoreline to see what Elias is talking about. For several minutes, he notices nothing and then it appears—a quick, fast-blinking light, flashing long and short in rapid succession. "What's that?" Petros asks.

"Our contacts," says Elias. "You don't think we came to get you without telling anyone?"

"There's the beach we're heading toward," says Stelios. "Not too long now."

But for Petros, the distance seems immeasurable; his body is already tiring. Part of the problem is the raft; where it had seemed to make swimming easier at first, it now feels like it is taking twice as much force to push it along. "Boys," he says finally, "I think there's something wrong with the raft." He pulls closer and pushes on it; it is half-deflated. He feels now on top; water is pooling on the surface.

Stelios feels it too. "It's taking water," he says despondently.

"We have to abandon it," says Petros. He thinks of the diary, the surveyor's maps; the last photo of Joanna's father.

"Your things," says Elias softly.

They continue, pulling and pushing the raft closer, in spite of the effort, but it is losing air fast now; soon it will be little more than a piece of floating rubber. Petros pats the top again and feels that his clothes in which the sheet and dairy are wrapped are soaked with seawater. He looks again at the blinking light in the distance, beaconing them ashore; they are at least a kilometer out.

"Let it go," he says, this time more firmly.

The three soldiers release the raft, pushing it away from themselves, out toward the sea; almost immediately it rolls over and sinks halfway under. Petros wonders if there is any hope that the diary might survive; perhaps it will be washed ashore and found by someone in the days and weeks ahead, he thinks, but he knows this is as much fantasy as any idea he has had on the journey so far.

Now, completely unencumbered, with no equipment or clothes—stripped of everything—they swim freely toward the shore. Petros paces himself, but fatigue has crept up on him nonetheless. It doesn't help that they swim to overshoot the beach so as not be carried backward by the current. *Dear God*, Petros thinks, *will we ever get there?*

Then, just at the moment when he really begins to wonder if he can continue, Elias shouts: "I'm touching!"

Petros pulls his legs under himself desperately, but he is shorter than Elias, and has to make a few more strokes before he can stand, and as he tries, he feels himself slip again, and his head go under one more time, but this time Elias grabs him and pulls him forward; he spits out the water and they wade toward the flashing light on the beach. In the end, Petros can barely walk; he lets the rolling waves pull him in. At the last second he sees the rescue party; three soldiers, his friends, rush into the surf, grab him by the arms and pull him to shore.

All of them are laughing, cheering; one of them slaps Petros on the back, making him wince. "You bastards!" shouts the soldier. "I can't believe it! You did it! You made it!"

And so, Petros permits himself to smile.

Chapter Twenty-Six

Two weeks out of the army, Petros sits on Joanna's balcony, looking out at the remnants of the village of Dhikomo, buildings that lay as tiny dark spots scattered up the side of the mountain, just under the apocalyptic symbol of the Turkish flag.

It has taken him a few weeks to fully awaken from his self-created dream/nightmare—weeks of potential court-martials, and hushed meetings with government officials, threats and threats of threats from bureaucrats and the appointed keepers-of-the-peace. They feign anger at him, but in the end they are not really angry, he has tried to do what so many others wished they could. They browbeat him, but in the end decide to do nothing. He signs papers agreeing to abide by a weakly-fabricated story about a bureaucratic mistake in which he had gone to visit relatives without obtaining a proper leave of absence. The mistake, they all agreed, was blown out of proportion by the media, and the Turks had used it as an opportunity to settle scores in their own ranks and blame the Greeks.

Behind closed doors the Turks rattled their sabers, and threatened reprisals, and Petros took a phone call from the president of Cyprus, who cursed him and told him he had almost started another invasion. *And what do I say to this?* Petros wondered, *I'm sorry?*

Joanna joins him, stepping onto the white veranda with a tray of iced coffee and sweet watermelon rind preserves. *Here she is again,* he thinks, watching as she leans over to place it on the table. Her white dress brushes against his arm, her neck is close, she smells of something he can't place, some mix of olive oil, lemon, fresh line-dried linens …

They are in some kind of strange period of reconciliation that he doesn't understand. The first time she saw him after he returned, he smiled crookedly at her and asked if she'd missed him.

She had hit him, hard—a slap, but with enough force that it popped his jaw. Then she said, "you were gone?"

He left angry that night; but now he is back to apologize.

Petros looks down at his drink now, a tall glass, swirling with brown and white, the cream and coffee still infusing each other as the foam crawls over the rim of the glass and trickles down its side. It is hot for September, around forty degrees centigrade. He takes a sip of his drink and a bite of the preserved watermelon. Too sweet, he thinks.

"Have you seen Elias?" Joanna asks.

"Not for a few days," said Petros. "When did you last talk to him?"

"I tried to call him," she said absently, "But I haven't seen him since he got out of the army."

To many people's surprise, two weeks earlier Elias announced to his family and friends that he had decided to become a monk, that he would be taking the tonsure in a few weeks, and that he was retreating to Kykkos monastery for the rest of the month. Another overdramatic gesture, Petros thinks, but maybe for the best.

Neither Petros nor Joanna speak for several minutes. There is nothing more to be said about Elias, just as there is nothing more to be said about Petros' ill-fated journey.

He looks at Joanna again, and imagines tears in her eyes. "You're crying," he says.

"No, I'm not," she says.

"I have aged at least ten years in the last few weeks," says Petros.

"Ah, but that's the thing," she says. "So have I."

Another pause, and then Petros speaks: "I found him," he says. "Your father. A photograph."

Joanna's eyes widen, but only for a moment; she seems less surprised than he expected.

"But I lost it," he adds.

A long silence falls between them again. She shrugs.

"I wanted to bring you something," he says.

"What?" she asks. "What could you bring me that would make a difference?"

"In the end, nothing," he says. "I am not sure it is possible for me to bring you what you need."

She nods, and sits back in her chair. She bites her lip for a moment, and then says, "What about you? What's next for you?"

"I don't know," he says. "I don't know where to go." The army is over, university is deferred, and he has put off working for his uncle.

"Maybe you could stay here?" she says. "I mean, at your mother's house?"

He raises an eyebrow.

"I mean, I will be around," she says. "I got word that they are finally closing my school."

"I'm sorry," he says. "Will they find you another position?"

"Eventually," she says. "Maybe a better one, in town." She seems unconcerned.

"I would like to stay here," he says. "To be here ..."

Then she reaches and takes his hand; takes his hand with her beautiful, wise fingers, and squeezes.

"What are we going to do then?"

He grabs her, covering her hand with his own, and pulls her toward him. And for a moment, the thin, uncrossable line separating them is breached.

Series Continues with Book 2, Fall 2015

Thank you for reading *August in the Vanishing City*. Look for Book 2 of the Cyprus Chronicles, which takes place in the 1950s when Greek Cypriot rebels staged an audacious guerrilla war to liberate the island from colonial rule.

Join my mailing list at http://lakispolycarpou.com to get advance notice of upcoming releases.

If you enjoyed the book, please leave a review!

Independent authors live on reviews. If you enjoyed the story, please consider offering your thoughts at Goodreads.com.

Author's Note

I have been thinking about Cyprus for most of my life, and writing about it on and off for more than two decades. *August in the Vanishing City* has its roots in a project started in the early 1990s, when, as an undergraduate, I received a grant to go to Cyprus and collect oral histories from ordinary people who had lived through extraordinary times. At the time, I imagined I would turn these stories into a multi-generational epic that would tell the story of a place that (it seemed to me) few people had heard of but where much had happened.

Needless to say, the project proved to be more challenging than I had anticipated. I returned to it over the years, but it wasn't until I realized that what I had was in fact three distinct but interconnected books that the story began to fall into place. Chronologically, *August in the Vanishing City* takes place after the other books in the series, even though it was written first.

I have been living with these characters and their story in one form or another for years. It's difficult to say goodbye! My consolation is the hope that my readers will enjoy meeting them and experiencing their stories.

About the Author

Lakis Polycarpou was born in Nicosia, Cyprus, but grew up in Colorado, USA. He now lives in Tarrytown, New York, with his wife and three children. Connect with Lakis and follow his work at: http://lakispolycarpou.com.